Praise for We

Summertim

"At first glance, *Summertime Guests* is~~~~~~~~~~~~~~~~~~~~~ly
restored Boston hotel where a guest fa~~~~~~~~~~~ death. But in the
chorus of voices exploring who died and what led to the plunge, Francis
explores the myriad facets of marriage—the little joys and banal failures,
the kindnesses and physical attraction, the ways we neglect and support
each other. A smart read with plenty of meat for book clubs."

—BARBARA O'NEAL, *Washington Post* bestselling author
of *When We Believed in Mermaids*

"In prose as glittering as the hotel in which the novel is set, Francis shines
as a master storyteller. A must-read for anyone who could use an escape."

—KRISTY WOODSON HARVEY, *USA TODAY* bestselling author
of *Feels Like Falling*

"The best kind of page-turner... This seductive novel will draw you into
the fascinating backstories of characters sipping cocktails poolside, and
you won't stop reading until you know what really happened... Kept me
guessing until the end."

—BROOKE LEA FOSTER, author of *Summer Darlings*

Best Behavior

"With warmth and humor, *Best Behavior* delivers a delicious family drama;
look no further for your perfect poolside read!"

—JAMIE BRENNER, bestselling author of *The Forever Summer*

"Francis writes with grace, depth and humor about complex family dynamics
and the joy and heartache of watching young adults spread their wings
and fly from the nest."

—MEG MITCHELL MOORE, author of *The Islanders*

"Wendy Francis captures all the joy and pain of being an (almost) empty-
nester in her latest novel. A terrific summer read."

—AMY POEPPEL, author of *Small Admissions*

Also by Wendy Francis

Three Good Things
The Summer of Good Intentions
The Summer Sail
Best Behavior

Summertime
GUESTS

WENDY FRANCIS

GRAYDON
HOUSE

GRAYDON HOUSE®

Recycling programs
for this product may
not exist in your area.

ISBN-13: 978-1-525-89598-2

Summertime Guests

Graydon House
22 Adelaide St. West, 40th Floor
Toronto, Ontario M5H 4E3, Canada
www.GraydonHouseBooks.com
www.BookClubbish.com

Printed in U.S.A.

"Summer afternoon—summer afternoon; to me, those have always been the most beautiful words in the English language."

—Henry James

"Blameless people are always the most exasperating."

—George Eliot, *Middlemarch*

Summertime
GUESTS

The Boston Globe
April 6, 2021
Seafarer Hotel Reopens
after Winter Overhaul

Boston's legendary hotel, the Seafarer, reopens this spring after having shuttered its doors since last November for a major overhaul of its interior. The hotel, established in 1886, has long been one of Boston's finest gems, attracting world dignitaries, Hollywood darlings and New England's literati. Now with new general manager Jean-Paul Savant at its helm, the landmark has been refurbished with modern flair while maintaining its historic elegance. New linen-upholstered sofas round out the oak lobby while the wraparound porch (a perennial favorite) sports a fresh coat of white paint and comfortable new chaise lounges. Guest rooms boast warm blue and cream hues, creating the effect of being suspended in the sky while overlooking the sparkling harbor below.

Says Savant, "We were striving to maintain the historic features that so many of our guests have come to know and love over the years while bringing the accommodations into line with modern expectations for hotel comfort." Perhaps it's Savant's French roots that we have to thank for the elegant touches, such as fresh flowers in every room, but whatever his secret is, we have to say it's working.

Friday, June 11, 2021

ONE

It wasn't as if Riley could have anticipated what would happen later that day. None of them could. Because when you're at a tasting for your wedding reception at one of Boston's ritziest hotels, trying to decide between crab cakes or lobster quiches, no one thinks of anything bad happening. Or at least, this is what Riley tells herself later. Why she—and no one else there—could possibly be to blame.

At the moment, though, Riley is sitting at a table by the window, half listening to her future mother-in-law while she sips gazpacho the color of marigolds. Something about wanting to know if the outdoor terrace can be transformed into a dance floor, assuming the weather cooperates. If Riley were asked to gauge her interest in planning her own wedding, she would characterize it as mild at best. Her only requirement being that she and Tom marry in July—and that the flowers are pale pink peonies from Smart Stems, the shop where she has worked for the past three years.

It was Tom who'd suggested the Seaport District for their reception, Boston's new up-and-coming neighborhood, and Riley had happily agreed. It's an easy spot for guests to travel to, and the setting is over-the-top gorgeous with views of both the city and the water. Not to mention the promise of fresh seafood—an almost impossible request if they were to wed in Riley's hometown of Lansing, Michigan, where everything remains hopelessly landlocked.

But she hadn't counted on Tom's mother wanting to be so, well, *involved*. Maybe it's the fact that Riley's own mother passed away a few short years ago, and so Marilyn feels compelled to step up and fill her mother's shoes. A retired schoolteacher, her mother-in-law-to-be still tackles each new day with the necessary energy for a classroom of boisterous second-graders, a gusto which she now seems to be funneling into her son's nuptials. At first, Riley was grateful, but while she sits listening to the hotel's wedding coordinator drone on about the Seafarer's rich history, she's beginning to feel as though she has stepped into one of those horrible, never-ending lines at Disney for a ride she doesn't particularly want to go on.

Riley is well aware that the Seafarer is one of the most coveted venues for weddings, especially in light of its recent renovations. It's no secret that New England's most glamorous, its most fashionable clamor to stay here and that the Seafarer's well-appointed rooms are typically booked months in advance. She should be grateful that they're even considering it as an option. Rumor has it that everyone from Winston Churchill to Taylor Swift has been a guest (as the saying goes, if you want to appear in the society pages of the *Boston Globe*, then spend a few hours at the Seafarer's exclusive summer cocktail hour from four to six). As for out-of-towners hoping to take in the full scene that Boston can be—with its attendant snobbishness and goodwill and weird accents wrapped into one—the Seafarer, Riley understands, puts you in the heart of it.

Not that she has anything against tradition, but if it were up to her alone, she would probably choose a smaller, more modest setting, a wedding with no more than fifty guests. There'd be a justice of the peace and rows of white chairs lining the harbor, the wind whipping her veil in front of her face. Naturally, she'd want a reception afterward, but Riley counts herself as the type of girl who'd be equally content with trays of fish tacos and margaritas under a tent as with oysters on the half shell served in a tony hotel restaurant.

"I can't reveal everyone," the coordinator is saying in hushed tones, "but it's no secret that some of Boston's greatest legends have celebrated their nuptials with us." Riley shoots Tom a sideways glance, as if to say *Is she for real?* but her fiancé's chin rests firmly in his hand, his attention rapt. He's eating up every word.

"Well, Gillian, it's all very impressive," Tom's mother says, slipping her reading glasses back into her pocketbook after a review of the menu. Her hair is pulled back in a severe ponytail, her lips coated in her trademark color, fuchsia. "It's no wonder Boston's finest flock here for their special occasions. The view alone is to die for." She gestures toward the expanse of crystalline water out the window, the romantic outline of the city's financial district in the distance. "Kids, wouldn't it be something to come back here every year to toast your anniversary?"

Marilyn shoots Riley a wink, as if the two of them are in cahoots to convince Tom that *this* is the spot, meant to be. There's no need to point out that she and Tom could never afford such a venue. They already discussed it over dinner the other night when Marilyn revealed that she'd gone ahead and booked an appointment for a tasting at the Seafarer on Friday and how she hoped Riley wouldn't mind. "I don't want you to worry about money, dear," she instructed. "Tom's dad and I would be honored to host. Tom is our only child after all."

And Riley had breathed a tiny sigh of relief while swallowing her pride. Not because she wants an extravagant wedding but because it means that she and Tom can now channel the nest egg they've been building toward a mortgage on a new home instead of toward an elaborate one-day celebration. It's a much more sensible use of their money, and Riley, having grown up poor verging on destitute, is nothing if not sensible.

Can she really imagine herself celebrating her marriage here, though? Tom keeps missing her not-so-thinly veiled comments about the food on the menu, which leans toward the bite-size variety that he hates (precisely because it never fills him up), but he has said nothing. Maybe he's just being polite. Riley quickly scans the room for other future newlyweds, but most of today's diners appear to be here for business lunches—buttoned-up men in suits and women in sharp blazers with silk shifts underneath. A few couples, perhaps away for a romantic long weekend, and a group of older women sharing a bottle of wine, sit wedged into the corners. It's a lovely space, but is it *too* lovely?

She shifts in her seat and tries to picture her dad here, wearing his familiar old sports coat that's nearly worn through at the elbows, his khaki pants and penny loafers, pretending to feel comfortable when he wouldn't know which fork to reach for, which glass to use.

When Marilyn turns to her and says, "Don't you agree, Riley?" Riley feels her cheeks flushing because she hasn't been paying attention. She has no idea what her future mother-in-law is referring to.

"I'm sorry. What was the question again?" She's slightly annoyed that Tom can't—or won't—decide on a few things himself or at the very least rein his mother in. Especially because they talked about this very thing—not letting Marilyn take over the tasting—last night! They're discussing the appetizers, apparently, and all Riley knows is that she doesn't want crudités. If there's one rule she's abiding by, it's that her wedding menu will include only those foods that she can pronounce.

It seems there should be a box on a list that they can check for the Standard Reception—something not overtly cheap but not insanely expensive, either. Tom squeezes her knee beneath the table, though it's unclear if it's meant as encouragement or as a reprimand for her not giving this conversation one hundred percent. What Riley really wants to know is this: How can she avoid attending any more tastings with Marilyn? Should she just agree to the Seafarer right now and be done with it?

"Mom was wondering," Tom says in complete seriousness, "if you thought it would be better to have cold and hot hors d'oeuvres or just cold since the wedding will be in July?"

"Oh, right." Riley pretends to consider her options. "Good point. It's bound to be hot, so I wonder—"

But somewhere between the words *so* and *wonder*, a loud whistle of air followed by a deafening blast socks through the room like a fist, sending Riley to grab the table and Tom to reach for her hand. Marilyn's fork drops from her elongated fingers, clattering onto her plate, and the room seems to shake for a brief moment. There are shouts followed by an eerie hush while the dining room settles back into itself. Riley watches the other diners who begin to mumble to each other across their tables, asking if they're okay and spinning in their seats to better determine the source of the blast. The woman at the adjacent table hovers on the edge of her chair, as if considering diving underneath the table.

When Riley glances over at Gillian, she looks equally alarmed and as surprised as the rest of them, which means this isn't some kind of bizarre emergency testing by the hotel. Whatever they heard was real. Significant. Riley's eyes slide toward Tom, then Marilyn, whose face has turned a shade as pale as milk, then back to Tom.

"What on earth was *that*?" Marilyn gasps, her voice an octave too high, her fingers fluttering to her necklace. It's a silver chain studded with azure stones, the kind of jewelry that Riley has come to associate with women of a certain age.

"I'm not sure." Gillian's voice cracks. "It almost sounded like some kind of explosion, didn't it?" And then, as if re-membering her wedding-coordinator cap, she rushes to re-assure them. "But I'm sure it's nothing like that. Maybe a blown transformer?"

But both Riley and Tom exchange glances because no matter how ill-versed they are in loud noises, that definitely was not a transformer. It wasn't so much a popping sound as a crash, she thinks. Did the massive chandelier in the lobby fall? Did it come from the kitchen? Construction work out-side maybe? It's hard to tell.

"Not to be overly dramatic, but it almost felt like an earth-quake," Riley says. "The table actually shook, I think." And although she understands that the curiosity sparked inside her is somehow inappropriate, she wants an explanation. "Whatever it was," she says, lowering her voice, "it sounded awfully close."

"Yes, very close," Marilyn agrees, still fiddling with her necklace.

And that's when the screams begin. Not from the kitchen at the back of the restaurant, not from the lobby, but from outside, just beyond the elegant bay windows peering out onto the terrace that fronts the water, the ocean seemingly close enough to dip a hand into. Riley's glance swivels toward the small crowd that's beginning to form outside near the firepit and hot tub.

"If you'll excuse me?" Gillian says, as if emerging from a fog, and rises awkwardly to her feet before heading toward the row of windows.

Riley's gaze follows her, and suddenly, she, too, feels compelled to get up, as if an invisible string tugs her toward the window. She hurries forward and angles around Gillian for a better view. But when she does, she immediately regrets her decision. Because it's not a collapsed scaffolding or an awning or even construction work that has caused the sudden shaking, the loud blast.

But a woman, lying facedown on the terrace, several yards beyond the window.

The body lies completely still, the woman's legs scissored like a rag doll's, her left leg angled upward awkwardly. A curtain of muddy blond hair shields her face from view. Riley watches while a few bystanders move hesitantly toward the woman, as if afraid of startling her, until someone kneels down and grasps her wrist, presumably to check for a pulse. A man in blue running shorts and a Red Sox T-shirt yells for someone to call 9-1-1.

To Riley, it looks as if the woman was perhaps reaching for a glass that slipped from her hand, her arms still outstretched above her head. Her body is long, lean, even elegant. Riley holds her breath, waiting, and feels Gillian stiffen beside her when a youngish man, nicely tanned and formally dressed, parts the crowd and gently encourages everyone to take a few steps back. He assures them that an ambulance is on the way and speaks with an authority that suggests his importance.

"That's Jean-Paul, our manager," Gillian says quietly as they watch him crouch down next to the woman and brush her hair away from her face.

Just then, a young man in the crowd throws his hand to his mouth and rushes off, and Riley stands on her tiptoes for a better view. And that's when she sees it, too—the wild splash of bright red she hadn't noticed earlier that lies at the far edge of the woman's hair. And in that awful moment, Riley—and everyone else watching—understands. An image of a woman in her yellow summer dress, cartwheeling through the air from somewhere up high, perhaps her hotel balcony, spirals through her mind.

"Oh, my God." It hits her all at once, a hollow pit forming in her stomach.

"Jesus," says Tom, who has come up beside her to rest a hand on her shoulder. "She's not moving."

"No."

It's obvious to them both, but somehow still needs to be said, as if by acknowledging it aloud, the woman might hear their words through the open window, might somehow will herself to move an inch, if only to give them a sign—a flutter of a hand, the shifting of a foot—that she's going to be all right.

But her body remains completely, horribly still.

TWO
Earlier that day

Jean-Paul wakes feeling as if something is off, the same feeling he gets when he has left the burner on or forgotten to lock the front door at night. When he pushes up out of bed, a sense of uneasiness pulls at him, and he tries to recall if the baby slept last night. A faint memory of Isabella crying and Marie going to hush her before Jean-Paul fell back asleep is what comes to him.

He realizes all too well that Marie is doing the heavy lifting with their three-month-old. Not only because Marie insists on breastfeeding (even bottles of breast milk are mysteriously verboten in their house) but also because Jean-Paul has spent most of the last several months at the Seafarer, overseeing the renovations and now tending to the swift uptick in reservations since it reopened in April. Being general manager of the prestigious hotel has turned out to be every bit as challenging and exhilarating as he'd hoped. He only wishes he didn't feel so guilty about leaving in the morning and chagrined when he returns home, excited to tell Marie about a successful day, only to sense resentment jumping off her body like sound waves.

Marie has no idea what his job entails—how could she? Since they set foot in the States, nearly a year and a half ago, arriving on a red-eye from Paris, her days—at least before the baby—were largely spent exploring the city while Jean-Paul versed himself in Seafarer protocol. Occasionally, she'd stop by the hotel, poking her head into his office to say hello and tell him where she was headed—off to the Museum of Fine Arts, the Christian Science Monitor Building, the Institute of Contemporary Art. But more often than not, she'd set out as soon as Jean-Paul left for work only to burst through the door at dinnertime, brimming with news about the paintings she'd seen, the quirky people she'd met. One day she'd gotten lost in the South End for hours and had the most delightful time asking strangers for directions, laughing at their funny accents, their oddly dropped *R*s.

Each day presented a fresh chance for his wife to explore, as if her new city were an elaborate set of nesting dolls to disassemble and admire. That she'd adjusted so well pleased him. He'd been afraid she'd long for her friends back home, maybe hunger for their Parisian cafés or miss her job as a motivational speaker. To the contrary, though, she'd been thrilled by the idea of Jean-Paul's taking the Seafarer job from the very beginning.

"What an honor!" she'd exclaimed when the call came. "You must accept, yes? Out of a hundred candidates, they picked you!" Her eyes had gleamed with pride, and Jean-Paul allowed himself to bask in the accomplishment for a brief moment.

"You wouldn't mind? Packing up and leaving behind our lives here?" Already he'd been promoted to assistant manager at Le Bistrol, one of Paris's most opulent hotels. It was quite possible that one day he would ascend the ranks to manager; as his friends liked to say, no one left Le Bistrol willingly unless, perhaps, he were being wheeled out in a casket. But the Seafarer position held a particular sway over Jean-Paul, as if it were built into his muscle memory: ever since he was a young boy, his father, an international banker, would whisk the family away to Boston for a week, where they'd stay at the Seafarer.

For Jean-Paul, the Seafarer encapsulates everything magical about his childhood—having his parents all to himself for a week, being able to partake in the theaters and ballparks and boiled lobster. Even now, a Red Sox banner from Fenway, where he and his dad watched the Sox defeat the Yankees 3–2 in a nail-biter, hangs on the bedroom wall. He remembers jumping from his parents' king-size bed to his own double in the hotel room, recalls sitting by the pool where waiters in crisp whites delivered meals to their lounge chairs and where Jean-Paul would unfailingly order a cheeseburger with fries and a Coca-Cola, the most American meal he could think of.

The opportunity to manage the hotel of his boyhood dreams, to *bring it into the next century*, as mandated by the board, had been too good to pass up, as intoxicating as the first scent of summer in the air.

"Mind? *Mais non!*" Marie said. "It's the perfect opportunity for you. As for me, I can learn to speak American," she teased. "At least, better than I do now." She'd pulled him into an embrace and pressed her soft lips against his. "And I will teach those American women the French secret to staying skinny."

"Ah, and what is that exactly?"

"Walking, fresh air, lipstick and sex."

"It sounds so simple," he said, loving that she seemed keen to join him on this new venture.

"Which is precisely why it works." She clapped her hands together, insistent. "You must call them back immediately. Tell them that you're honored to accept."

Which was how they'd found themselves, one month later, on American soil, living in a two-story brownstone in Boston's Seaport District, selected for them by a realtor who, in turn, had been recommended by the hotel. Their lives unspooling exactly as they'd imagined.

And then one day Marie stepped into his office holding a surprise behind her back: a tiny white stick bisected by two pink lines.

Soon enough his wife's days were consumed with setting up the nursery (that is, after Jean-Paul had dragged an untold number of unpacked boxes and crates from the spare room into the garage) and painting the walls a soft pink. Along the top near the ceiling, she stenciled tiny bluebirds for a border. "But what if she hates birds?" Jean-Paul asked, and Marie had shooed him away, saying what did he know about little girls anyway?

Those had been their salad days, when they joked with each other easily, when a pregnant Marie might page him at the hotel to tell him to bring home a pint of Ben & Jerry's Half Baked ice cream if he had any intention of not sleeping on the sofa that night. Together, they watched as her belly grew and grew, until his petite French wife looked as if an enormous basketball were attached to her front, and yet Jean-Paul still thought her the most enchanting woman he'd ever met.

When Isabella arrived at last, five days past her due date, it was with a holler and a bang—practically pushing herself out into the world as the medics wheeled Marie across the hospital entrance. Jean-Paul remembers the exquisite little toes, the dainty, crinkled fingers, Isabella's tiny face scrunched up in rage during those first few minutes. But when the nurse laid the baby on Marie's chest, she'd instantly settled, as if recognizing her own mother's scent.

Besotted, that's what they were.

But somewhere in the last few weeks (or maybe months?) Marie has grown quiet, sullen. Work now demands that Jean-Paul arrive at the hotel by seven most mornings and that he often stay as late as seven or eight in the evenings. Especially now that the renovations are complete, reservations have soared. And while technically he's on call only for the weekends, inevitably a small crisis—an angry, belligerent guest; a leaky pipe; a broken generator—will arise, and his night manager, Oliver, will call to wrench him from the depths of sleep.

Sometimes when the phone rings in the middle of the night, Marie will give him a swift kick under the sheets, as if Jean-Paul isn't answering quickly enough (though, she claims to never remember the call—or the kick). Inevitably a tender bruise will pop up on his calf the next day, proof. When he left this morning, she was particularly petulant, shooting him dark looks across her coffee mug while the baby—dear, sweet Isabella, with her enormous brown eyes and plump belly sticking out deliciously over her diaper—shifted fitfully in her arms. His wife is convinced that their daughter suffers from colic, but their pediatrician has reassured them that she's a typical three-month-old, if a tad sensitive.

"Sensitive?" Marie had come home raging. "How about every little thing sets her off?" Jean-Paul didn't know what to say to make things better. He felt as if he'd already exhausted all his best material: *It's only a stage. The baby will grow out of it. Maybe she's going through a growth spurt?* But the comment that really sent his wife into a whirlwind of rage was when he inquired if maybe they should switch to formula to help calm Isabella.

Was it possible, he asked foolishly, that Isabella was allergic to Marie's milk? Well, he might as well have accused Marie of poisoning their own daughter! For two whole days, she refused to speak to him.

How, Jean-Paul wonders (to himself), does she expect him to provide for his family and do his job well on practically no sleep at all? *At least Marie can nap during the day while the baby sleeps.* He'd actually said this aloud over dinner one night, another comment made in grave error when he was delirious from lack of sleep himself. Marie had practically snapped his head off like a sprig of broccoli. As if he'd suggested that taking care of the baby was akin to checking into a lavish spa for the day! He'd meant no such thing, naturally, but why is it that *his* fatigue never seems to matter? Marie claims her exhaustion exists in another realm that he can't possibly imagine, a realm that is sanity-robbing.

Whenever he rushes through the door at seven or even, on occasion, six thirty (six thirty!), her disappointment still greets him. Always, Jean-Paul takes Isabella, cradling her in his arms and cooing to her until she finally quiets.

"See, she likes you," Marie said one night. "She hates me." Jean-Paul clucked his tongue, dismissing it for the nonsense that it was. But before he could entirely reassure his wife, she vanished, the sound of her feet already tripping up the stairs to the tub, where she treated herself to a long soak, no one allowed to disturb her. Sometimes, he thinks, his wife acts as if the baby is an inconvenience, an ill-timed guest dropping by the house who can't leave soon enough.

What Jean-Paul doesn't say, but occasionally feels, as he lays his precious daughter down to sleep at night, is that their dear, sweet baby whom he adores, has ruined them.

It's seven thirty in the morning when he finally swings through the hotel's revolving door and tries to tamp down the rushed, panicked feeling in his chest. The lobby already bustles with activity. The oak floors have been freshly polished, and a fresh bouquet of lush purple lilacs sits on the marble table in the main vestibule. From the back windows that open onto the harbor, the morning sun pours in, bathing the lobby in an early-morning glow. Jean-Paul takes a moment to appreciate the splendor of the newly renovated space, a delicate balance between old and new, before approaching Tabitha and Rachel at the front desk.

"Good morning. All's well?" he asks.

"So far, so good," says Tabitha. "One hundred and three new guests arriving today, mostly for the wedding."

"Ah, right. The Saltonstall nuptials." Jean-Paul makes a mental note to check in with Gillian, his wedding director, later this morning to ensure that everything is set for Saturday's reception. The Saltonstalls represent old money in Boston, and if there's one wedding the hotel wants to get right this summer, it's this one. There's certain to be a flock of photographers. Across the way at the concierge desk, Clive is already assisting a guest, busily unfolding brochures to suggest a dozen possible tours for the day.

When his night manager, Oliver, strides by, Jean-Paul joins him to grab a cup of coffee and inquires how the evening went.

"Nothing too egregious to report. No one walking naked in the hallways," Oliver jokes, though this has happened once or twice in the Seafarer's storied history. "Only a few rooms that were a little too loud. Had to shut down a couple of parties."

Jean-Paul raises an eyebrow, the sinking feeling of the morning returning. He understands guests come to vacation at the Seafarer, but he also understands that *vacation* means something different to everyone and that the hotel's more subdued guests, in particular, don't appreciate a late-night party in an adjacent room. "No police, I hope?"

"Nah," says Oliver. "Pretty tame stuff. Some kids in their twenties, it looked like."

"Floor?" Jean-Paul asks. He'll double-check the rooms for any damage after Housekeeping finishes up. Already, he's anticipating the complimentary dinner cards he'll have to pass out as an apology to any neighboring guests.

"Fourth. Rooms 405 and 407, I think. Tabitha can confirm it for you."

Jean-Paul helps himself to a cup of coffee at the breakfast buffet. "Anything else I should be aware of?" The cream pools in his coffee, and he stirs it with a spoon.

"Not that I can think of. My nightly report is on your desk."

Jean-Paul nods his thanks, scoops up a glazed Danish and lets his gaze wander over the early-morning diners in the restaurant. Many are already dressed for touring Boston in the summer heat—sneakers, sun hats, water bottles. There are families with small children, a smattering of couples, and a few individuals who dine alone. One woman, her plate piled high with waffles, scans a magazine. When she glances up, Jean-Paul recognizes her and tries to avoid catching her eye—but it's too late. Ms. O'Dell gives him a small wave.

He manages to return a weak smile and a nod. Dealing with Ms. O'Dell so early in the day is an interaction that demands at least one full cup of coffee, and Jean-Paul has only had a few sips. A guest since Monday, Ms. O'Dell has made herself known to the entire staff because she has called the front desk thirty-four times. Thirty-four times! Requests for extra towels, a pitcher of water with fresh lime slices (not lemon), someone to show her how to work the television (never mind the detailed instructions on the card by the bed) and a more comfortable chair from which to enjoy the view from her balcony (a chaise lounge from the porch was dispatched).

There have, in fact, been enough requests for extras that Jean-Paul wonders if she might be someone famous, a movie star, perhaps. She'd mentioned that she was a reporter for the *Providence Dealer*, but perhaps it's a cover. Is she a celebrity traveling in disguise, only no one has bothered to alert him? It seems unlikely. Most stars, he knows, travel with an entourage, and if nothing else, their outrageous demands, typically outlined in all caps (e.g., MUST HAVE ROOM-TEMPERATURE EVIAN AVAILABLE UPON CHECK-IN; ABSOLUTELY NO FLOWERS IN SUITE DUE TO ALLERGIES) preceded their arrival weeks before. Still, seeing her this morning makes him think he should google her on the off chance that she *is* someone important. Something about her seems vaguely familiar.

When she turns back to her magazine, Jean-Paul makes a quick exit, winds his way back through the lobby and arrives at his office. He sets down his coffee and clicks on the computer to check emails before morning meeting at eight o'clock. There's a note from Housekeeping (they're running low on towels) and another from Maintenance about a faulty shower on the fifth floor, a burned-out hallway light on the seventh. By the time he has culled through the most important ones, Jean-Paul has forgotten all about Claire O'Dell, and when an advertisement for something called NannyTime pops up on the screen, he clicks on it randomly.

The website features a photo of an attractive young woman, presumably the nanny, smiling at a happy, contented baby in her arms. NannyTime Equals *Mommy*Time says the caption. Underneath, it reads:

Do you need a break? Let our fully certified, loving nannies come to your rescue. They'll watch your precious one while you nap, shop, work or do whatever your heart desires. Give yourself MommyTime by signing up for NannyTime today!

It dawns on Jean-Paul that not once have he and Marie discussed hiring a nanny. Someone who can visit for a few hours, give Marie a chance to nap or take a solitary walk. Knowing his wife, he suspects she'll protest, but given time, he might persuade her otherwise. Slowly, the possibility turns over in his mind while he reads on. There are multiple candidates with résumés rivaling Mary Poppins's. One talks about her work as a nanny for a former governor; another describes how she helped raise six kids under ten (Jean-Paul shudders; he can't imagine). As he scrolls through the friendly, confident faces, the wisp of an idea begins to take on more definite shape. A nanny might solve all their problems, might be precisely the ticket to break Marie out of her momentary funk.

He decides then that he'll make a point of discussing it with her over dinner tonight, assuming that he makes it home in time, and grabs his notebook for morning meeting. Of course, it's Friday, which means they're about to kick off the hotel's busiest forty-eight hours. As he saunters down the hallway, he considers his pep talk for his various directors; maybe he'll pull an inspirational quote from Charles de Gaulle or Charlemagne—something about fighting nobly to the very end or bucking up when the stakes are high—because one thing is for sure: they'll need every ounce of energy and poise that they can muster for the weekend ahead.

Earlier that week

THREE

On Tuesday morning, June 8, Claire finds herself driving by the house of her boyfriend of thirty years ago. She's on her third loop around, as ridiculous as it is, despite the fact that she's starting to feel like a stalker and vaguely worries that a neighbor will see her and call the police. What she's doing here, she can't exactly say. Hoping to catch a glimpse of her former lover on his way out the door to work? Satisfying a morbid curiosity to see if he has aged well or merely somewhat well, like herself? Claire has already decided that if she spots him but he doesn't recognize her, she'll take it as a sign from the universe that she should keep on driving. Right back to the hotel. Maybe right back home to Providence. Her stomach is a mess, butterflies, or *botherflies* as her late husband, Walt, used to call them.

"Stop it," she says aloud, scolding Walt for sneaking up on her, on this of all days. "You're always getting in the way," she tells him, though, to anyone else it would appear as if she's talking to the glossy interior of her Subaru. "So can you please be quiet for once?"

She waits for a sign, maybe a bolt of lightning skewering the sky above, a flat tire, some indication of her late husband's displeasure with her plan. But there's nothing. Only the automatic sprinklers switching on in the yard at the adjacent house, the hum of the air conditioner and NPR on the car radio.

It was easy enough to find Marty's home address, even though nearly three decades have passed since last they spoke. He'd skipped every one of their high-school reunions, to the point where Claire wondered if he were doing it to avoid her personally. Also he seems to be the one person on earth who lacks any social-media presence. Still, Claire, a journalist at the *Providence Dealer*, could have found him over the years if she'd really wanted to. She could have picked up the phone, tracked down an email address. But after all this time, something about calling Marty or emailing him out of the blue didn't feel right. No, tracking him down in person, she'd decided, made the most sense.

Which is why she has driven the fifty-eight miles up to Boston and checked into the Seafarer Hotel for a week. She's on a mission, even though it's bizarre to think that Martin has been so close, only a stone's throw away, all these years. She hadn't allowed herself to search for him online until Walt passed away, almost a year ago now, because what was the point? Marty could have been in Seattle, or in Katmandu for that matter, and the result would have been the same. Getting together with him under any other circumstances would have felt like a betrayal, a mockery of her marriage. And Claire, for all her romantic notions, isn't one to cross that line.

Martin, she thinks. The man has continued to take up space in her mind, like an old, comfortable recliner she can't bring herself to throw out.

Claire's children, Ben and Amber, didn't like the idea of her driving up to Boston from Providence all by herself—in fact, they'd vehemently disapproved—even though they've no idea about the real reason for her trip. Claire promised them that she'd be absolutely fine. "Good grief," she protested. "Just because I'm sixty-one doesn't mean I'm helpless. Even a two-year-old could find her way to Boston with a GPS!"

But she understands they have other concerns on their minds.

Well, she'd made it to the hotel fine all by herself. Even managed to check herself in. And guess what? No one recognized her. Not one person asked her if she were Claire O'Dell from the *Providence Dealer*, the journalist who'd been asked to take an indefinite leave of absence. Providence news, it seems, doesn't travel as swiftly or as easily to Boston as her children might believe. She even called Amber to tell her so, promptly after the cute bellboy deposited her suitcase on the bed. "People here could care less about my little debacle," she said into the phone. "Like I told you, I could be anyone here."

"Okay, Mom, but please promise me you'll still be careful."

"Cross my heart," Claire said, running her finger in an invisible X across her chest. (Sometimes the speed with which their roles have reversed takes her breath away, her children now insisting she check in with them whenever she travels.) She appreciates their concern, but, really, what harm can one middle-aged woman do in the world? Or the world do to her, for that matter?

On her fourth loop, Claire pulls up across from Marty's house on the other side of the street. It's a modest gray Cape, two dormer windows on top, a two-car garage. In a few places, the paint shows signs of peeling, blanched wood poking out from behind it. Redbrick steps ascend to a blue front door with a *Welcome* sign. It's a tidy enough house, Claire decides, possessing a certain amount of charm, even if a bit worn-looking. The small front yard appears well-tended, and beneath a wide picture window an avalanche of pink Cape roses tumbles to the ground. Attached to the house's left side sits an odd little room capped by a sloping roof.

Marty could have done worse, Claire thinks. Though somehow, a part of her expected him to do better. Maybe one of those new minimansions that sits on two lots. Or a New England saltbox with a wide yard and breathtaking views of the sea. That her old boyfriend's house is none of these deflates her spirits unexpectedly. Of course, thirty years ago, when she first imagined Marty's house, his life, it included *her*. Marty's home, *their* home together, would have reflected Claire's own eclectic style. Rooms with high ceilings and sunlight spilling onto hardwood floors, hallways that ended in an inviting window seat, a wide front porch with a swing and maybe a rocking chair or two.

The driveway sits empty, the garden hose neatly coiled around its spin handle. When she'd searched for him online, she'd discovered that Marty's wife, Audrey, had passed away three years ago. Claire met Audrey once during a chance encounter in Boston years ago, the streets gray and slushy with old snow. She and Walt had bumped into them at a Legal Sea Foods downtown, where both couples were waiting to be seated. "What are the odds?" they kidded loosely with each other, but when Marty introduced Audrey as his fiancée, Claire was struck speechless. Somehow, she'd always assumed Marty would seek out her approval before moving on to another woman, past their memories together.

That he was engaged to someone so slight, so waiflike and soft-spoken, someone so much *the opposite* of Claire, surprised her. During the entire meal, Claire kept snatching furtive glances at the lovebirds while she barely touched her own meal, flitting in and out of conversation with Walt. When Marty reached across the table to clasp Audrey's hand, Claire quickly excused herself to the ladies' room, tears stinging her eyes.

Hadn't Marty told her she'd always be the one for him? And hadn't she secretly, foolishly believed him? That Marty would never find another girl like her and so would wait for Claire for the rest of his life, even if she married someone else. Even then, staring at her reflection in the washroom mirror, it occurred to her that, yes, she had, on some level, always assumed Marty was *hers*. And that if life with Walt didn't pan out (had she suspected it even then?), Marty would always be available. How unfair of her, how presumptuous! How very selfish!

Especially when she was the one who'd broken things off. They'd dated for seven years—two in high school and four in college (Marty at UNH; Claire at Northeastern), plus a bonus year afterward. But somewhere along the way, Claire began to doubt their bond together. When he started tossing around words like *marriage* and *family* and *kids*, she could feel herself shrinking ever so slightly, Marty's grasp feeling increasingly like a strangle. Because the truth was the life he was proposing didn't particularly sound like the one she wanted—three kids, two vacations a year, life as a stay-at-home mom. For Claire, motherhood represented the last stepping stone toward full-fledged adulthood—a big white rock that would one day lead her to the solid shore of grown-upness.

A rock she wasn't quite prepared for.

The more Marty pressed her about getting engaged, the more she distanced herself. When she fell into an editorial-assistant position at the *Boston Globe*, Claire felt her world expanding, a fledgling planet in full orbit for the first time. It was a chance to establish herself in the writing world, the place where she felt most comfortable, and perhaps to be with a few other men (Marty had been her first and only, which her girlfriends said made her either a hopeless romantic or a prude).

Then, one winter evening, after Marty got off his wait shift in Faneuil Hall, he grabbed her wrist a little too tightly, demanding, "If not now, then when, Claire? When can we get married?" Never one to respond to ultimatums, Claire decided then and there that they were through. "What?" he'd sputtered in disbelief. "What about our plans?"

As if he didn't quite understand. As if they'd signed a binding contract, sealed in blood.

She shrugged off his question like bad poetry. "People change," she said. "I don't want this anymore." And then, as if the pain she'd already inflicted hadn't been enough, she added "I don't want *us* anymore, Martin. Don't you see?" She'd been so cruel, their breakup as clean as a fresh snap in the femur. But it was the only way to ensure her freedom, to become the journalist she so desperately wanted to be. Martin thought it would be okay if Claire wanted to go back to work part-time after they had kids, but Claire wasn't about to let a man set the parameters of her career, her life.

So, *onward*.

When, a few weeks later at a conference in Providence, Walt appeared, Claire was easily charmed by the two tall yards of him, his generous wit. He was a grown-up, thoughtful and sensible in ways that Marty had never dreamed of, bringing Claire egg-noodle soup when she came down with a horrible case of strep. Compared to Walt's mature gestures, Marty's love-struck pleas seemed foolish and juvenile. A year and a half later, she and Walt were married.

And yet. If she'd realized how her relationship with Walt would evolve, one tied up more in practicality than passion, would she have still chosen him? And how ironic that Amber, her first, had been a honeymoon baby: all that worry about becoming a mother too soon with Marty had played out anyway—but with another man.

She stares at the house, giving herself a moment to gather her thoughts, and a soft laugh escapes her. What on earth is she doing here? There's no point in driving circles around the man's house, especially when it appears he's already left for the day. Maybe, she thinks, she can come back later tonight. Or tomorrow.

The butterflies begin to settle in her stomach. She has a full week to find Martin, to see if she can set things right. There's no need to rush. After all, there's an entire list of places to visit and things to do while she's in town, a list that she now pulls up on her phone:

Visit the MFA.
Eat a cannoli from Mike's Pastry.
Have dinner in the North End.
Walk along the Greenway.
Visit the aquarium.
Get a massage.
Enjoy a cocktail.
And, of course: *See Marty.*

If she heads back to the hotel right now, maybe she can book a massage appointment and relax by the pool. Already the car thermometer reads seventy-five degrees, and when she'd traipsed by the pool earlier this morning, where a dozen or so older women were vigorously performing water aerobics in the shallow end, it struck her as the perfect place to sip margaritas. On impulse, she digs in her purse for a pen and her notepad before she begins to write:

Hello, Marty! Surprise! I hope you won't mind my leaving a note, but I'm in Boston. For the week. Would love to catch up. Call me. I'm staying at the Seafarer. Yours, Claire

She adds her cell phone number in a postscript, then folds the note over and scribbles his name on the front. Before she loses her nerve, she hops out of the car and aims for the black mailbox sitting at the bottom of the driveway. In the note goes, her heart pounding as she hurries back to the Subaru.

She shifts the car into gear and sets out in search of a Starbucks and, more specifically, a chai latte. It's comforting to think that no one will judge her today, that there's no need to worry if she has misstepped or said something out of line. Which, when it comes right down to it, is largely what her life has become these last few weeks.

Not once does she notice the black sedan trailing her, about two blocks behind.

FOUR

"What's with you lately? It's like you're mad at the world," Gwen says.

Jason stares across the table at his girlfriend and tries to decide how best to answer. It's Tuesday, the 8th of June, and the events of the next four days (e.g., that a woman will come crashing down at the hotel where they're staying) aren't even a flicker in his thoughts. Jason can hardly read his girlfriend's moods, let alone the future.

Does Gwen *want* to start an argument, or is she inquiring in a concerned, caring way? Some days it's hard to tell. Just because he changed his order twice and then reprimanded the waiter for bringing him nachos instead of the shrimp cocktail doesn't mean that he's mad at the world, does it? Maybe a little annoyed with their waiter, but mad at the world? That seems unduly harsh. Maybe he's still trying to get his head around the fact that his girlfriend has spent a small fortune on his thirty-third birthday present—four nights at the Sea-farer Hotel—and frankly, he's not sure he deserves it.

"I thought you could take a few days off now that the se-mester is over," she'd said as she rolled over on top of him this morning, the bedsheets twisting around her body in a seductive bow. "Your dissertation can wait. Check-in time is at one o'clock this afternoon."

"Wow—that's amazing," he'd replied, too surprised to react otherwise. The truth is, he can't remember the last time he actually worked on his dissertation. Lately he's been spending large chunks of time at the library taking long naps and working toward the world record for fastest comple-tion of the *New York Times* crossword puzzle. Typically, he comes home, tosses his briefcase on the couch, cracks a beer and listens to Gwen talk about the students in her freshman English seminar. "I mean, you'd think these guys had never heard of Shakespeare," she complained one night. "Do you know one told me he thought Shakespeare was overrated because all he wrote was clichés?" Jason had groaned sym-pathetically. Gwen, a teacher's assistant, is working toward her master's at the same small New England college where Jason is an adjunct professor and earning his PhD.

She also happens to be five years younger, which on most days seems like no big deal, but on other days feels like light-years, as if she won't ever catch up to Jason's slightly jaded worldview. Not that it's necessarily a bad thing: Gwen's ebul-lient overtures have often provided a welcome counterpoint to his more dour moods at dinner parties. But sometimes he wonders if they're compatible for each other in the long run. More specifically, he worries that she might be too good for him. Gwen is head-turning gorgeous, tall and blonde and smarter than any other woman he's ever dated. What she's doing with him is a bit of a mystery, but if he probes too deeply, there's a chance she'll recognize her mistake. So for the moment, he focuses on enjoying their time together.

"Nah, I'm fine," he says in response to her question and twirls the ice in his scotch. "Just recalibrating to vacation time, you know?" He has yet to tell her that this vacation may be more permanent than she knows, that he may not go back to finish his PhD or teach next year.

A few Fridays ago, while he stood lecturing about the Bolshevik Revolution, his students had stared back at him with what he interpreted as disinterest and, quite possibly, disgust. And that's when it hit him: these kids didn't give a shit about the Bolsheviks. They could barely remember what someone had texted them a few hours ago, let alone an event from one hundred years ago.

So, he'd lost it, in front of twenty-one kids, breaking the cardinal rule of teaching: never let your students see you sweat.

"You know what? If you guys don't give a damn about what I'm teaching you, why should I?" he'd demanded, rousing a few of them from their stupor. No brave hands went up, however. "I can't force you guys to be interested." His eyes darted around the room, daring someone to challenge him, to restore his faith, but not one kid met his gaze long enough to return it. His books and lecture notes went sailing into his briefcase. "We're done here," he said, "until someone can prove to me that you're actually interested in learning." Well, that got their attention. A boy in the back row who'd yet to say a word the entire semester raised his hand. "Yeah?" Jason practically shouted.

"So does that mean, like, we automatically pass, or do we have to take the class again next semester?"

And he'd thought *I'll be damned. They really* don't *care.* He grabbed his briefcase and spun around. "Enjoy the rest of your semester. Finals are in two weeks," he said. "You dudes have my email if you want to be in touch."

That was nearly four weeks ago. Now finals are over, grades have been passed in and while he has heard some murmurings on campus, he assumes none of his students dared to rat him out to the administration. Because they don't care enough; for them, canceling class was probably a godsend. And even though Jason thinks he might have handled the situation better that day, it was a tipping point: he'd been growing weary of teaching entitled, unengaged students. Now the thought of doing it for the rest of his life makes him want to rip his fingernails out. Before he tells Gwen, though, he needs to figure out what's next. Because he's pretty sure he wants to call it quits on academia altogether. The teaching, the dissertation. The whole kit and caboodle.

"Well, I'm glad to hear that's all it is," Gwen says and leans over to kiss him lightly on the mouth. Her lips, sticky, taste like strawberry daiquiri. "For a minute there, I thought I was going to have to find someone else to have wild sex with this weekend."

"Ha. Fat chance," he says and grins. They've already dropped their bags off in their room overlooking the harbor. It's on the tenth floor, and there's a giant king-size bed that Jason can't wait to roll around in tonight, and maybe, if he's lucky, later this afternoon.

"But first," she says, raising her glass, "I'd like to propose a toast. To the birthday boy!"

"I'll drink to that." He clinks her glass, and the Johnnie Walker goes down smooth and smoky.

"And cheers to our first vacation away without having to worry about the dog," she adds. Jason sets his glass down. He's not ready to toast the dog's departure quite yet.

About three months ago, they'd adopted Muddy, a chocolate Lab, whose temperament had turned out to be a cross somewhere between the Terminator and Rocky. Muddy devoured everything: grass, leaves, rocks, pens, Kleenex. A brand-new set of AirPods, reading glasses, the fireplace brick. A cashmere wrap that he'd bought Gwen for Christmas. No matter what bitter-apple spray they coated their belongings with, nothing prevented the dog from chewing it to shreds.

After a few weeks Gwen was on her last nerve. When she walked Muddy, it looked as if she were water-skiing across the grass, the dog yanking her along. They tried everything, going so far as to throw a few hundred bucks at a trainer for a weeklong, so-called in-residence program. But even the trainer seemed baffled, surprised by what he described as the dog's *strong will*. He went on to explain that some breeders overbred their dogs with poor results and suspected that such was the case with Muddy, a well-meaning canine who was slightly off in the head, thanks to crappy genetics.

Which only made Jason feel more sorry for it.

"I hate to say it," Gwen pauses, then smiles as if it doesn't pain her *that* much, "but it's kind of nice not to have to think about the dog. Those were some of the most stressful months of my life."

Jason's lips curl into a half smile. "Admit it. You're not really sorry, though."

She shrugs and fiddles with her rings. There's a silver one on her middle finger, two on her thumb, and, on her pinkie, another slim ring with a star and a moon. "Does that make me a horrible person?"

"Probably," he teases. If it were up to him, he would have kept the dog, but then again, he was fine leaving it outside while it barked for four or five hours, which Gwen said bordered on animal abuse. The fact that he still thinks of Muddy as an *it* and not a *he* probably says a lot about how Jason treated the dog in the first place. Still, he'd felt like a jerk giving it away, as if Muddy had failed some kind of IQ test.

"But, hey, not everyone's a dog lover," he says now, willing to move on.

"Right." She snakes the lime wedge off her glass and squeezes the rest of the juice into her glass. "And I'm sure Muddy's a lot happier with his new family. Those kids really adored him."

"Yeah, seemed to." He understands that his job at the moment is to reassure her that they've done right by Muddy, that he'll be fine without them and happy in his new home, a friend of Gwen's.

"I suppose it means we won't be good parents, though." She sets down the vanquished lime beside her glass.

"Wait, what? How do you make that leap?"

Her shoulders rise, as if it's obvious. "It's what people say. You know, first you have your dog baby, and then, once you can handle that, you're ready for real babies."

His eyes narrow, and he wonders if she really believes this or if she's trying to bait him, feel him out about kids.

"Huh," he says, noting a certain dreaminess that's crept into her eyes. They haven't talked about kids in any meaningful way before, despite the fact that they've been dating for a year and a half. Hell, they're not even engaged. "Well, we're not most people, are we?"

Her gaze settles back on him, its wistfulness evaporating as quickly as it arrived so that Jason can't be certain it was even there in the first place. "No. We're not," she says succinctly, as if that might be a bad thing instead of good. Her fingers work to fold her cocktail napkin into miniature squares, and Jason gets a funny feeling that those squares might soon turn into angry shreds of paper. Gwen flips her ash-blond hair over a shoulder, a punctuation mark on their conversation.

What unspoken words have just passed between them he's not sure, but he hopes he hasn't already screwed up the vacation. His eyes roam around the bar, taking in the mostly older guys in polo shirts and loud shorts. A few sit with their wives or, Jason supposes, girlfriends. He and Gwen are by far the youngest couple here, which makes sense, given that it's a weekday and most people are probably working on a Tuesday afternoon. The Seafarer definitely caters to a particular clientele, which is to say the ridiculously rich. Back in the dead of January, when it had been snowing for seven consecutive days and they were climbing the walls of their apartment, Gwen had clicked on the hotel website and scrolled through the photo album, calling him over to take a look. It was impossible not to be impressed—all that marble, the dark-paneled lobby, the sweeping staircase, the views of the water. The history of the place.

"We should go sometime," she'd said nonchalantly. "You know, for a romantic getaway. Or a special occasion. Once it reopens."

"Yeah, sure," he agreed—and then promptly forgot about it.

Now he reaches over to run his hand along her tanned arm, her skin, remarkably smooth. For a split second, he debates telling her right here—how he walked out on his students, how he's been wasting his time at the library, hasn't written a word in weeks. How he's turned out to be a huge disappointment but doesn't care because any whiff of idealism he might have possessed—that he might actually influence the next generation of students for the better—has vanished. But he shakes the thought off. Gwen is killing herself to make this getaway special, and in typical fashion, Jason can only think of ways to screw it up. Why can't he appreciate a good thing when it's within his grasp?

"Buy you another daiquiri, darling?" he says instead, slipping into the Southern drawl that sneaks up on him from time to time, usually when he's had too much to drink. (Jason hails from Virginia but he'd be loath to call it home.)

Gwen holds up her drained glass and grins. "Thought you'd never ask."

When he attempts to flag down their waitress, the sound of church bells—his ringtone—goes off on his phone. He flips it over to see it lit up with a text from a number he doesn't recognize.

Dude, I can't believe you failed me. You're such an asshole, especially for someone who can't teach.

"Can you please put that thing away?" Gwen's tone telegraphs mild annoyance. "I don't see how you can possibly relax with your phone going off every ten minutes."

"Sorry," he says and shuts it off. *The little fucker*, Jason thinks. Final grades were posted yesterday. Only two people could have sent that text, and it's sure not the young woman he failed. She'd never have the balls to address him as *dude*. It can only be Charlie—contemptuous, fall-asleep-in-the-back-of-class Charlie. Jason is tempted to fire back a response immediately, something like, *Well, Charlie, what did you expect? When you don't do the work, you don't get an automatic pass.*

Instead, he slips his cell into his shorts pocket and thinks he'll deal with Charlie later. Much later. Like maybe never later.

Friday, June 11, 2021

FIVE

When he questions her later, Riley tries to think if, in fact, she saw anything out of the ordinary. While it's true that they were all sitting at the table adjacent to the window—the table that would have provided the best view (had one of them been glancing out the window at that exact moment)—Riley can't recall any relevant details. Her hands are still shaking while the officer sitting across from her, probably midfifties with a sizable belly and kind brown eyes, waits patiently for her to say more. She knits her hands together in her lap, willing them to calm.

"Take your time," he says gently, as if he's accustomed to interviewing perfect strangers about perfectly morbid events.

Riley closes her eyes briefly, trying to conjure up an image across the black scrim of her mind. Tom and her future mother-in-law were debating something at the time. What was it again? *Oh, right.* Whether or not they should serve only cold hors d'oeuvres since the wedding will be in July. But then that would mean that they wouldn't have Tom's favorite—pigs in a blanket. She'd been thinking to herself what a ridiculous conversation it was to be having when the crash stopped everything.

What does a person see when someone falls from the sky? How do you fathom the unfathomable? The questions dart around her mind like birds fluttering through the low branches of a tree. Was there a glint of yellow that crossed her field of vision when she gazed at her fiancé at that precise moment? The man whom she loved very much, but with whom she was losing patience for failing to rein in his mother? She knows that the stranger was wearing a yellow dress, but did anything catch Riley's eye when she fell? A flash beyond the window that she might have mistaken for something else? But, no, there's nothing. Just more nuthatches flying around in her mind. Riley shakes her head, defeated. "I'm sorry." It comes out sounding apologetic, as if she should be doing a better job of being a star witness. "I can't think of anything."

"It's okay," the kind officer reassures her. "Sometimes details come back to us later." He uncrosses his legs and leans back in his chair like it's already been a long day. "Especially after something this traumatic."

"Her hands," Riley says suddenly, without thinking.

His dark eyebrows flicker upward. Unlike his thinning hair, they are robust and thick, as if they decided long ago to be the wild child of the family. He bends forward again. "What about her hands?"

"Oh, nothing," Riley says, embarrassed that she's gotten him excited about such a trivial detail. "I just remember noticing her hands, like they'd been grabbing for something. And they were freckled, I think. And rings. She wore several rings." She watches as the officer scribbles notes on his spiral pad and nods, as if he suspected as much.

"Any chance you remember seeing her in the restaurant before…before the incident?" Riley's eyes flicker in mild surprise. So, he's being careful not to call it a suicide. Maybe the woman with the blond hair didn't jump at all. Maybe she fell by mistake. Or, maybe, she was pushed.

Riley shoves away the image stuck in her mind, that of the dead woman's body lying several yards away, and shakes her head. "No," she says. "I don't think so. I mean, I don't remember seeing her in the restaurant. I only remember the sound."

"The sound?"

"Um, the sound of, you know." She swallows, struggling to get the words out. "When she hit the terrace, I guess." Riley's stomach contorts into a knot as she says this, the ear-splitting blast of a human body colliding with the earth still ringing in her ears.

"And what was that like? The sound?" Riley stares at him as if he's crazy. He really wants her to *describe* it?

She holds out her hands, palms up, unsure of what to say. "I don't know. I thought the chandelier in the lobby had crashed. Or that there'd been an earthquake. Or someone had shot off a gun." It's weird to think that now. But the noise was so loud, so sudden, not at all how she'd imagine the sound of a body falling. "Everyone jumped. I think we were all so startled. No one knew what was going on."

The officer nods his head and makes a few additional notes. Riley imagines he was probably handsome once and might still be to a certain type of woman. He's the kind of man who presents himself with a certain heft, sturdy and unflappable. His hands are rough and cracked, but his fingernails are neatly trimmed, clean.

"It must have been frightening," he says now, throwing her a bone.

She gives him a timid smile, grateful for this small kindness. "There was a lot of screaming. But that was right afterward. At least, I think so. It was total chaos, you know?" He nods again.

"And what happened immediately afterward?" Riley is unsure what he's driving at. "Did you see anything suspicious? Anyone moving away quickly from the scene?"

She bites her lower lip sharply, so much so that she thinks she tastes blood, and tries to remember. There was the jogger, the man who took the woman's pulse, a small group of people huddled around. And then the general manager had arrived, encouraging people to back up while he crouched down beside the woman to help. Riley didn't see the woman's face, turned away from the restaurant window, when he'd brushed back her hair, but she'd gathered from the manager's expression that it wasn't good. "Um, nothing suspicious that I know of," Riley offers now. "The manager was on the case pretty soon afterward. It looked like everyone tried to help. Until he pushed her hair away and you saw all the blood. You kind of got the sense that they weren't going to be able to do anything after that."

The officer, saying nothing, continues to write in his notebook. Riley pauses to sip from the water bottle that Gillian handed her earlier. "And I think it was the manager who got the tablecloth, you know, to cover her up." Riley thinks back to that moment, how her heart dropped when she realized that the woman was, indeed, beyond saving. Her stomach rumbles, though whether it's because she's hungry or upset, she's not sure. "The paramedics came shortly after that."

Her eyes wander back to the window, where she notices a dinner roll lying on the floor. Probably knocked off the table in the commotion after the fall. Or jump, or whatever they're calling it. Beyond the window, someone has strung a ribbon of yellow police tape around the terrace's perimeter to prevent pedestrians from passing through. The woman's body, Riley knows, has since been removed, but a yellow tarp has been erected over the place where it hit near the firepit. A small team of policemen hovers just beyond it.

Her lips begin to quiver, and the officer fetches a napkin from a nearby table for her.

"Thank you." She dabs at her eyes, blows her nose. "I'm sorry. It's just that…it's just that today was supposed to be wonderful. I took the afternoon off from work so my fiancé and I could sample a menu for our wedding day, and well…" She hesitates and gives a feeble laugh. "And well, this wasn't quite what I imagined."

"No, I wouldn't think so." His eyes crinkle sympathetically while he waits for her to continue.

"I'm so sorry. I'm a terrible person. Here I am talking about how my day has been ruined, and that poor woman lost her life. Does her family know yet?" Riley's mind suddenly spins with questions.

The officer shakes his head. "We're hoping someone on staff can identify her. We should know soon enough, though."

When she searches the room again for Tom, he's sitting about a hundred feet away, talking to a policewoman. His brown hair is tousled, his shirt untucked, which means Riley probably looks like she flew in on a hurricane herself. She reaches up to smooth her hair, then gives up and weaves it into a loose braid. It occurs to her that she hasn't seen her mother-in-law-to-be since Marilyn started hyperventilating and a young man from the waitstaff had to escort her out of the dining room. A mix of worry and sympathy bubbles up inside her. She doesn't know if Marilyn will ever recover from this day—but then again, will any of them?

"I'm sorry. I don't know how else I can be of help, and I should really check on my fiancé and my mother-in-law. Do you mind if I go?"

The officer flips his notepad shut and says, "Not at all. I think we're done here. I appreciate your time. You've been very helpful, Miss…" He double-checks his notes.

"Thorton," Riley supplies.

"Thorton." He tilts his head and gazes at her with a funny expression. Riley's afraid of what might be coming next. Will he want her to go down to the station, even though she has nothing more to offer? She's watched enough true-crime shows to understand that the police want to record everyone's memories while they're still fresh. But Riley didn't really see much of anything. "I'm sorry," he says finally. "I don't mean to stare. It's just that you look so familiar, and I'm usually good with faces."

Riley smiles, stands up and smooths her skirt. "I get that a lot. Memorable in an unmemorable kind of way."

He chuckles and shakes his head. "No, that's not what I mean. I'll think of it eventually. Here, in the meantime, let me give you my card, in case you remember anything else." In her hand he places a white rectangle that reads *Detective Dale Lazeer, Boston Police Department*. A telephone number and an email address float below it. "Give me a call anytime. Day or night."

"All right, thank you. I will."

Halfway across the dining room, Tom is breaking free of his interview, and she pushes through a press of people to meet him. "You okay?" he asks and pulls her into his arms. Riley nods, but she knows she's not okay, and he's probably not, either, and his mom most certainly isn't, and that they should find Marilyn as soon as possible, but instead of saying all this, tears slide down her cheeks, salty and hot, while the image of the woman in the yellow dress lodges in her mind. Because, God, how could something so horrible have happened on such a beautiful day?

And Riley knows one other thing: she and Tom can't possibly get married here now.

SIX

Jean-Paul understands that the Seafarer has seen its fair share of drama over the years, largely due to the kind of clientele it caters to—the wealthy, the famous, the self-indulgent. Those most likely to make unreasonable requests or inappropriate use of the hotel simply because they're unaccustomed to being told *no*. He's familiar with this kind of guest because his old hotel in Paris, Le Bistrol, catered to the same class. But sometimes the brashness of Americans surprises even him. Their assumption that the world revolves solely around them, that they're infallible (at least the French have the decency to mask their entitlement with good manners). The other day, his night manager, Oliver, recounted a story of how, a few years ago, a famous American actor insisted on flying his helicopter to the hotel. Even though the hotel had advised him that they had no helipad, the actor had insisted, setting his helicopter down on the hotel's front lawn, its whirling blade giving it the virtual finger.

Then there was that time, back in the eighties, when a few Hollywood stars invited everyone in the bar up to their suite for an Ecstasy party. Guests wandered the halls naked, and the Boston cops had to herd them like drunken cats into their patrol cars. There were also the husbands and wives (and mistresses) who occasionally had run-of-the-mill spats down in the lobby. Rumor had it that a spurned mistress once hurled her lover's clothes and laptop off the balcony and that they'd landed with a satisfying *crack!* on the water. And every so often, a fistfight breaks out in the bar. But such incidents are par for the course, to be expected in the hospitality business. Jean-Paul knows this.

But never has the Seafarer experienced anything like what occurred today—a deceased guest, her body strewn out on the premises for all to see. According to Oliver, only a handful of travelers staying at the hotel have passed away on-site, and all of those were due to natural causes. "There were a few heart attacks, a couple of strokes, I seem to recall," Oliver says while he debriefs Jean-Paul (Oliver has been kind enough to stay on for the day shift given recent events). Now that the ambulance has taken the body away and some semblance of order has been restored, Jean-Paul is trying desperately to reach the hotel's PR manager, Julie Morgan. Because the story must be controlled at all costs, spun the right way before the press swoops in and gets ahold of it. "Though, come to think of it, one of those might have been a drug overdose. Rumor had it someone in Housekeeping found the dude curled up in bed, a needle hanging from his arm. But that was probably ten years ago," says Oliver.

Jean-Paul hits the redial button on his phone repeatedly (it keeps going to voice mail) and simultaneously tries sending his PR manager a text: NEED TO SPEAK WITH YOU IMMEDIATELY. Julie will know how to handle such a debacle, how to stomp down any speculation, not to mention calling in a hazmat crew to clean up the area once the police are finished with their investigation. It unnerves Jean-Paul that his night manager seems calmer than he is, that the scene that occurred half an hour ago beyond their dining-room window doesn't appear to faze him. How is this possible? Jean-Paul decides it must be because Oliver never actually saw the woman's face when Jean-Paul brushed her hair away, a face that was, for lack of a better word, *unrecognizable*. And when the image of it pops back into his mind, Jean-Paul quickly pivots toward the wastebasket and vomits.

"Whoa, boss," Oliver says behind him. "You okay?"

Jean-Paul holds up a hand while still bent over the trash can, making sure nothing else is about to come up. The sour taste of this morning's coffee and Danish coat his mouth. He allows himself a moment before straightening, then wipes his mouth with the back of his hand. Thankfully, a travel-size tube of toothpaste and mouthwash are housed in his bottom desk drawer, items he'd purchased in case he ever needed to spend the night at the hotel for an emergency. So far, this hasn't happened. Tonight, however, may be the first. He frowns, remembering Marie and his earlier idea—that he'd surprise her with NannyTime over dinner—and realizes it will probably have to wait.

"Thanks, I'll be all right," he says, covering his mouth with his hand. "If you wouldn't mind checking in on the guests in the dining room—see if they need more water, anything at all—that would be appreciated. I'll just take a minute here to wash up."

"You got it, boss." He watches the door close behind Oliver, retrieves his toiletries and hurries to the private bathroom abutting his office. In the bathroom mirror, his skin appears jaundiced, his eyes rimmed with red. His usually impeccable hair sticks up at odd angles. He quickly dabs some water on it and smooths it down. Then he brushes his teeth and swishes the mouthwash around. Holding it together for his staff today is of the utmost importance.

Back in his office, he pulls the blinds closed to ensure a few more precious minutes of privacy before true chaos descends. Already, he can sense the hotel staff buzzing to answer questions from the guests who've come downstairs late, wondering why an ambulance was pulling away from the hotel. Jean-Paul paces his office, twenty steps across, twenty steps back, and reminds himself that a few casualties are to be expected when you're running one of the premier hotels in a major city. But something so categorically awful—a death that guests have witnessed firsthand? No, nothing has prepared him for this.

It's going to be one hell of a publicity ride, that's for sure. Already, on his short trip from the dining room, where he'd been running triage with Oliver and the cops, to his office, the hallways were humming with concern. He'd overheard a woman in Housekeeping speculating that the hotel might need to close after such an awful tragedy, which had prompted an immediate call to his head of staff. "Please remind your staff that we're not in the business of fueling rumors. As unfortunate as this accident is—" and, yes, he'd been very careful to call it an *accident*, knowing all too well how quickly one misspoken word could ignite a legal firestorm "—the Seafarer will remain open and continue to serve its guests in the stylish manner they're accustomed to." Shortly after that, his head chef had pulled him aside to say that his crew was running around like "birds beat out of a bush," uncertain if the dining hall would be closed indefinitely.

Jean-Paul stretches out his arms and cracks his knuckles,

a nasty habit that Marie has been trying to break him of. He'll need to call a staff meeting to debrief everyone—to warn them not to talk to the press under any circumstances. But not until he speaks to Julie in PR and gets his marching orders. He suspects they'll be issuing a statement along the lines of *There's been an unfortunate, unexpected incident at the hotel. Our condolences go out to the family who've lost a loved one, and right now the proper authorities are handling the investigation. We'll update you as we know more.* It's only a matter of time before the television crews start showing up on the front lawn.

He thinks uncomfortably of the conversation he'd overheard among the officers at the watercooler, who were speculating about whether they could be dealing with a possible homicide. The last thing the hotel needs is a witch hunt during the rush of summertime guests. And then he remembers: they've got a wedding this weekend! How on earth will they manage to handle all the guests arriving within a few short hours? On his notepad, he scribbles *Talk to Gillian!*

A sharp dart of pain shoots through his chest, right beneath his rib cage, and he rubs at it with his palm while considering the logistical nightmare that awaits him. Even if, as he suspects, it's a suicide, this unfortunate event cannot be quietly swept under the rug, as much as he's tempted to do precisely that. There are witnesses, a potential crime scene. What if it was a lovers' spat? A slip off the balcony? What if, God forbid, somehow the railing on the balcony had cracked and gave way? When was the last time they'd had the balconies inspected for safety?

His mind spins with the possibilities, none of them good. The police will want the room number of the guest who fell. They'll probably need to cordon off the area, perhaps the entire hallway. He'll need to double-check that none of this weekend's wedding guests are booked for that floor.

Slowly, the domino effect begins to settle in. Without asking, he already knows that the hotel is fully booked for the weekend. Two hundred and fifty-two guests. Where can he move people? He'll have to call in a favor, maybe his pal, Frederick, over at the Four Seasons, see if he can walk the guests over, as they say in the business, to his hotel.

But first things first. He needs to figure out who their mysterious guest is. Already officers are knocking on doors, checking rooms one by one with Housekeeping. Any room on the side of the building facing the harbor. Above the fifth floor. That leaves five floors, up to floor ten. Because about one thing there is no question: that woman fell from a considerable height.

It feels, Jean-Paul thinks as he bravely opens the door to his office, like waiting to hear which guest drew the shortest straw upon checking in.

Earlier that week

SEVEN

"Daisies or lilies of the valley?" Riley asks.

"Lilies of the valley." Tom probably doesn't have the faintest idea what the flower, a delicate chain of tiny white bells strung along a green stem, looks like. "What?" he says when Riley shoots him a look. "I like the sound of them," he says. "Daisies seem kind of, I don't know, boring."

They're jogging along the Charles River, the narrow ribbon of blue-green water unspooling to their right. On this Sunday morning, June 6, a few early rowers skim the water in their shells, attempting to get a head start on the heat forecasted for later in the day. Already the morning air is thick, swollen with humidity. Sweat beads on Riley's forehead, and she regrets having forgotten to grab her baseball cap before heading out. At the very least, she could have slathered sunscreen on her face, which will, in all likelihood, explode into a million freckles this afternoon. Riley's fair Irish skin is no match for Boston summers.

"Good choice," she huffs, her breathing growing more labored now that they've passed the mile-and-a-half marker. Her footfalls try to match Tom's, whose stride is about twice as long as hers. Yesterday, she'd been debating which white flower would complement the pink peonies in the bridesmaids' bouquets, and lilies of the valley, she agrees, are the best choice. Although she suspects Tom could care less about the flower selection, bouncing the random wedding detail off him every now and then is important. Not only so that he feels involved but also so that Riley can assure her mother-in-law, who's certain to ask, that Tom has been consulted on every detail.

Riley had always assumed it was the bride's mother, not the groom's, who would be interested in all the details. And the very fact that her own mom isn't around to help her with dress-shopping or picking music for the church or choosing her bridesmaids' dresses only underscores that—no matter how fantastic her wedding day might be—it will always be somehow less than. *Less than* all she'd hoped for. *Less than* what her mother would have wanted for her. *Less than* because her mom won't be there to walk her down the aisle with her dad, which is how she'd always imagined it.

It's a fact that Riley keeps trying to ignore because there's nothing in her pink wedding handbook or her oversize binder filled with fliers and pamphlets (mostly from Marilyn) that advises a bride on how to proceed when her mother has died. She supposes Marilyn is only trying her best to fill that huge void, but it's almost laughable. Because no one else can come close to filling the shoes of Libby Thorton, world's biggest hugger, easiest laugher, most loving mother ever. If her mom were still here, Riley would be having an engagement party with all her friends and neighbors back in Michigan. There would be an announcement in the local Lansing paper. There would be darling little gifts her mom would be sending to her bridesmaids, saying what special friends they were and how much she loved them, even thought of them as her own daughters. If Libby Thorton were around, this wedding would be about love in all its forms, and the planning part—the logistics of it all—would take a back seat.

But there's no way to explain this to Tom or his parents. To make them understand. They never had the opportunity to meet Riley's mom, so they only know what Riley has told them and what they've seen in pictures, usually her mom's arms wrapped around Riley or her dad. There's no way to capture the bigger-than-life essence of her. That ebullience. The gift she had for making everyone feel as if they were the most interesting person in the world while she was talking to them. No, trying to capture Libby Thorton for someone who has never met her is the equivalent of trying to explain the rush of skydiving to someone who has never tried it.

So, alternatively, Riley has been pushing any thoughts of her mom further away, to a place where she can guard them like precious heirlooms, where they'll be accessible to her when she needs them most. In the back of her mind.

When a handful of runners heading in the opposite direction approaches them, Riley and Tom have to jump out of the way before hopping back onto the asphalt path. Now that the weather has turned warmer, the running route along the river fills up quickly. It's annoying, especially when she and Tom have grown accustomed to having it mostly to themselves in the early mornings. She thinks back to over a year ago, to the jam-packed road race where they first met near this very spot. The weekend of the Earth Day festival. The race had wrapped up at the Hatch Shell, and all the sweaty runners suddenly found themselves rubbing elbows with the horde of environmentalists gathered on the grassy lawn. They were easy enough to spot in their hemp shorts, their Birkenstock sandals, a *Save a Tree* or *Save the Whales* sticker affixed to their T-shirts. Everyone was waiting to see which band would take the stage next.

Riley and her best friend, Hannah, were part of a larger runners' group that had signed up for the race, and after crossing the finish line, they'd steered their way over to the white beer tent nestled among the row of environmental booths. Dotting the way were kiosks highlighting the merits of solar panels and wind energy. An Adopt-a-Turtle tent and companies promoting environmentally conscious products, like reusable silicone straws and socks made from recycled plastic. At another tent you could sign a petition protesting elephant poaching and alligator skinning. There were gorgeous, luxuriously soft blankets fashioned from bamboo.

Riley was probably a little bit drunk by the time Tom bumped into her. A race number was safety-pinned to the back of his T-shirt, and when he spun around in Riley's direction, his entire cup of beer splashed over her front. He'd been ridiculously apologetic as he tried to mop up the mess with napkins, which had required a fair amount of dabbing at her boobs. Riley tried not to laugh at his earnest efforts. "I'm so, so sorry. I'm such an idiot. I didn't even see you there," he said.

After a few minutes of casual chitchat, Hannah pulled Riley aside and said, "If you leave here without that guy's number, I will never forgive you." Duly warned, she'd marched back in and found Tom, who'd just returned with fresh beers for them both. She asked for his number.

"Why do you need my number? Are you going to make me reimburse you for that shirt?" he said jokingly while

Riley tapped the digits into her phone and Hannah excused herself to go investigate other booths. While they talked, Riley discovered that they both lived in Cambridge (*convenient*). A Boston College grad, Tom worked in a homeless shelter downtown (*i.e., he had scruples*) and had grown up around Boston. She teased him about his accent.

"He's hot," Hannah said later on the subway ride home. "You know, in a Hugh Grant kind of way with that floppy hair and toothy grin and comical eyes." And Riley had burst out laughing because what did Hannah mean by *comical eyes*, exactly? But on some level, subconsciously perhaps, she understood what her friend was driving at—and Tom *did* have nice hazel eyes, framed by thick, dark lashes. If they weren't comical exactly, they were mischievous. Riley wanted to learn more about those eyes—and everything behind them.

The very next day, he'd called (she'd given him her number as well) and asked if she wanted to grab a bite to eat. The chance to redeem herself, to see him when her body wasn't drenched in sweat, when she was wearing a little makeup even, was tempting. That he'd still called after having glimpsed her at her most unattractive seemed promising. She assumed things could only go up.

He was waiting for her in front of the Border Cafe, and even though Riley was five minutes early, Tom was earlier. A case of nerves suddenly seized her. Maybe this was all a huge mistake. Why hadn't she suggested a double date, something where the stakes weren't quite so high? They'd both consumed a lot of beer yesterday (a disastrous decision for work the next day), and it was possible, even likely, that her radar had been off. By this point, she'd gone on enough online matchups to know that the person you *thought* you were meeting was usually a few steps removed from the actual guy, a rough facsimile.

But Tom had broken the three-day rule and texted her the day after the run, which she took as a good sign. By the time she'd walked down the block to the Border, she'd convinced herself there was no harm in sharing dinner with him.

"Hey, there. Look at you. You're even prettier when you're showered," he said, and she laughed, the earlier tension draining from her body as swiftly as water down a drain. The rest of the night turned out to be the most fun Riley had had in months. They devoured way too many enchiladas, drank three margaritas each. Tom told her about his work at the shelter, which involved checking men in and ensuring they had a cot and a freshly laundered blanket for the night. Somehow she'd assumed he was on the administrative side of things. That his work was hands-on helping impressed her.

Unlike so many other guys she'd met, Tom didn't seem obsessed with making boatloads of money, a fact that Hannah later pointed out (correctly) probably meant his family was loaded. But that didn't render his work any less noble in Riley's eyes. Tom loved that she grew up in Michigan and quizzed her on things like whether she'd ever tipped a cow (*no*) and if she was a Wolverines fan (*of course*). Each question she considered seriously, lobbing her answers thoughtfully across the table like a well-aimed Ping-Pong ball.

Much later, when he asked if he could walk her back to her apartment, Riley felt a drunken swell of infatuation. Since Tom lived entirely in the other direction, Porter Square would be a trek. But she'd said yes only too gladly. If she'd been expecting him to spend the night, however, it soon became apparent that his intentions were different. Up the stairs, he helped her to her attic apartment, looked the other way when she changed into her sweats and brushed her teeth, and tucked her into bed.

All she got was a cool kiss on the forehead.

That night she dreamed of Tom strolling into her flower shop and handing her a dozen pink peonies. The following morning, a cup of coffee in hand, she'd called her father in Michigan. "So, Daddy, I'm pretty sure I met the man I'm going to marry."

That she'd met Tom at a time when she'd been considering a move back to Michigan was slightly ironic. With her mom gone, she sometimes worried that her dad sounded lonely when she called. It seemed he might benefit from some company, especially since Riley didn't have any particularly compelling reason to stay in Boston, aside from her job and Hannah, who kept threatening to move back to Michigan, anyway. And there were dozens of floral shops in Lansing where Riley could land.

But Tom was an unexpected, welcome road bump. A genuinely good guy. He read voraciously, titles like Howard Zinn's *A People's History of the United States* and Matthew Desmond's *Evicted*, worldly, sophisticated books. On occasion, he'd walk over to her and say "Stop whatever you're doing because you have to listen to this." And he'd read aloud whatever passage it was he'd stumbled across. At night, he cleared away the dinner plates and rubbed her back. When she asked for the remote, he'd hand it over willingly so she could switch from the sports channel to a cooking show. When he knew she'd had a long day, he'd stop off at the corner store on the way home from work and grab a bottle of Kendall-Jackson.

Hannah fretted that maybe Tom was too good to be true. "I bet he's a vegan, right?" she asked, eager to pronounce him a fraud.

But Riley had laughed and said "No, actually, he loves nothing better than a big, fat juicy steak."

To which Hannah replied, "Oh, well, I guess he does

have a *few* flaws, then. I was worried for a minute. I guess that makes him all right, you know, if you're thinking of marrying him."

To which Riley had screamed "Stop it! First he has to propose!" But she'd been secretly thrilled by her best friend's stamp of approval. She and Tom had only been together for three months at that point.

"Sounds like wedding bells to me." Hannah shrugged, as if it were obvious.

And then one day in May, Riley arrived home from work to an apartment flooded with four hundred white tulips, representing the number of days that she and Tom had been dating.

"I rounded up," he said. "Technically, it's three hundred and eighty-six days. But I've known since day one, back at that horrible beer tent, that you were the girl I wanted to marry. I don't think there are any more white tulips left in New England." And Riley had hugged him so hard that she could feel his rib cage pressing against hers.

"This is the most beautiful thing anyone has ever done for me," she told him.

"So does that mean yes?" he asked.

"That means absolutely."

If she could, she would have married him then and there.

She checks her watch and sees they're on a seven-thirty-minute-mile pace. Some days she can feel Tom champing at the bit, ready to take off on the last mile. But not today. Today he seems content to run along beside her.

"So, my mom says she wants to have us over for dinner sometime this week. I was thinking maybe Wednesday? Or even tomorrow?" he says.

Riley focuses on the sound of her sneakers hitting the pavement, her mind suddenly spinning with the multiple ulterior motives that her mother-in-law might have for suggesting a midweek dinner. She likes Marilyn well enough, but there's something about the woman that makes Riley feel as if she's constantly being taken measure of, as if she can't possibly live up to Marilyn's expectations for a future daughter-in-law. Though Marilyn is much too tactful to say so, Riley imagines she was probably counting on her son to marry one of his well-to-do classmates from Boston College. A girl who would come with a set pedigree, who'd be accustomed to tennis matches at the country club. Someone who already owned her own set of golf clubs, complete with cute pink golf socks on the drivers. Although that type of girl doesn't appear to be the type Tom would ever be attracted to. (In fact, sometimes Riley wonders if Tom lives his life in direct opposition to the path his parents have imagined for him.)

The fact that Riley plays neither tennis nor golf and hails from the uncouth state of Michigan (which Marilyn always confuses with Wisconsin) must be slightly jarring for her mother-in-law, who has already told her how appalled she was by the Netflix series *Making a Murderer* (though, Riley suspects that she and Marilyn were appalled by very different things about this show, which is set in Wisconsin, not Michigan). And when Marilyn inquired what Riley's parents did for a living and Riley revealed that her mother had been a stay-at-home mom (a swift nod of approval from Marilyn) and that her dad worked in sales, Marilyn had appeared satisfied.

"Your father must be a very charming man to succeed in sales these days. What does he sell? That software technology stuff I can never understand?"

And Riley, while appreciative of Marilyn's interest, sensed that her mother-in-law was on a bit of a fishing expedition.

Maybe to ascertain if Riley's gene pool would be suitable for her own grandchildren? Riley elaborated.

"Actually, my dad sells washers and dryers. Maytags." And the expression on Marilyn's face had dropped so swiftly that Riley had been tempted to reach over and physically lift the woman's chin up off her chest. But Marilyn recovered swiftly, shifting her expression to one of mild surprise.

"Oh, really? How nice," she'd said evenly, while reaching for the bottle of Cabernet sitting on the dinner table. It would have been so tempting for Riley to add *I know! I always had clean clothes as a child! Can you believe it? It was great!* but she suspected that even Marilyn would pick up on her sarcasm. Tom grabbed her hand under the table, squeezing it in solidarity.

Riley understands that, for her future in-laws, money is no object. (How very nice for them and especially for Tom while growing up!) But she also recognizes that the only reason the Cantons are well-off is because Tom's father works as an attorney at one of Boston's most prestigious firms. The whole superiority card Marilyn likes to play is ill-gotten. Because Marilyn's job as an elementary schoolteacher certainly didn't cover the bills, their sprawling house in Newton where Tom grew up, their new tony brownstone on Newbury Street. Raising her eyebrow at Riley's upbringing is most definitely an example of the pot calling the kettle black.

"Okay," Riley says now, instantly wary. "Is something up that would require a midweek get-together with your parents?"

Tom shoots her a sideways glance. The Harvard Bridge stretches out before them, and they bound up the steps until they're on the bridge proper. "Why do you always assume the worst, Ry? Maybe she just wants to cook a nice meal for us during the week so we don't have to think about it."

"Maybe," Riley allows, wondering if Tom really believes this. When they crest the bridge, the Prudential Center and the slender finger of the John Hancock Tower come into view, a sight she never tires of, no matter how many times they've run this route. "I suppose you're right," she says, striving for affability. Arguing about Tom's mother doesn't fall high on her list of priorities at the moment, especially on a Sunday morning that typically ends with a brunch of eggs Benedict and sex back at their apartment.

"Look, I know she's been a little overbearing these past few weeks with the news of the engagement and all, but I honestly think she's excited for us and wants to help. Now that she's retired, she's looking for something to fill her hours. Maybe you could give her a couple of jobs to do, stuff that you don't care too much about?"

Riley grins. So her fiancé *does* understand the awkward dance that she and his mother are involved in! Riley wants a simple affair with only their closest friends and family in attendance, which Tom agrees would be ideal. Marilyn, however, keeps hinting that they should aim big and consider every possibility.

Riley would be glad to cede a few nuptial tasks to her mother-in-law, jobs like coming up with centerpieces and party favors, so long as Riley and Tom retain the ultimate power of approval. More than a few of her friends have already warned her about the giant time-suck that wedding planning can be, which is precisely what Riley wishes to avoid. She's not the type of girl who spent her childhood clipping wedding-dress photos from magazines, and she would just as soon get the day over with so that she and Tom can get on with the rest of their lives. An elopement is still not entirely out of the question, at least in her mind.

So yes, Marilyn's helping out might not necessarily be

such a bad thing. If only Riley weren't so concerned that her mother-in-law might lose her shit and turn it into the wedding of the century.

"Sure," she says finally when they reach the end of the bridge and turn right, heading back into Cambridge. "I'm sure I can come up with a list of jobs for her. No problem."

EIGHT

At the elevator on Wednesday morning, the 9th of June, a couple is already waiting, the down button illuminated by a faint yellow glow. Claire exchanges smiles with the tallish young woman who's dressed in a sharp, white tennis skirt and a dark blue top, a racket case in one hand. Her yellow hair hangs down her back in a thick braid. On her right bicep hovers a tiny tattoo, a delicate Chinese symbol, which Claire guesses means serenity or balance or another one of those new-agey mantras. Her boyfriend (they're holding hands, so it seems a safe assumption) is dressed in baggy khaki shorts and a Bruins T-shirt. There's a grungy, drummer aura about him. When the bell dings for the elevator, though, he surprises her by holding the door and saying, "After you."

"Thank you," Claire says, pleasantly surprised. In general, she finds the next generation to be appallingly lacking in good manners. She's noticed this around the office, especially among the young interns, who show up to work with an automatic sense of entitlement. As if they're too smart to work the copy machine, too important to skip lunch even while the senior staff races around to meet a deadline. Somewhere along the line, Claire thinks to herself, the Golden Rule has gotten lost, replaced with a cool indifference. Being nice has fallen out of fashion. Which is unfortunate because she'd much prefer to live in a world where strangers remember to stop and hold the door. Where people make an effort to say *please* and *thank you* every now and then and ask *How can I help?* instead of *Can I have that?*

Walt and she used to discuss this very thing. "What's so old-fashioned about kindness?" she would demand after some particular affront by a stranger.

"Nothing," Walt would say. "We used to call it common courtesy." Walt, she thinks, would have liked this young man on the elevator.

"Enjoy your match," she tells the young couple when they all step off the elevator, and they say thanks, wave goodbye.

Claire heads straight for the pool, where the dozen or so umbrellas scattered around the perimeter bring to mind a field of brightly colored poppies. A cabana boy materializes by her side and offers to fetch a chaise lounge for her, and Claire thinks *Oh, yes, please. How wonderful!* After lugging the chair over, he asks if she'll be needing another, if she's expecting company, to which she curtly replies "No, thank you," before slipping him a modest tip.

She shakes the hotel's red-and-white-striped beach towel out over the chair and sets her bag down on a side table. It's funny, she reflects, how it was almost easier traveling with Walt. Simply because then she was part of a couple, and most people, she has discovered, are more comfortable when they can slot a person into a particular category. With Walt, she'd been a wife, part of a pair, in a twosome, a Biblical Noah's ark duo. Easy to explain and file away. But After Walt (the time which she now thinks of as AW), it has become apparent that some people don't know how to handle her solitude, whether they should acknowledge it or avoid it like a pesky pothole.

It's as if she, a slightly older woman flying solo, suddenly presents a conundrum to the rest of the world. Is she divorced? Widowed? Or, even worse, single? She watches while strangers' minds whirl through the possibilities, trying to place her. And though her wedding band, a tiny diamond on a thin silver ring, now dangles from a small chain necklace around her throat, she'll occasionally slide it back onto her ring finger to let strangers know that yes, indeed, she was married once. *Please don't pity me!* is what she really wants to say. The constant urge to explain her oneness to others—still a surprise to herself some days—can grow tiresome. She's joked with Ben and Amber that maybe she'll start wearing a name tag, like the ones she used to at journalism conferences, that identifies her as *Claire O'Dell, widowed at 61. Still happy!*

She plunks down on the chair and takes a moment to rearrange her swimsuit cover-up, a pretty white eyelet that could double as a dress. She'd found it on the sales rack at Macy's along with some other vacation wear, as Amber called it. From her bag she pulls out a magazine, her eye snagging on an article entitled, "How to Spice Up Your Marriage When He's All Vanilla." She grunts to herself. Do people actually read this drivel? Before she's a sentence in, though, a young mother trying to coax her daughter to jump into the shallow end interrupts Claire's concentration. She watches while the little girl, probably three, tiptoes over to the pool's edge and bends her knees. Her face scrunches up in willful determination—

or maybe it's fear (it's hard to tell)—before she chickens out and races back to her dad.

Claire can't help but smile because oh, how she remembers those early years with Amber and Ben! As if they were only yesterday. Probably because those days were all about pure survival—both for her and the kids. Surviving multiple rounds of strep, pink eye and then the chicken pox. The interminable struggle to get the kids into their winter jackets, the battles over teeth-brushing and hair-combing. Endless hours spent negotiating with tiny people who marched around her house as if they were Napoleon (but with high, squeaky voices). It was all she could do to wrestle her children into bed at the end of each day—and keep them there.

When Walt would arrive home around eight or nine from work, disdain would sweep over her, and Claire would demand "Where have you been?" even though she knew full well that his job as an accountant demanded long hours. He always apologized, but beyond that, he had little to offer in the parenting category. Especially during the preschool years, which were so exhausting, so hard. It was then that the first kernel of jealousy was planted, Walt getting to pursue his career while Claire neglected hers to care for the kids. She'd missed the buzz of the newsroom, the adrenaline surge of chasing a story. That her days were suddenly filled with feeding schedules and nap schedules and bath time…well, the sheer boredom of it could be mind-numbing.

Her reward had come in the relatively peaceful stretch that followed, the kids falling into the easy rhythms of elementary school and Claire going back to work once again. Likewise, her relationship with Walt, like a river that had nearly run dry, found its way back almost to its original level. They went out to dinner again, just the two of them, even enjoyed an odd movie together. Babysitters were cheap, and when Claire thinks back to some of the young girls—not even teenagers—she'd left Ben and Amber with! Well, it was a good thing child protective services wasn't checking up on her. But those dates had been necessary, critical to her sanity.

And then the middle-school and high-school years hit—at least, that's how she thinks of them. As if a giant meteor collided with her marriage, her family. Awkward, stressful, soul-sapping years. Walt was constantly working, Claire was trying to get ahead at the paper and Amber, for some reason, had decided to stop eating. One day her daughter had lifted up her shirt to go shower, and Claire, hovering at Amber's bedroom door, could discern the alarming, gentle curve of her ribs beneath the skin. Three years and thousands of dollars of therapy later, Amber began eating again, as if nothing at all had happened, leaving Claire to wonder if they'd really lived through that hellish time or if she'd dreamed it.

The little girl has returned to the pool's edge, but before her mom can even outstretch her arms to catch her, she scurries back to her dad again. Claire's eyes connect with the mother, who shakes her head and lifts her hands, as if to say *What can you do?*

By the time Ben left for Columbia (Amber had already graduated from Bates), Claire was leading her own team at the *Dealer*, her name creeping up the masthead. And she and Walter were barely talking to each other. Still, she supposes it was marginally better than those years when the kids were in high school and they'd mostly argued. Oh, he could make her so angry! Like no one else in the world.

Especially when it came to Ben, the boy whom Claire loved with a ferociousness but who could never seem to measure up in Walt's eyes. Naturally a quiet child, Ben wasn't prone to the big gesture or to being the big man on campus. Unlike his father, who'd been an all-star athlete on both the basketball and baseball teams in high school and then at the University of Rhode Island, Ben was miserable at sports. When he managed to get cut from the high-school JV soccer team (a team almost everyone made), Walt had made some callous remark about how even Amber could have made the team. How furious Claire had been!

"Words have meaning," she'd shouted at him in their bedroom later that night. "You are destroying your son one word at a time. Why can't you just let him be?"

And then when Ben called home freshman year of college to say that he was choosing health sciences and agriculture as his double major, Walt had nearly lost it. He'd wanted Ben to follow in his footsteps and major in economics.

"What? So you're going to be a farmer, now? What are you going to do with a major like that?" And Ben had patiently, calmly explained that he was interested in health food, that he hoped to one day open his own health-food store. Walt couldn't hang up the phone soon enough, but Claire had stayed on, listening to the quiet excitement in her son's voice. It was the first time she could remember him sounding that happy in months. And really, wasn't that the most any parent could hope for for their child? That they'd be happy?

She'd given Walt another earful that night, too. "I don't understand why he can't choose a normal major, get a normal job," Walt told her. "He doesn't have to be an accountant, but why not a lawyer or a doctor? Something more traditional that will pay the bills? I mean, he's going to Columbia, for Christ's sake. How's he ever going to pay off his loans by working at a health-food store?"

"I think the idea is that he'd own the store. You know, manage it."

"Well, it's less than ideal," Walt had concluded.

And Claire had come so close to saying the other thing on

her mind, which was why did he have so much trouble getting on the Ben-train? Why was it so easy for him to support Amber getting her graduate degree in anthropology and not Ben earning his degree in health sciences? She didn't exactly see Amber setting off for an anthropological dig anytime soon, so why was he so hard on their son? It made no sense to her. Ben was a constant disappointment to a father who'd apparently been hoping for a son who'd work at the same firm as he did, a son who'd want to throw back a few beers and watch football together on a Sunday afternoon. But if he'd taken any time to get to know Ben over the years, he'd understand how ridiculous that was.

"You're such a hypocrite," she'd screamed at him on one particularly bad night, when a conversation between Walt and Ben had resulted in Ben charging up to his room in tears. "Here you're always telling Amber she can be anything she wants, but with our son, you basically spend all your time telling him all the things he can't be. Or that you don't want him to be. Why can't you just let him *be*?" She'd stormed out of the house and walked probably three miles, well past the outer reaches of their neighborhood and into some parts of Providence she'd never seen before. When she crawled into bed later that night, Walt had offered a half apology.

"I'm sorry I lost my temper with Ben. I shouldn't have." But there was no acknowledgment of how wrong he'd been, how unfair his wildly different expectations were for his two children.

"Well, I think it would be best if you tell him yourself in the morning," she'd said.

So many years of running interference between the two of them! No wonder she'd been utterly exhausted back then.

When Walt died, she'd been shocked, naturally. And sad. It was hard to believe that the man she'd shared a home with for thirty-six years was gone, taken from her as quickly as a snap of the fingers, his heart closing up. She remembers sorting through his closet with Amber a few weeks later, their knees covered in dust bunnies as they pulled out his myriad plaid shirts, some still unopened, his multiple pairs of tan chinos and shoes. Packed them up and toted them off to Goodwill. And as they drove away, a surprising sense of lightness had drifted over her, as if she'd been carrying around that damn closetful of shirts for thirty-six years.

But the empty space in her bed, the vacant seat across the dinner table, those voids still feel unfamiliar to her. She'd gotten accustomed to having Walt around. Like the leaky faucet or the ancient dining-room table that she's forever banging her knee into, he'd become a permanent fixture in the house. Occasionally annoying, but familiar.

Plus she can't shake the feeling that he might show up any minute and announce he's been away on a very long trip. If he did, she wonders what advice he might give her? About Amber. About her newfound solitude. Even about Ben.

When her phone chimes, she glances at the unfamiliar number and debates answering. Probably a telemarketer calling to offer her a deal on insurance, a burial plot. She picks up, ready to be annoyed. "Hello?"

"Claire? Claire, is that you?" The voice is familiar, and for a second, she almost thinks it's Walt calling, but then it comes to her, a flood rushing in. *Marty.* "It's Marty," the voice says.

When he hadn't called last night, hope had cratered in her, and she'd considered that maybe he'd had no interest in reconnecting. But now that his voice is on the other end, she can't quite believe it.

"Marty. Hello!" she says loudly enough that the statuesque woman sitting three seats down and reading *The Silent Pa-*

tient looks up from her book. "I'm so glad you called," she says more discreetly. "I wasn't sure that you would."

There's some throat-clearing on the other end, then, "To tell you the truth, I wasn't sure I would, either. It's been such a long time, you know?"

Clare nods her head. *Oh, how she knows.*

"Anyway, I was sure surprised to get your note, and I thought, hell, if you wanted to talk, why not? Is everything okay, I hope?"

She stands with her phone wedged between her shoulder and ear, wraps her towel around her waist and heads toward the pool gate to gain a sliver of privacy. On the adjacent lawn, a young boy with floppy blond hair and his father, lean and tall, swat at croquet balls. She watches while the man rearranges his son's hands on the mallet. "Oh, everything's fine," she lies. "I'm taking a little time off from the paper, treating myself to a vacation at the Seafarer Hotel, and well, I thought since you were in Boston I should reach out and say hello. Seeing as you never come to any of our reunions. You like to make yourself scarce, don't you?" Her thoughts unspool in a meandering ramble, and she regrets that her last comment sounds like a criticism or, worse, a suggestion that she's been on the lookout for him for the last thirty years.

But he laughs on the other end, a big-hearted, generous chortle that she didn't realize until now how much she missed. "You know me. I was never into that reunion stuff. So how the heck are you? I see you're a bigwig at the *Providence Dealer*. What else is new?"

She debates launching into all that's happened, wondering how much she needs to bring him up to speed. Has he read her entries in their high-school alumni magazine that catalog the various milestones in her life, such as Ben's and Amber's births and graduations, the birth of her grandchild,

Fiona, or her promotions at the paper? "Well," she begins, pausing for time to better arrange her thoughts, "I guess you know I've got two grown kids now, Ben and Amber, and I'm a grandmother now, if you can believe it. My oldest, Amber, has a three-year-old. And what else? Oh, Walt passed away about a year ago." She hadn't meant to deliver this particular piece of news over the telephone, but it slips out, as easily as air.

On the other end, there's a beat of silence before Marty says, "Oh, Claire. I'm really sorry to hear that. He seemed like a good guy for you."

Hearing those words is like cracking a walnut right open, her old boyfriend's admission that her husband had been a good match. But there are too many pieces to pick up at the moment to address the matter head-on. Instead, she hurriedly says, "Thank you. We had a good thirty-six years together." She pauses. "Listen, not to change the subject, but I was wondering if you wanted to get together while I'm in town. Maybe over dinner? Or you're welcome to come sit by the pool with me here. It's quite lovely."

What she really wants to ask him is: Why hasn't he called all these years? Does he still think about her? If Audrey passed away three years ago, then why didn't Martin pick up the phone to seek her out? There's nothing in the old-boyfriend rule book that says you can't still be friends.

But she stops herself, bites her tongue. She mustn't play all her cards at once. "Patience," Walt would coach her, the one thing that has never come naturally to her. Claire always had to chase the story, whereas Walt preferred to sit with an idea for a while, turn it over like a rock in his hand. "Sometimes the biggest stories come from waiting, not from breaking the news first," he'd say, and she'd tell him that he should stick to accounting. *Not right now, Walt,* she thinks involuntarily.

He's not here at her side, of course, but the fact that he still insists on worming his way into her head from time to time annoys her. Especially when lately it seems to be whenever she's thinking about Marty.

"Well, wouldn't that be nice?" Marty says now, and Claire waits for him to say more while she watches a handsome pool boy, dark wavy hair, tan as a chestnut, deliver lunch to her chair. A grilled cheese-and-tomato on rye along with a generous margarita. There's one of those festive paper umbrellas, bright pink, poking out of it.

"I'm working till four thirty most days at school," he continues. "But I suppose I could cut out a little early tomorrow. How's Thursday night?"

A knot of relief (he said yes!) and disappointment (she'll have to wait till tomorrow) forms in her chest. "Thursday's perfect. Where shall we meet?"

Another beat of silence follows while presumably he thinks on the other end, and Claire takes the opportunity to wander back to her lounge chair, swerving around a brother and sister who swat a Pro Kadima ball dangerously close to the pool. When the tiny red ball lands in the water, they play rock, paper, scissors to see who has to jump in; the sister loses and cannonballs into the deep end. Claire drops into her chair, fishes the pickle spear off the white china plate and tilts the phone upward to better mask the sound of her crunching.

"How about our old haunt? Bricco in the North End?"

A shudder ripples through her as soon as he suggests it because Claire has been thinking the exact same thing. "I'd love that," she says finally. "Five thirty? Six?"

"Six o'clock," he says. Then, "And Claire?"

"Yes?"

"It will be really good to see you."

"You, too, Martin." Her heart cartwheels across her chest. "See you tomorrow."

After tapping off, she watches the young girl with a dark ponytail, probably eight or nine, pull herself out of the pool, the tiny red ball in hand. Claire attempts to tamp down her excitement. The man she nearly married will be sitting across from her tomorrow night! It's almost impossible to believe.

Martin, Martin, Martin, she thinks. *Can a flame be rekindled? Do you still have feelings for me?* She thinks back to how Marty used to be able to tell exactly what she was thinking, even when she was trying her best to hide it. He always knew when she was upset or worried or scared. They used to joke that he had ESP. Does he still have this second sense, she wonders? (Walt, on the other hand, always seemed entirely unaware of her moods, even when Claire thought she was conveying them quite directly. He'd stare at her as if her expressions were inscrutable.)

The question of what to wear skitters across her mind, but then she recalls the outfit already packed in her suitcase, a blue-and-white polka-dot sundress. All this time wondering how her old boyfriend's life has taken shape, and tomorrow she'll find out. All this time wishing she'd chosen differently, and now perhaps she'll have another chance. The margarita, when she sips, is heavy on the booze and light on the fruit—she'll be bombed in no time, which, given the circumstances, probably isn't such a bad thing.

She searches for her reading glasses and finally locates them on top of her head (Oh, if only her kids could see her now, misplacing her glasses: they'd have a field day!) and slides them down on her nose. Her mystery book sits on the table, and when she opens it to the thumbed-down page, it takes her a minute to familiarize herself with the characters once again. Another few minutes pass before her mind sufficiently quiets to read.

★ ★ ★

Meanwhile, a few chairs down, a man dressed in pink Bermuda shorts and a Tommy Bahama button-down shirt lowers his newspaper to make a quick call to his boss. He reports that Claire O'Dell is relaxing by the hotel pool and, for all intents and purposes, looks as if she'll be here for the duration of the afternoon.

NINE

Jason had posted something funny on Facebook last night about the current mess of the world—or at least he thought it was funny—but when he checks his account before stepping onto the tennis court this Wednesday morning, he's disappointed to see that the post has received only a handful of likes. Why are people so sheepish when it comes to calling out corrupt politicians on the terrible things they do? He's much more likely to get a positive response to a post of a puppy chasing its tail (an easy hundred likes, no problem). But say one thing about how people should be held accountable for their actions, and suddenly, all those so-called friends have crawled under a rock.

Not that everyone has to agree with him, of course. And yet, more often than not, he's surprised when they don't. Because he's usually posting about tough-to-argue-against ideas, things like saving the environment or being a responsible citizen. If he were pressed, he'd probably admit that he posted as a distraction from what he really needs to do—which is to call his department head, George, and alert him to the harassing text he got from a student. It's university protocol. Nearly twenty-four hours have passed since Charlie's text. But there've been no follow-up messages, which Jason interprets as a good sign—the kid probably just needed to blow off steam.

Next to the tennis net, there's a white chair (*very Wimbledon-like*, he thinks), where he tucks his phone underneath a towel and out of the sun. It's ten thirty-five. They've reserved the court for an hour, which should be plenty of time for his girlfriend, a former junior tennis champ, to crush him. Next to the court is a mounted brass plaque that Jason steps over to read. It says *In July 1921, the 30th president of the United States, Calvin Coolidge, also known as "Silent Cal," played tennis with his wife, Grace, on this court. They were honored guests of the Seafarer several times during his presidency.*

"Hey, did you know President Coolidge played here?" he shouts over to Gwen, who's already on her side of the court and stretching, her legs in an inverted V, her hands flat to the ground.

Her blond ponytail bounces when she lifts her head. "No. Cool," she says, as if she's not really all that impressed.

Jason goes to uncap the can of fresh tennis balls, purchased for a princely sum at the hotel gift shop this morning (because even though they'd remembered their rackets, they'd somehow managed to forget tennis balls). Each ball is stamped with the Seafarer emblem, a modern outline of the hotel with three wiggly lines for waves underneath. As they tumble out of the canister, the familiar chemical scent whisks him straight back to childhood when he and his little sister, Ruth, used to hit balls back and forth at the end of their narrow street. He stuffs two into his pocket and trots over to his side of the court. Gwen's already in position on the service line, and they swat a few back and forth, warming up. When Jason hits three consecutive balls out of bounds, she yells, "Don't worry. I'm not judging!"

"Ha! Right," he calls out, his thoughts returning to when tennis was his get-out-of-jail-free ticket. Whenever their dad was having one of his nights, as his mother used to call them, he and his sister (now happily married and a financial adviser in Manhattan) would grab their rackets and play until the sky grew dark, by which time his dad would have usually passed out on the couch. His father's moods back then were volatile, unpredictable, hard to read. One minute the family would be sitting around the dinner table and talking about high-school football, and the next thing he knew his dad's hand would wrap around his wrist in a vise grip after Jason had asked for the potatoes to be passed. "Think you might want to add a word to that request?" he'd demand, and Jason would squeak out "Please?" Even after he'd acquiesced, his plate would sometimes end up on the floor, and Jason, in tears, would have to sweep up the shattered, jagged pieces.

Inexplicably, his father's wrath never fell on Ruthie, only on him and, by default, his mother. Sometimes when his mom tried to intervene on Jason's behalf, his father's face would flush crimson before he'd stand up and slap her across the face, the lingering imprint of his hand still visible on her cheek hours later.

Quickly, Jason learned the skills of an artful dodger, and later, as his body began to assume the bulk of adolescence, the punches of a fighter. He'd read up on what it took to emancipate yourself, how old you had to be. In Virginia, a teenager could request emancipation at sixteen, which seemed like a million years away when he was only thirteen. He thought about running away, but where would he go? He didn't have any relatives he knew of besides his dad's brother, who was also a drunk, wandering in and out of jail. And there was a small piece of him that worried that by leaving, he'd be abandoning his mom and sister. Because what if, when his father discovered Jason was no longer around, he decided to turn his rage on his sister? Every time he packed his bag to leave, the image of Ruthie sporting a black eye—instead of him—made him unpack it all over again. He must have packed that bag twenty times.

He's told Gwen some of this, but not the worst, not the unforgivable parts. Like how he came home from middle school one day, and his mom's arm was in a cast. "Fell down the stairs," she said, but he could read the lie behind her hooded eyes. He knew his dad, a telephone-line repairman, had been home for lunch that day.

And then there was that January night when he returned home from basketball practice and two police cars, their red lights circling, were sitting in the driveway. The neighbors were standing on the front curb, wrapped in blankets, not coats (Jason remembers this strange detail), and they'd cast him worried looks but said nothing. Jason had never run so hard in his life, darting across the yard in his sneakers up to the house, his heart pounding, certain that his dad had done it this time, gone too far. But when he burst through the front door, his mother was sitting on the couch, a bag of frozen peas covering her left eye, and Jason's dad was sitting on the couch beside her, his hand gripping her knee while he chatted amiably with the cops.

The officers—there were two—were talking about grouse hunting with his dad as if they'd stopped by to have a casual chat. When Jason asked what had happened, his dad answered for the cops. "Oh, we had a little misunderstanding. Seems our neighbors called the cops on us. They heard your mom and me arguing. Geez, can't anybody have any privacy in their own home these days?" The cops stared down at their shoes. He can still recall his mother's eyes, full of fear, and the slight shake of her head when he turned to her. As if to say *Let it be, Jason*. At the top of the stairs, Ruthie, probably no more than nine at the time, cowered. No one took domestic violence seriously then—the husband was king of his castle. Still, to this day, Jason gives credit to those officers, who asked his mom if she wanted to press charges.

But his mother had held her head high, the bag of peas still on her eye, and said "No, thank you. I'm fine, Officers. Just a little disagreement, like my husband said." And Jason had recoiled at that awful lie. It was then that he understood exactly how petrified she was.

When he was fifteen, his dad took off for good.

The visceral memory resurfaces like a punch to the gut. Five years ago, his aunt—a woman he'd never met—called from California to say that his dad was gone. Cirrhosis of the liver, she reported, and Jason had thought *Serves the bastard right*. For Jason, there's no easy point of reference when it comes to being a decent husband, a good father. His dad was a bully, a tyrant in the house, plain and simple.

Another ball zooms past, bringing him back to the present moment. "Hey, go easy on me, would you?" he shouts. "Not all of us are former tennis champs."

"I *am* going easy on you," Gwen says with a laugh.

He pauses to wipe his forehead with the bottom of his T-shirt. The air has already turned muggy, cut only by the faint breeze off the water. But it feels good to sweat, to be using his body again and not standing in front of a classroom or sitting in the library, his dissertation staring back at him and daring him to finish. Plus there's something satisfying about swinging a racket and hearing the ball's *thwack!* against the sweet spot.

They begin a proper match, and before Jason has even fully woken up, he's fallen behind two sets. The third set starts off well enough, but then Gwen makes a couple of killer returns and pulls ahead so that they're even.

"Out!" Gwen calls when his ball lands somewhere near the white line on a return.

"C'mon!" he hollers. "That was in!"

"You know the rules." She trots over to fetch the ball out of the bright pink begonias hemming in the court. "Person on the side of the court wherever the ball lands gets to call the shot. Besides, there's no way you could see it from way back there."

He shakes his head in resignation and gets back into position for the next serve. When she tosses the ball up in the air, her body bent into an alluring reverse S, Jason allows himself a moment to appreciate the graceful arc of it, but it's a moment too long because his racket misses the ball as it goes sailing by.

"Try to stay awake!" she yells, clearly delighted. Jason bounces on the balls of his feet, twirls his racket, tries to refocus. He's down 40–15 already in what might well be the last set. His mind flashes back to when he visited Gwen's parents' house in Chestnut Hill for the first time and he saw her girlhood bedroom, an entire wall littered with trophies and ribbons among faded posters of Justin Bieber and James Van Der Beek. At one point in junior high, she'd even considered going pro.

She leans over and bounces the ball a few times in quick succession before serving. Fortunately, there's not much spin on it, so he's able to return it across the net with a quick forehand. Gwen scoots toward it, slams it back and Jason sprints to the opposite side of the court, backhanding it over. They've almost got an actual volley going, and he swats it back again to win the point.

"Lucky shot," she calls out.

"Call it whatever you want. I'm still in the game." The next point he wins as well, bringing the score to an even deuce. And then it's 40–40, advantage Jason. But his semi-victory is short-lived. Gwen slams one, then two more aces, slicing them down the middle. "Yes!" She trots over to the net in victory.

"Didn't anyone tell you you're supposed to let your boy-friend win on his birthday weekend?" he teases. She grabs her towel off the chair and blots her face, leaving behind a tuft of white terrycloth on her cheek. He reaches over to pluck it off and blows it into the air. It floats away like dandelion fluff.

"Funny, no." She uncaps her water bottle and grins. "Hey, check it out. That's someone, right?" She nods in the direc-tion of the adjacent court where a man with a mop of dark hair and a goatee and a woman with auburn shoulder-length hair unzip their racket bags.

"Yeah, it's someone," Jason confirms.

"No, you know, as in someone famous. I'm sure of it. His name is on the tip of my tongue. You know him, he's funny. On TV."

"Seinfeld?"

"No, no. The one with the crazy family. Remember, he sticks the smelly cheese in the suitcase to try to get his wife to carry it upstairs?"

"Oh, Ray Romano?"

"Yes! That's it. That's who it is. I'm positive."

Jason narrows his eyes, tries to get a better bead on the guy, who's now staring back at them. Jason's about to look away, but then the dude lifts his racket in a half wave and smiles. Gwen squeals. "Oh, my God! It *is* him. See, I told you! He's waving at us."

Even Jason allows himself to be impressed for a brief moment. It does appear to be Ray Romano and, presumably, his wife. "Do you have anything he can sign?" Gwen asks, digging through her racket case. "How about a pen?"

But there's only his racket, a towel, a water bottle, their room key, a tennis-ball canister. Gwen's face falls for a second, then brightens. "I'm going to ask him to sign my racket," she announces, and before he can remind her that she doesn't even have a pen, her white tennis skirt goes flouncing across the court to say hello. It's all Jason can do not to call her back, to tell her to hold on. But then he hears church bells. Another text.

He snatches up his phone, but this time it's not from that Charlie kid. This time it's the head of the history department, George, writing.

Jason, please call me at your earliest convenience. Charlie Wiggam (a freshman in your class) has filed a complaint against the university. Let's talk.

He flops down in the chair. The little prick. He's actually going to contest his grade? Jason can't believe it. Maybe he's the son of some bigwig, an alum who has donated millions to the school. Jason should have thought to check before he flunked him. But the kid hadn't lifted a finger all semester! And his final exam, a piddly two-paragraph response to one of five different questions, was a joke. Underneath the other four questions, Charlie had drawn big, loopy smiley faces that winked up at Jason, as if he already knew: the joke was on him.

TEN

What does Riley want from marriage?

It's Saturday, June 5, and Riley and Hannah are shopping for a wedding dress at a boutique in Hingham. "You're not like other brides," Hannah says, sorting through a rack of ivory gowns that reminds Riley of a giant, poufy cloud. "So your dress should be unique. You know, it should say *Riley*." When Riley raises an eyebrow, Hannah hurriedly clarifies. "Well, not literally, of course, but it should fit your personality. Kind of quirky and cute and sweet." It's this description that makes Riley smile for the first time since they've set foot in the store. If it were up to her, she'd order a handful of gowns online and choose whichever one fit best. The whole wedding-gown industry strikes her as a colossal racket, another chance to make frazzled brides feel even worse about themselves.

"Hey?" Hannah asks, turning back to Riley. "Are you

okay? You know, we don't have to do this today if you're not feeling it." Riley loves that her friend has given up her afternoon to brave the upscale shops along the South Shore to search for a wedding dress. That she has picked up on Riley's ambivalence (more like reluctance) is further testament to what a true friend she is.

"Yeah, of course. Let's do it." Riley slips her arms through her tiny backpack straps and begins sifting through the trough of dresses with laser-beam focus. That Hannah looks nothing like your stereotypical maid of honor—combat boots, a romper that's a touch too short for her Rubenesque figure, frizzy red hair done up in a scrunchie, makes Riley feel as if she's surrounded by a secret force field. One look at Hannah, and the rail-thin, makeup-laden, perfumed salesclerks will, Riley hopes, steer clear of them.

"So tell me about your hopes and dreams. You know, for your wedding, your marriage, your life," Hannah elaborates, after Riley shoots her a long, hard look.

"You're joking, right?"

"What? No. We might as well make good use of our girl time."

From the rack, Riley has pulled off a white satin dress, which Hannah now plucks from her hands, frowns at and returns to the rack. "Not you." She reaches in and pulls out two other gowns, one a sexy low-cut that might be better suited to a 1920s flapper and another that can only be described as a gushing river of sequins. For a second, Riley's heart performs a flip. Even though Hannah is her best friend in the entire world and she would step in front of a bus for her, it's possible that her friend's sense of style when it comes to formal wear leaves something to be desired.

Riley crinkles up her nose, says "Mmm...don't think so."

The funny thing is, when Riley considers Hannah's question, she's more certain about marrying Tom than she has been about pretty much anything in her life. She may not have dreamed of her wedding day like most girls, but when she considers what she wants from her *marriage*, well, she wants it all—the fairy tale of happily ever after. She wants the sweet house and babies and a dog (probably a golden retriever), and family pictures flecking the stairway wall. She wants out of their dingy apartment and into a place where they won't have to drag their groceries up three flights of stairs every week. She wants a garage, where they can park their bikes without worrying about locking them up, and a wide, expansive yard with a small vegetable garden and trellises of morning glories. She wants a lifelong companion who will laugh at her jokes, agree with her political views (at least most of them) and maybe give her a massage after a long day at the flower shop. She wants romance and dahlias for no special reason. She wants to sneak upstairs to the bedroom to make love while the kids are napping or are away at a sleepover. She imagines a husband who, when he gets home from work, will come up behind her and wrap his arms around her waist while he plants delicate kisses along her neckline. She wants to know that she's loved and to love someone back.

She imagines years of school photos tucked away in albums and attending her children's softball games, maybe coaching their soccer team. She wants a neighborhood not so unlike the one where she grew up in Lansing, where the kids can ride their bikes around safely or trek through the woods, so long as they're home in time for supper. She wants sit-down dinners and nighttime stories while the family monkey-piles on top of each other by the fire in the deep of winter. She wants hand-holding and maybe a few stern words exchanged about too much TV-watching or no more video games. She wants backyard barbecues and Neighborhood Watches. Someone to bring her tea when she's sick, someone to grow old with, who won't drive her crazy.

Riley may not be greedy about her wedding day, but when it comes to her future spouse, her life, she most certainly is. "What do you think of this one?" she asks, holding up a simple A-line gown, a pretty satin ribbon encircling the waist.

Hannah tilts her head in serious consideration. "Not bad. It's a little…something, though. I don't know, plain, maybe?"

Riley returns it to the rack. They've been here for fifteen minutes and already she's growing bored. A slim, attractive salesclerk, her dark hair pulled up in a tight knot, follows a few paces behind them and begins asking Riley questions about her Big Day, whether it's a formal or an informal event, what month. Riley tells her July, explains she's looking for a simple yet elegant look and burrows back into the rack of dresses. She doesn't care for this person's help, but she doesn't want to be rude, either. She has Hannah, Hannah who has already promised she won't make Riley squeeze her body into a gazillion gowns. They've agreed to three dresses—five, tops—to try on today. Riley refuses to make this process into a circus, will not buy into the patriarchy that says women need to look a certain way on their wedding day and spend countless hours worrying about it.

The clerk reappears holding a gown that would look lovely on someone with an hourglass figure, which is to say definitely not Riley. "How about this one?" she inquires. "We have the cutest shoes to match." Her voice trills upward on the mention of the shoes.

Riley pretends to consider it a moment before admitting, "I don't think it's quite right for me. I was thinking more of an A-line, maybe?"

When the salesclerk wanders off, Riley shoots Hannah a

desperate look. "Shoes? I have to get special shoes, too? You mean, I can't wear my Birkenstocks under the dress?" She's not kidding. On her perusal of the few wedding magazines in her possession, all the gowns appeared to hide the bride's shoes. Riley was hoping to excise at least this one expense from her bridal budget.

"You should probably have some nice shoes for the ceremony," Hannah advises. "But don't worry. You can change into your Birks afterward for dancing."

Riley nods, takes shallow breaths.

"Hey, I meant to tell you, Tom and I looked at stationery last week."

"You did? Wow, you're ahead of the game, Riles. You don't even have a firm date set yet."

"I know, but I thought looking at stationery might help us pull everything together, figure out what kind of style we want for the wedding."

"See anything you liked?"

"I think so." It was, Riley has to admit, the one task she's enjoyed so far out of all the wedding preparations. Combing through various card stocks and textures, debating over different typefaces had actually been kind of fun. Initially, they'd been planning to design the invitations on their computer at home, but Marilyn had quickly shot down that idea. "Nonsense. You two don't have time to do it yourselves. You have to go to Cranes in Copley Plaza. They have the best stuff. Top of the line." Then added helpfully, "And don't worry about the cost. It's my treat."

Marilyn's offer was a pleasant surprise, especially once Riley scanned the price tags. It seemed the more you ordered, the cheaper the cost of an individual invitation, but she intended to keep the guest list small, no more than seventy-five people.

"Do you know how many people your parents are thinking of inviting?" she'd asked Tom as nonchalantly as she could.

"Oh, I don't know. My mom said something like a hundred and fifty, I think."

Riley's hand had stopped turning the pages in the binder of samples. "You're kidding."

Tom peered up from his binder. "No, why? Is that a problem?"

Riley didn't know where to begin, whether she should start by saying that her family was so small—as in, infinitesimally small—that she could probably narrow her entire guest list down to thirty people, including her closest friends. That aside from a few cousins whom she saw once every decade, it was only her father, a handful of aunts and uncles, and if Tom's family had one hundred and fifty guests at the wedding, then the tables would be embarrassingly lopsided. Not to mention that every guest meant another meal to pay for, another party favor to be ordered and a hell of a lot more booze.

"Honey, that could easily turn into a two hundred–person wedding."

Tom shrugged and went back to scanning the invitation samples. "Guess I hadn't given it much thought."

Which was fair. They hadn't focused on the particulars yet. But had her fiancé forgotten all they'd talked about when they first got engaged? How they'd imagined a simple, intimate wedding? They'd even considered eloping, and now suddenly a wedding for two hundred people was possibly in the cards.

Riley struggled to keep her voice from trembling. "I get it. Neither of us has given this day as much thought as your mother has," she said jokingly. "But, seriously, we're going to have to rein her in, trim that number substantially." She hated the way she sounded. Like a drill sergeant.

"All right?" His eyebrows furrowed in seeming confusion. "Whatever you want, honey. It's your day."

"But it's not just my day!" she'd exclaimed, setting the book down on the table as if it were suddenly too heavy to hold. "That's my whole point. It's *our* day, and I was kind of hoping you'd be a little more heavily invested in it."

"Okaaay." He set the binder down. "I'm listening. Talk to me."

Riley shook her head. "I'm sorry. I don't mean to get all wedding-hysterical on you, but I feel like I'm stressing out—which is precisely what I promised I wouldn't do—and we're a good year away from the wedding. What's going to happen when we're only a few months or weeks away?" She stopped, filling her lungs with air. "I guess what I'm trying to say is that I'd love some more input from you, so it's not me making all the decisions."

He reached across the table and took her hand. "I'm here, aren't I? That's what I'm trying to do. We're looking at invitations today, right? Figuring out what we like and don't like?"

She nodded, bit her lip.

He leaned in and whispered, "Have you been reading that awful pink book again?" And with Tom's mention of the dreadful pink book, the balloon of sudden panic growing inside her had burst with a satisfying *pop!*

"Maybe?" When they first got engaged, Tom's mom had gifted Riley one of those bride-to-be manuals, complete with a built-in planner leading up to I-Do Day. It was filled with annoying checklists of what to do when. "You're right. I'm sorry. I'm freaking out for no reason. I guess this just makes it all seem very real."

She picked up the binder again, and after a few minutes,

paused on a Save the Date card with a pleasingly guileless typeface, a font similar to that of the *New Yorker* magazine. Not a single, girly curlicue in sight. Below the type was the emblem of the peace sign.

"It's okay, I guess," Tom said when she showed it to him. "Seems a little artsy-fartsy, though. I mean, aren't these things supposed to have a theme?"

"But that is a theme," she protested. "Peace, love, harmony. All those things."

"I suppose." He appeared unconvinced. "How about something nautical? Maybe a sailboat, considering we're planning to marry near the water."

"You don't think that's, I don't know, cliché?"

"How should I know?" He laughed. "Listen, this is crazy. We don't even have a date yet—or a place. Why don't we just agree on the color and typeface for now?"

"Deal," Riley had said, relieved to have that much decided.

"No peace sign," Hannah says now when Riley fills her in. "Definitely not." She helps Riley step into a dress with reams of tulle, like an inverted flowerpot. For the moment, they've eluded the saleswoman and have hidden themselves away in the last fitting room at the back. "Trust me. You don't want to make a statement on your wedding invitation. Keep it simple." Three years ago, Hannah and her boyfriend had married in a small Unitarian church, followed by a reception at the Sheraton Hotel in Norwood.

This is another reason Hannah is Riley's best friend: she always tells her the truth. "Now, spin," Hannah instructs.

When Riley turns around to gaze at herself in the mirror, she groans. "Ugh. This is exactly what I was afraid of. I look like a mushroom."

"You were afraid of looking like a mushroom?" Hannah

asks, her head tilted while she considers the dress. But then she nods. "You're right. It's not for you. There's something a Little Miss Muffet about it." Riley laughs.

The next gown, an A-line with a satin bodice, a sweet-heart neck and a lace train, is an improvement. "Not bad," Hannah says while Riley does a twirl.

"It's better than the last one, that's for sure. A little snug. Might have to go up a size. How much?"

Hannah fishes out the price tag, which is wedged between Riley's skin and the back zipper. "Seven hundred and fifty."

"Also not terrible."

"So a possibility?" When Riley nods yes, Hannah fishes out the notepad from her backpack and writes down the dressmaker's name and the style. "See, now we're getting somewhere."

"Ladies, how's it going?" Riley shoots Hannah a panicked look. Despite their best efforts to lose her, it appears the sales-clerk has found them in their fitting room.

"Oh, fine," Hannah calls out. "We're good."

"Need any different sizes that I can get for you?"

"Nope, all set," Hannah says spritely. "Thanks again." But Riley is bent over, gripping her sides and trying to suppress the laughter that's bubbling up inside her. The poor salesclerk is only trying to be helpful—she understands this—and even Riley can't say exactly why she finds this whole exchange so funny. But there's something about the day, the fact that her dress-shopping has turned into a cat-and-mouse game with the salesclerk that makes her laugh.

"What is so funny?" Hannah loud-whispers after she peeks around the curtain to check that the clerk has gone.

Riley can't begin to explain it to her, though, and she slides down the wall, still wrapped in the satin dress. "I don't know," she says and giggles. "Leave it to us to turn wedding-dress shopping into a hide-and-seek game with the salesclerk. It just seems wrong somehow, doesn't it? I mean, clearly I'm not invested in this process as much as I should be. I should *want* her help."

"Why? So she can dress you in a fancy gown that's totally not you? Nonsense. I'm your best friend. I have your best interests at heart." Hannah flops down beside her.

Riley sighs. "What would I do without you?"

"You'd be a disaster," Hannah says simply and pats Riley's head. Then she says, "Hey, Riles, I'm sorry it's me dress-shopping with you and not your mom. She would have loved to be here, you know."

Riley picks at her cuticles, which are in worse shape than her eyebrows. "I know she would." She's been careful not to let her mind wander to that dark, difficult place. "But she also would have made me try on at least a dozen dresses. So there's that."

"Good point," says Hannah. "You'll have a much more efficient shopping experience with me."

"Yup. That's why I chose you." Riley leans over to hug her friend, but when she does so, the sound of the zipper popping open at the back makes her instantly straighten. "Oh, no!" she gasps, her fingers fumbling for the broken clasp.

Hannah's eyes go wide after she peeks at the damage. "Well," she says, stifling a laugh. "I guess it's decided, then. You're buying this one!" And the laughter Riley has been trying to swallow bursts out, a wonderful, crazy river gushing forth. Because she realizes that whatever happens, whatever dress, ceremony, invitation or cake she ends up with, it will all be fine. Better than fine. Because she has Tom, not to mention the best friend in the world a girl could ask for.

ELEVEN

Claire sits on the Seafarer's wraparound porch while enjoying a Madras cocktail and people-watching. It's been a pretty taxing Wednesday, she thinks with amusement, having moved from napping by the pool to now drinking on the porch. After the young girl finally jumped into the shallow end (and Claire had applauded her courage), Claire had dozed off for a good hour or two. Now behind her wide-rimmed Jackie O sunglasses, her eyes are peeled for anyone famous.

Last night after dinner she'd paused to study the photos lining the hallway leading into the hotel restaurant. Almost all of them autographed. There was Winston Churchill and Calvin Coolidge, Robert Redford and Judy Garland. Gabriel García Márquez and Ernest Hemingway. Audrey Hepburn and Shirley Chisholm and Lorraine Hansberry. Remarkable, really. Claire wouldn't mind spotting Mia Farrow or maybe Dustin Hoffman at the famed Seafarer cocktail hour today.

She'd like to ask Dustin what it was like working with Meryl Streep in *Kramer vs. Kramer*, one of her all-time favorite films. Or how difficult it was to transform himself into a matronly woman every day on the set of *Tootsie*, another favorite. She bets they'd have a fascinating conversation. And rumor has it that later in the week, the daughter of a Boston Brahmin will be hosting her wedding reception here.

The fact that she's seen no one famous, though, won't detract from Claire's pleasure. She sighs contentedly and gazes out on the side lawn where various croquet matches are taking place. There's the cute couple she met this morning on the elevator. The fellow has his arms wrapped around his girlfriend while he tries to show her how to shoot her red ball through the wicket. The young woman, her long blond hair hanging down past her shoulders, is even prettier than Claire remembers. She throws her head back and laughs when the red ball goes sailing right past the wicket. "Let's go back to playing tennis!" she shouts playfully. The whole exchange makes Claire think fondly of those first years with Walt, when they'd been in so in love, every outing an opportunity to flirt, to have fun. When it seemed that the whole world was ripe with possibility. Yes, she's quite sure that once, a long time ago, she and Walt were a lot like this couple.

She doesn't want to spoil it for them, but she does have half a mind to march over and warn them. That things won't always be this easy. That life is difficult, and even if you think you've done everything right—lived by your moral compass, loved deeply—the world doesn't owe you a thing. So beware.

But what is she? A total killjoy?

She scolds herself for being petty. If she's not careful, she'll turn into one of those old biddies who give out unsolicited advice, *that woman* whom people try to avoid at the grocery store. All she needs is a pair of sensible sneakers and a sun hat with a wide brim to complete the stereotype. But no, tonight she's dressed in a very pleasant-looking blue linen skirt and a white blouse that she hopes will signal to strangers that she's sophisticated enough for engaging conversation. After the pool, she'd headed up to her room to shower and change, in the event that she *did* happen to bump into someone famous at the cocktail hour, say, Michelle Obama. Because if they ever got around to talking, Claire is confident that she and Michelle would become instant best friends.

So far, though, she's only seen couples—everyone annoyingly paired off, who shoot her kind looks and say hello but quickly move on to the next chair, never mind that there are two empty seats right beside her. When a waiter stops to offer her tomato and mozzarella on a skewer, she helps herself to two and places them on the elegant white plate handed to her. There are worse things in life, she reasons, than enjoying a cocktail and hors d'oeuvres on the porch, even if it's by herself.

For a moment, she considers calling Marty—she has his number now, clocked on her cell—just to see if he might want to hop over to the Seafarer, join her for a quick drink. But then she thinks better of it. There's a reason he suggested tomorrow for dinner, not tonight. He's probably busy.

She watches while a Mercedes, a Porsche and then a bright yellow Lamborghini pull up to the hotel. She's no car expert, but she recognizes money when she sees it. This is clearly the place where the well-to-do come to summer. Other guests wander about in their Vineyard Vines polo shirts and shorts, their sockless loafers. The women—tanned, Botoxed and predominantly blonde—all look twenty years younger than the men. They also all appear to be carrying either an Hermès or a Louis Vuitton handbag. Claire gives her wicker summer purse a swift kick under her chair, out of sight. No need to highlight the fact that she's alone—*and* middle-class.

She's never understood some people's need to be show-offy about money. She and Walt always had enough to live the lives they wanted, and frankly, she couldn't imagine why anyone would need more. It seemed people were always divorcing over money or getting into even worse trouble. That the two of them had been able to buy a house, put the kids through college and take the odd vacation had always seemed plenty. Plus, there was something unseemly about being a rich journalist, as if your sources couldn't be trusted. Claire had always taken a certain pride in the fact that her family was solidly middle-class.

But this young couple in front of her, whacking croquet balls, doesn't want to hear her theories about how they'd be better off if they didn't spend their lives chasing money. Or her theories on relationships, or marriage, for that matter. They don't want to hear about how quickly marriages can take a turn for the worse. Besides, she barely knows them! No, she'd best keep her opinions to herself.

She drains the rest of her drink, retrieves her purse and asks the concierge to call her a cab. Because Claire has plans for this evening, including a trip to the Museum of Fine Arts. She's looking forward to wandering among the Monets and the Renoirs, getting lost in the winding halls of all that artistic grandeur. And so, when she slides into the cab and her driver asks if she's waiting on someone else, she refuses to let his question discourage her. Instead, she tells him sharply, "No, just traveling for one this evening. Thank you very much."

TWELVE

On the evening of the 9th, Jean-Paul returns home to discover Marie pacing the floor with a crying, inconsolable Isabella. He sets his briefcase down by the door and goes to take the baby from her. "Do you think she might be coming down with something?" His palm rests on Isabella's crinkled forehead. It's cool to the touch.

Marie glowers at him, deliberating over each word when she says, "No. This is how she gets every day from five to seven." It's five fifteen (he has raced home), which means he has arrived for the baby's witching hour. And perhaps, it occurs to him, his wife's, as well.

"When did she last eat?"

"About fifteen minutes ago. What? You think I'm not feeding her? I'm telling you, she's a colicky, petulant baby. Wait until she's a teenager. We're doomed." Jean-Paul takes a moment to study his wife. Bags hang like tender bruises beneath her eyes, and her dark hair is pulled up in an angry, messy ponytail.

He sighs and strides around the living room, bouncing the baby in his arms, while Marie flops down on the brown leather couch. Already one of the armrests bears the imprint of the Baby Boppy, where Marie feeds Isabella every night. Beyond the brownstone's casement windows, he can glimpse the edge of the water, the harbor shimmering in the distance. Their street is one of a handful in the neighborhood recently landscaped with young saplings, and the new swath of green reminds him of a giant caterpillar inching down the block. That Boston is a melting pot of city and nature, parks and harbors, bustle and serenity conjures up his beloved Paris. But as much as he misses the view of the Seine from their old apartment, the view out their new window easily rivals it.

In his arms, the baby has quieted, her eyes, edged with thick dark lashes, mercifully closed. Soft breaths escape from her delicate lips, and Jean-Paul pads over to his wife to give her a glimpse of a serene, sleeping Isabella.

"Peace," Marie says. "Finally." And then, "She really is a sweet baby when she's asleep."

And Jean-Paul smiles because it's a glimpse of the Marie he remembers from the hospital—a mother besotted by her child—and an idea seizes him. "Let's go out," he announces.

Her eyes narrow. "Now? Are you crazy? We should put her down in her crib. And where would we go, anyway?"

He thinks for a second. "The Museum. The MFA. You're always talking about it, and I haven't been yet. I overheard Oliver telling a guest that it's open late tonight, till seven or eight, I think. We still have plenty of time. We can plop Isabella in a stroller, and she can sleep while you show me your favorite paintings."

His wife regards him for a moment as if he's lost his mind,

and then slowly her face begins to brighten. "Give me five minutes to put on some makeup and comb my hair."

Before long, they're stepping into the Art of the Americas wing at the MFA. The museum is surprisingly crowded for a Wednesday night, but Marie steers them expertly through the lines until they come to a painting entitled *The Daughters of Edward Darley Boit*, by John Singer Sargent.

"Isn't it beautiful?" she says. "I spent half an hour looking at it when I was here last time." Four young girls, dressed in their white pinafores, stare back at them from the dark foyer of the painting. On either side, two unusually large white-and-blue ceramic vases tower over the girls.

Jean-Paul studies the painting for a moment. "It has an Alice in Wonderland feel to it, doesn't it, where the two older girls are hiding behind the enormous vase? As if everything is out of proportion."

Marie tilts her head, considering. "I'd never thought of it that way, but you're right. I spent most of my time trying to figure out if the girls were happy. Their expressions are so cryptic, don't you think? I think they look almost sad."

Below the painting is a plaque, which explains that the Boits were friends of Sargent's and that Edward Boit, a former lawyer turned painter, hailed from Boston before moving his family to Paris. "Apparently the Boits were quite well-off," says Jean-Paul.

"Well, I should think so. Look at the size of those vases!" Isabella fusses in her stroller for a brief moment, and Marie bends down to tuck a yellow blanket more firmly around her bare feet. "Do you suppose our daughter will sit for a portrait like this one day?" she asks when she straightens.

"Maybe," Jean-Paul says. "But it will have to be while

she's sleeping," he says, which elicits a wonderful laugh from his wife.

It feels like forever since they've done something like this, the two of them wandering the halls of a museum and discussing art, talking about something other than Isabella's feeding schedule or bowel movements. In Paris, they'd go to the theater midweek (!), and on Saturdays they'd spend leisurely afternoons strolling through the Louvre followed by a romantic dinner along the Seine. Perhaps these are the things, he reasons, that weigh on Marie most heavily. Not Isabella's crying fits, but the fact that their old way of life has fallen away so suddenly, so completely. And although his work at the Seafarer keeps him tethered to the real world, Marie has only the baby and the narrow four walls of their brownstone. The claustrophobia of what her days must feel like hits him in a way it hasn't before.

He remembers one Friday back in Paris when he'd taken the afternoon off from work and they'd gone to Shakespeare and Company, the bookstore made famous by American expatriates like Ernest Hemingway and Gertrude Stein. As soon as they stepped inside the iconic shop, the intoxicating scent of pastry intermingling with that of dusty, antiquated books greeted them. (As a result, this is how Jean-Paul expects all bookstores to smell now and is disappointed when they don't.) He and Marie had spent a few idle hours there, combing through the bookshelves, comparing various editions, enjoying a cappuccino. At one point, she'd rested her head against his shoulder while she read from *Madame Bovary*. The memory of this tender moment surprises him. He can't recall the last time his wife has laid her head on his shoulder to read.

Afterwards, they'd stumbled out into the rose-lit evening, the whole night ahead of them. Marie twisted his arm to go into a chocolate shop, where they'd bought up an entire row of dark-chocolate turtles, the cashews protruding like miniature feet at the bottoms. And then she'd dragged him into a lingerie shop, the thought of which, even now, sends bright color racing to his cheeks. There had been other men lolling about the store—so it wasn't as if Jean-Paul stood out completely—but he kept casting sideways glances at the coquettish salesclerks who, he was quite certain, looked on with amusement while Marie held up various scanty panties, a pair of garters, a bra that appeared to be made only of silver chains. She'd purchased several undergarments, none of which, Jean-Paul thinks, he can recall seeing recently.

"This is nice," he says now. "Spending time with you outside of the house."

"Yes."

"It's been a while, hasn't it?"

"Yes."

"Sometimes I miss spending time together, just the two of us." And as soon as the words escape from his mouth, he regrets them. Because what kind of father admits that he wishes he could spend time without his daughter around?

Marie surprises him, though, when she grabs his hand and says, "Oh, me, too. You've no idea."

Maybe, he reasons, they should choose one night a week for a date night, a time that they could both look forward to. Surely someone at the hotel could recommend a babysitter. Would a few date nights be enough to get them back to where they were, though? Because that's what Jean-Paul misses the most, their life as it was, but with Isabella neatly tucked into it. The flirtatious exchanges, the lazy Sunday afternoons reading the paper, making love on a weeknight just because they felt like it, going out to dinner on a Tuesday because Marie had read a review in the paper about a fantastic new restaurant. Talking about the books they'd read (Jean-Paul can't even remember the title of the last book he read!). Their lives used to be overflowing with culture, with intimacy. And now there's hardly any. By the time he arrives home from work, they're both too exhausted to do anything but eat dinner, feed Isabella and crawl into bed.

He's been thinking of this year as a year to be gotten through—until the renovated hotel is up and running at full speed, until the baby gets through her colicky stage. Life, he tells himself, will improve. But meanwhile, he's left Marie to deal with the here and now, to help them over to the other side. And it feels as if she's mentally keeping track of all the time she tends to the baby while he's at the hotel, like she might be tallying up her total hours and will one day hand him a bill.

They've arrived at another painting, *Le Verre de Porto*, where a melancholy woman, cradling an aperitif, stares out at them, while her husband, his back turned, enjoys a smoke. When did he and Marie start to keep score? he wonders. When did they forget to go searching for those pockets of joy hidden in their daily lives? The trips to the bookstores and museums and chocolate shops that were so readily available to them in Paris? And are also available to them here in Boston. Somewhere along the way, probably with sweet Isabella's birth, they've let those moments fall by the wayside so that lately their marriage feels more like a competition, a game of scorekeeping. *Only when someone grows afraid of being left behind. That's when the scorekeeping begins.* The answer comes to him unbidden, as if the woman in the painting has spoken directly to him.

He spins away and lifts Marie's hand to his lips. "Let's do this more often."

And Marie, his lovely, smart wife, turns to him, a smile

playing across her lips, and says, "Yes, all right. Good idea. How about every day, then?"

Before he can respond, she leads him to a Mary Cassatt painting of small children playing in the sand. Maybe, he thinks, he can persuade her to throw away the scorecard, to get back to the way they used to be. He'd almost forgotten their outings together, how much he enjoyed them. And he feels a stab of guilt that he hasn't thought sooner to grab his wife by the hand to go exploring their new city together. That's what they need to do to get their lives back on an even keel, he thinks. More exploring. More pockets of joy. And preferably, as soon as possible.

In the Old Masters wing, Claire peers at a dark, somber painting by Rembrandt. It's part of a study on the Dutch Golden Era, as the free leaflet informs her, and she pauses to read the label: *Artist in His Studio*. So, it's a self-portrait, then, but Rembrandt looks surprisingly unassuming, a wee little man dressed in tattered clothes, his brown hat tipped at an angle. Claire imagines that if she were to paint a self-portrait, she'd err on the side of embellishment, not modesty, as Rembrandt seems to have done. He really isn't much to look at, even though she understands that's not the point.

On the museum map that she consults, the Impressionist wing (her favorite) appears to be located farther down on the second level, and Claire goes in search of it, bypassing the Caravaggios (overly dark and religious) and the Bruegels (slightly more cheerful town scenes). Outside the Rubens room, she pauses for a moment, taking in the huge canvases bathed in dark scarlets, rich tans and creamy browns. In one, a baby's hands are so exquisitely rendered that Claire is inclined to reach in and touch it, imagining the pudgy fingers entwining with hers. How marvelous, she thinks, that a few brushstrokes can add up to create an image so realistic, so three-dimensional. (Although, to be honest, she could do without quite so many naked women frolicking about in Rubens's paintings.)

Walking among all this extraordinary art makes her think that she's missed out on what could have been a dynamite piece about the MFA for the paper. Of course, Providence has its own museums to tout—the RISD Museum, the Children's Museum, the John Brown House Museum and the Museum of Natural History, to name a few. They'd run articles on all of them. But it wouldn't have killed the *Providence Dealer* to expand its reach a little, highlight this mecca of art that's less than an hour away. And now, when it seems the paper might not even welcome her back, it's unlikely she'll get a chance to pitch the idea at another editorial meeting.

When Claire finally reaches the Impressionist wing, she drops down on the uncomfortable wooden bench in front of the foyer to catch her breath and gather her thoughts. A moment to be honest with herself. Because, really, isn't that the other reason why she's here in Boston? Not only to find Marty but also to escape? *To take a little break*, as her boss Julian suggested.

So she'd flubbed a story. But one botched article in thirty-some years wasn't so terrible, was it? Granted, it was a big story, maybe her biggest yet, alleging that a Providence politician (and alleged mob boss) was dipping into taxpayers' money for personal gain, but Claire had made certain that every statement was impeccably sourced. Artie McKinnon's assistant, the woman who shared unlimited access to his emails and accounts, had turned on him, and Claire had given her word that she'd be protected.

But now McKinnon, of all people, was threatening a lawsuit against the paper, claiming defamation of character, and

Claire's boss had recommended that she take a temporary leave of absence while, as he said, "the brass figured things out." Which Claire had interpreted to mean *Take a long vacation until we can turn this into your early retirement.* Ordinarily, she'd protest, fight like hell to stand up to Artie McKinnon and his goons, but even Julian had seemed spooked. "He's at the top of the mob chain, Claire. We don't like to mess with guys like that." And Claire had thought *Well, it's a hell of a time to tell me that now, don't you think?* Without so much as a murmur of disapproval, Julian had signed off on the original idea for the article. Now, when things had gotten uncomfortable, he'd run off like a hound dog, his tail between his legs.

Maybe, she allows, Julian is truly concerned for her well-being. It's possible. Her own children, after all, have bought into the conspiracy theory, worried that she's gotten herself—and by extension, the rest of the family—into a pot of trouble by pointing her finger at the mob. Last time she spoke with her daughter, Amber had sounded positively ready to sign her up for the Witness Protection Program! But isn't this why Claire became a journalist in the first place? Why anyone becomes a journalist? To keep public officials honest and accountable? Artie McKinnon had been flexing his predatory muscle around Providence for years. It was only a matter of time before someone called him on it.

But for all their trailblazing bravado, the paper had retracted the article last Friday, offering a formal apology. Claire assumed it would be more than enough to call off McKinnon's goons. She knows her kids still worry, though. How many times does she have to remind them that she's a sixty-one-year-old woman who sometimes forgets where she left her glasses or her coffee mug? How much harm can she do?

Of course, there's the lamentable matter of a few messy

facts—that's the most unsettling part. She'd promised herself that if she ever lost her edge in the business, she'd cut out, shut down her byline. Her reputation for almost three decades has been unimpeachable. But when she'd been putting the final touches on the McKinnon article late at night, she'd found herself unable to reconcile a few contradictory items. In one paragraph, she'd written that McKinnon had swindled a dry-cleaning business out of $2,300,000; in the next it was $230,000—an alarming discrepancy. Which was it? To eliminate the figure entirely would unravel too many other allegations in the article. Claire had gone back to check her notes, scrambling for clarification, and had suddenly found herself spiraling down a rabbit hole of panic. The feeling wasn't unfamiliar exactly—it had happened a few times before—and she rested her head on the table, waiting for the spell to pass.

But when she resurfaced—a few minutes later? a half hour?—any recollection of what had upset her in the first place was gone. *Poof!* Sometimes the anxiety had this effect, swept her away on such a colossal wave that nothing remained when she resurfaced. A momentary blackout, a brain freeze, her mind empty. When she got up to get some water, the office was eerily dark, only the blue blink of screen savers lighting the path to the watercooler. Back at her desk, she'd felt an indescribable chill—because nothing was coming back to her. Piles of papers stared up at her from her desk. She searched her computer screen, her notes, anything to jog her memory.

Gradually, it dawned on her that she was staring at the McKinnon file, still open on her screen. She'd yet to send it! She quickly closed out of the document, hit Send, and off it went with only minutes to spare till press time.

Only later, when the piece ran the next day, did the inconsistencies and contradictions swim to the surface again. There was the money discrepancy, two different names referring to the same person (an alias, but still)—and who knew what else. Fear slid over her while she read. *This is bad.*

"Excuse me, ma'am, but are you all right?" Claire startles. The museum guard, an older man with a mop of gray hair and watery blue eyes, studies her, as if perhaps she's lost. She glances over at Monet's *Water Lilies* series. How long has she been sitting here?

"Oh, yes, I'm fine. Sorry, I just needed a minute to rest."

"No problem." The guard waits a moment. "Can I help you up?"

"No, no. That won't be necessary. Thank you, though." She nearly leaps to her feet. It's one thing to call her ma'am, quite another to help her up. She's not *that* old. "The Monets are lovely, aren't they?" She hopes she sounds semi-knowledgeable, not someone deserving of his pity, and she sets off determinedly for Renoir's *A Girl with a Watering Can*, another favorite.

In another wing, Modern Art, Jason grips Gwen's hand tightly. They've been here for over an hour, which by his count is an hour too long. But after their tennis match earlier this morning, Gwen insisted on going to the MFA. "Winner gets to choose what we do for the rest of the afternoon." This had included snatching an autograph from Ray Romano (who'd turned out to be a genuinely nice guy), lounging by the pool, playing croquet, and then visiting the museum in the evening. (The concierge at the hotel had tipped Gwen off that on Wednesdays the MFA stayed open late.) Jason would have been perfectly content hanging by the pool and watching his girlfriend slather sunblock on her legs, but she'd insisted on getting a taste of culture while in

Boston. "C'mon, it'll be fun," she'd said. "Take your mind off whatever's bothering you."

"Nothing's bothering me," he said.

"Yeah, right. Which is why you keep checking your phone."

"Mea culpa." (Jason still hasn't called his department head back. Why ruin his vacation completely? He can't delay it forever, though. He'll need to get his side of the story out there before Charlie tries to bully the university into giving him a decent, completely undeserved grade.)

So, he and Gwen had hightailed it over to the museum in an Uber, their driver nearly colliding with a Green Line train that ran on its own track with its own set of stoplights. There was, Jason thought, something unnerving about seeing subway cars out in the daylight, like trying to play dodgeball in a pinball machine. Too many moving parts. College kids, dressed in shorts and Boston University T-shirts, flocked the sidewalks. Their driver explained that a lot of students stuck around during the summertime. It was so unlike their small New Hampshire campus, where the inside joke was that the college was an island unto itself—once you were in, there was no way out. But they'd made it safely to the museum, and ever since, he's been counting down the minutes till they can leave and grab dinner. He'd spotted an Uno Pizzeria not too far away, a couple of bars that seemed like good options.

Jason's hands are stuffed deep inside his jeans pockets, and the sunburn on the back of his neck is beginning to throb. Something about museums always makes him twitchy. It's the same feeling he used to get as a young boy whenever he visited his grandmother in the nursing home. The smells aren't comparable (thankfully no urine or disinfectant here), but the sense of being surrounded by relics from the past makes him antsy. The irony isn't lost on him—a historian who doesn't care for museums—but nevertheless, the place makes him feel weirdly depressed, like everyone, no matter how famous, is going to die anyway, so why bother? If he were to share this view with Gwen, though, she'd say that's precisely why everything matters: because art survives life. But he doesn't feel like getting into a tautological argument right now, so he keeps his mouth shut.

At the moment, she's leading him by the hand toward a life-size bronze sculpture. "Cool, right?" she asks, and Jason offers a lackluster nod.

He thinks it looks like a couple of naked women hugging. When he reads the card, though, it says *Two Fish Jumping*. He laughs, shakes his head. "Sorry, I don't see it."

"I think you're supposed to be open to the possibility," she counters, "even if they don't *literally* resemble fish."

"But that's just it. Why make a sculpture of two fish if they don't look remotely like fish?" He doesn't mean to be difficult. Or, maybe he does.

In another room, there's a papier-mâché sculpture that reminds him of a bag of McDonald's french fries, but he knows better than to say so. The label identifies it as *Purse of Sorrows*. His eyebrows flicker upward, but Gwen ignores him. "Moving on," she announces without further comment.

Somewhere around the Andy Warhol paintings, Jason's attention swerves toward two guys talking near an enormous sculpture of a dog fashioned out of metal slats. They've spied Gwen on the other side of the room but haven't yet connected her with him. He watches while the taller one, dressed in jeans, a T-shirt and bright blue Nike sneakers, nudges his buddy and says something under his breath. Slowly, the guy inches his way toward her. She's studying Warhol's painting *Red Disaster* when the guy makes his move.

"You like it?" he asks, and Jason watches her back stiffen.

His girlfriend is distinctly attractive, and unsolicited attacks are par for the course. But Jason's typically not within viewing distance when they happen. Usually he hears about them after the fact.

"Yeah." She turns her back on the guy and quickly moves on to a painting of a double helix exploding. Jason leaves his corner. He can't get to her side fast enough, but when he does, he inserts himself in the narrow space between Gwen and the other dude.

"Hey, babe." He moves toward her, wrapping a possessive arm around her waist. Now that Jason's within striking distance, he sees the guy is younger than he'd originally assumed, probably midtwenties, with slicked-back dark hair and bright blue eyes. Jason bets his hands are soft like a baby's.

"Hey, man, sorry. I didn't know she was with you." Blue Eyes's hands are raised, palms open, apologetic.

Jason pretends to play it off. "No worries. I mean, how would you know, right?"

Blue Eyes nods, as if he's relieved they've reached a gentleman's agreement, as if Gwen is a piece of property to be bargained over.

"Jason, it's fine," she whispers, her hand clasping his, perhaps sensing his growing anger through the tight press of his fingers. "He was just asking about the painting."

"Mm-huh."

The next several seconds happen so quickly that even Jason's not sure he could recount them precisely. But when Blue Eyes's buddy approaches, Jason could swear he hears him whisper to his friend, "Bitch is already taken." It's a word that instantly triggers memories of his father shouting at his mom, and it's as if a switch that he wasn't even aware existed inside of him goes off.

He finds himself letting go of Gwen's waist, taking a lunge

toward Blue Eyes and swinging at his face. His fist collides with the bridge of the guy's hooked nose, as if in slow motion, and releases a sickening, cracking sound.

"Dude! What the fuck?" the friend shouts, dropping to his knees to see if his buddy, who's now moaning on the floor and cupping his bloody nose, is all right.

"Jason!" Gwen yells and tries to yank him away. "Stop it! What are you doing?" The rage in him is so fierce, so intense that it's all he can do to restrain himself from kicking Blue Eyes in the stomach. But his buddy quickly forms a body shield in front of him. When Gwen yells "Stop it!" a second time, Jason is swept back to his mother's screams, her voice ringing in his ears. *Stop it! Stop hitting him! He's only a kid! You're hurting him.* There are his father's punches landing on his stomach again, his body curled into a protective ball on the living-room couch.

He stumbles backward, unsure of what's just happened here. His right hand is bloody, the knuckles scratched up. In an effort to make sure nothing's broken, he tries to straighten his fingers, his thumb. A small group of people has gathered at the edge of the room, where someone is calling for a guard. And then, for the police.

"Jason, come on," Gwen urges, her eyes wide with fear, her little purple purse with tassels jingling against her waist. "Let's get out of here." He shakes his head, as if to dispel the reality of what's occurred, and follows her through an exit opposite the gathering crowd. They hurry down the stairs and out the museum's front doors.

In the taxicab's back seat, she turns to him, breathing hard. Red blotches bloom on her face and her neck. "What the hell was that all about?" There's a faint line of perspiration above her upper lip, and she's pushing her rings up and down her fingers, her tell-tale sign of distress. Seeing this sends an immediate pulse of regret through him. Defending Gwen has only served to frighten her further.

It's not the first time he's had no answer for her. "I don't know," he says and shakes his head, staring out the window. He understands he should try to reassure her, tell her everything's all right. But is it? His bloodied hand is wrapped in the hem of his shirt. The sound of the guy's nose cracking echoes in his ears. What on earth was he thinking? Whatever happened back there, he knows he's going to have to find the words sooner or later to explain it to Gwen.

Or else risk losing her forever.

Friday, June 11, 2021

THIRTEEN

Jean-Paul likes the mornings the best, when the hotel is quiet and the day still ripe with possibility. Before the hotel wakes up. He'll walk the property, check the lobby, stroll through the public spaces, rearrange the chairs on the porch and say good-morning to the staff, who are readying themselves for the onslaught of summertime guests—those out-of-towners who arrive to partake of the city's shows and restaurants and general swagger, hoping perhaps that some of the ephemeral glitter might rub off on them. That this exquisite building falls under his watch and key still amazes him. Every day it seems he discovers something new. A particular painting he's never noticed before. Crown moldings on the ceiling of the men's bathroom. A sketch of the Boston skyline that has been hiding in the pantry for who knows how long. The way the colors of the harbor appear to morph into different shades of blue throughout the day.

Sometimes he'll stand in the oak hallway leading to the dining room—known affectionately among the staff as the Walk of Fame—and study the photos of the New England greats who've stayed here. Pictures of E. B. White in a rocking chair on the porch. An autographed photo of Mick Jagger, picking at the guitar. Prince Rainier III of Monaco and Red Sox superstar Ted Williams. Elizabeth Taylor, floating down the ornate staircase, and Lauren Hutton, beaming her impishly gap-toothed smile. Rumor has it that the poet Robert Lowell once checked in for a week while working to meet a deadline, and his portrait hangs alongside authors like Louisa May Alcott, Oliver James, Emily Dickinson and John Updike. That Jean-Paul gets to be the steward of a place so steeped in history both awes and slightly terrifies him.

Around seven thirty, guests will typically start to filter down for breakfast. At eight o'clock, he'll call his brief, stand-up meeting with the staff outside the lobby, where he receives updates from his director of Housekeeping, the director of Food and Beverage and the director of the Front Office. They fill him in on what happened overnight and what to expect for the day. Were there any incidents at the bar last night? Are any VIPs checking in today? What's the number of arrivals and departures forecasted for the day? Because even though Jean-Paul can't be on the premises 24/7, the hotel, like a hospital, never sleeps.

What started out as a fairly normal Friday morning, however, has turned out to be anything but a typical day. More like a catastrophe. A full-blown disaster. He checks his watch. One thirty-five. So far, he has dealt with the immediate crisis: the paramedics have come and removed the body from the premises. The directly affected area has been cordoned off, and a small tent has been erected to hide the blood splotches from view. The police remain on-site to question anyone who might have been a witness. He has exchanged a few cursory words with their PR company and hosted an ad hoc staff meeting, passing along the warning that no one, under any circumstances, is allowed to speak to the press, which is sure to be descending like a kettle of vultures any minute. A fair amount has been accomplished, but mountains of work remain.

At the top of his list is a task he's especially dreading but that can't be postponed any longer: a call to Gerald Manley. Gerald is the patriarch of the Manley family and the owner proper of the Seafarer.

It's Jean-Paul's duty to alert him to the so-called situation. He imagines Mr. Manley lounging innocently by his pool this morning, maybe checking on a trade with his stockbroker while he basks in the Florida sunshine. Later, he'll head to the park to play pinochle with his pals. Jean-Paul knows this routine because once, before Isabella was born, he and Marie were invited to spend a weekend at Mr. Manley's mansion in Naples, Florida—a sunny yellow stucco with turrets on either side that sits maybe fifty yards back from the beach. And although Mr. Manley's wife has been dead for maybe ten years, it hadn't prevented him from hosting attractive young women who circled his pool at all hours of the day. Marie had joked it was a little like stumbling onto the Playboy Mansion.

So, no, interrupting Mr. Manley's pleasant day is not high on the list of items Jean-Paul would like to do. But it's his job.

When he calls, Manley answers as if in midsentence. "Yeah, hello? Jean-Paul?"

"Hello, sir. Yes, it's me, Jean-Paul." He knows that his name is included in Mr. Manley's Favorites list on his phone, should Jean-Paul need to reach him at any time, night or day. Likewise, Jean-Paul has Mr. Manley on speed dial.

"Well, what is it, son?" That Mr. Manley speaks to him as if he's part of the family (which includes two sons and one daughter) makes Jean-Paul feel proud, but he also can't help but detect a hint of condescension in this particular nomenclature. Mr. Manley is seventy-two to Jean-Paul's thirty-nine. If nothing else, the man gets straight to the point.

Jean-Paul manages a deep breath before launching in. "Well, forgive me, sir, for bothering you—"

"Nonsense," he interrupts. "No bother at all. I'm paying you to run my hotel, aren't I? I expect you to call me. Now what is it?"

He begins again. "Well, sir, I'm afraid there's been an incident at the hotel this afternoon."

"What sort of incident?"

"An unfortunate one."

"Well, hell," Manley says. "What happened now? Somebody croak by the pool?"

His boss's cavalier attitude catches Jean-Paul by surprise. Maybe this won't be such a big deal after all. "Um, no, sir. Not exactly. But a woman did fall—or maybe jump—from her balcony." He hurries to get the last sentence out and waits for Manley's reaction. Silence.

"Sorry. Say that again?"

Jean-Paul repeats his news.

"Well, I'll be damned. That's a new one. No fault of ours, though, I hope?"

"I wouldn't think so, sir. Although, that's for the police to decide, of course. At the moment, they're combing rooms, trying to figure out where she jumped from."

"Well, that's silly. Weren't there any witnesses?"

"Yes, but unfortunately, only on the ground as far as we know. She, um, landed right outside the dining room on the terrace, near the firepit and hot tub."

A sigh. "Well, that's damned unfortunate. What a mess." Jean-Paul can almost see Mr. Manley shaking his head while he sips his mimosa. "Any idea who it is?"

"Not yet, sir. We've narrowed it down to a couple of floors, though."

He sighs into the phone. "Probably a suicide. The world can be a damn depressing place."

Jean-Paul isn't sure how to respond to this comment and waits in an uncomfortable silence for Manley to say more.

"Any press yet?"

"Not yet, but I'm sure they'll be here momentarily."

"You can count on that. They're like a pack of hyenas, scavenging wherever they can get their next meal. Have you spoken to Julie yet?"

"Briefly. She's writing up a statement for release."

"Good, good. Julie's smart. She'll run it by our lawyers. She'll know how to handle this. Do whatever she says. And, Jean-Paul?"

"Yes?"

"Make sure you tell that staff of ours that no one is to speak to the press. Under any circumstances. Or there'll be hell to pay—both for them and us."

"Yes, sir."

"Thanks for ruining my nice day here."

"Sorry, sir. I thought you'd want to know."

He makes a sound like a grunt. "Keep me posted." And the phone goes dead.

When Jean-Paul looks up from his desk, Oliver is poking his head in the doorway. "You said you wanted to know when the TV crews showed up. Well, WBZ-TV is parked outside right now. Get ready, boss."

Jean-Paul feels the blood draining from his face.

"Want a shot of whiskey, a little jolt, before you face the cameras, maybe?" Oliver asks.

What Jean-Paul really wants is to crawl back home and into bed with his wife and child. Managing human tragedy is not his bailiwick. "Thanks, but I'd better not." He scoops the phone off his desk, grabs the printout of Julie's email and heads for the lobby, his heart leaping around in his chest. He'll need to get the police commissioner on board for this press conference before he does anything else.

Because Jean-Paul is damned if he's going to talk to the press alone.

Earlier that week

FOURTEEN

On Thursday, Riley places the last sprays of freesia in the delivery for Mount Auburn Street. One of the store's forty-eight signature bouquets, the *Sunshine* arrangement brims with cheerful yellow daisies. This one, in particular, is for a young woman named Joan, who's celebrating her thirtieth birthday. The flowers are from her parents, which Riley interprets as meaning Joan has no boyfriend. Not that she's judging, because Riley thinks it's sweet whenever parents send their kids flowers. Especially when they send them to their office. It surprises her, though, how often people order flowers for delivery to someone's house, when no one is home to receive them in the first place. Or gawk over them, which is really more than half the point.

Since Smart Stems always tucks the message card discreetly into an envelope, Joan can tell her coworkers whatever she pleases, such as that a secret admirer sent them. The bouquet will also serve to remind her superiors (in the likely event that they've forgotten) that today is Joan's birthday and that they should take her out for lunch or a post-work cocktail. It's the whole reason why Riley got into this business: the power to make people happy, to improve their lives just a touch, even if it's only for one day.

She walks the bouquet over to the front counter so it's waiting for the next delivery run. Smart Stems is located in the off-center of Harvard Square, which isn't really a square at all. More like a wheel, with the spokes of various streets shooting off from it haphazardly. A fixture in Cambridge, the store has been fulfilling the floral needs of its customers since 1953. It's a classic, a throwback, in the best sense of the word. Every arrangement has its own, slightly hokey name. *A Summer's Day. Starry Night. Springtime Song.* Sometimes in the shower Riley will invent new names, ones that carry a whiff of irony—*It's Freesia-n Outside! Glad(iola) You're Okay!* So far none has been adopted.

Her boss, Rick, is an avuncular, gray-haired man with a trim mustache, prone to wearing cardigans even in the summertime. His eyes crinkle upward at the edges, which gives him the look of someone who's always about to smile and which, Riley thinks, is entirely appropriate for someone in the flower business. Oftentimes, he'll recite poetry out loud, a sliver of Wordsworth here, a little John Donne there. Gentle, kind and knowledgeable, Rick has proven a wonderful mentor over the last few years, a sort of stand-in father or uncle. He'll definitely be invited to the wedding.

Across the street is Slices, a popular late-night pizza hangout for students. Whenever Riley closes on Tuesday nights, she watches the college kids file in, a blend of artsy teens, notable for their dyed hair and body piercings, and burly, athletic types. Pizza and sauce are apparently the ultimate unifier, and she thinks someone should tell that to today's politicians. Although only six years have passed since Riley graduated from the University of Wisconsin-Madison, in some ways it feels like decades. These kids aren't worrying about whether to hire a band or a DJ for their wedding, about whether they should limit their invites to a hundred guests (and risk offending distant family members) or invite two hundred people, many of whom are merely far-flung acquaintances. Sometimes she has to stop herself from stepping into Slices just to slip into one of its social circles and eavesdrop. A few sweet minutes of pretending she's back in school, where the most important concerns are tomorrow's exam or Friday's party.

Working in the Square, next to Harvard Yard, makes her job even more enjoyable because there's something appealing about being so close to all that brainpower. In theory, it seems she should be getting smarter through osmosis. Often a professor or a student will wander into the store looking for flowers and strike up a conversation. Usually, they're hopeless when it comes to knowing what they want, but Riley is only too glad to help.

She likes to think of herself as a matchmaker, bringing the right bouquet together with the right customer. Even those shoppers who have a good sense of what they want are often hard-pressed to tell a petunia from a begonia. That's where Riley comes in. "My wife, who's home sick, could use a little pick-me-up," a professor might say, and Riley will hurry to suggest massive pink peonies or a bouquet of cheerful yellow and white tulips. She's forever trying to steer customers away from roses (a popular choice), which, in her opinion, are the world's dullest flowers. Why on earth would anyone choose roses when so many other gorgeous blooms abound—colorful dahlias, lilies, lilacs or snapdragons?

Riley is tidying up the counter, discarding the chopped-off remnants of stems, when the bell on the front door jingles. When she glances up, it's not a customer, but Marilyn, her mother-in-law-to-be, and Riley's sunny mood instantly evaporates. As lovely as she seems, Marilyn is, Riley has learned, the kind of woman who often arrives under false pretenses. It takes a while before the true purpose of her visit reveals itself.

"Riley! So nice to see you," Marilyn says as if she's surprised to find her daughter-in-law here, at Riley's place of work, in the middle of the day. That she says this even though Riley and Tom had dinner at her house last night makes it even stranger. A dinner where Marilyn sprung the news that she'd booked lunch reservations at the Seafarer for this Friday to sample wedding-reception menus. Riley nearly spit out her shrimp scampi, knowing full well that she and Tom could never afford a wedding venue as lavish as the Seafarer. But Marilyn was quick to add, "Hugh and I insist on paying for the reception. Really. You kids should save your money for a house." And maybe for the first time in the entire stretch that she has known Tom's parents, Riley found herself agreeing with the woman.

"Hi, Marilyn," Riley says now with fake cheer. Her mother-in-law strides over and gives her a kiss on both cheeks. "What a nice surprise. What brings you in?"

"Well," Marilyn sets her purse down on the counter and glances around the store before continuing. Riley braces herself for whatever bomb she might be about to drop. "I'm so glad you asked, sweetheart. I was hoping to grab you for a minute, maybe a quick bite to eat?" She pauses when Riley doesn't respond. "But if you're too busy..."

As her voice trails off, Riley scrambles to come up with an excuse. Except for the two of them, the store is painfully empty. "I'm sorry," she says, inventing her story as she talks.

"But I can't step out right now. I'm the only one here." Rick will be back any second; he's around the corner grabbing a coffee. "But we can talk here, can't we?"

Marilyn sighs heavily, as if this is a huge disappointment, but plows ahead nonetheless.

"All right. Well, after dinner last night, Hugh and I got to talking." Riley can only imagine what Marilyn's latest plans are for *her* wedding. Swans parading across the lawn? Acrobats? The Boston Symphony set up on the terrace of the Seafarer? "And we both agreed that Tom seemed awfully quiet. It's not like him. And, well, we were wondering if everything's all right between you two?"

Riley feels her eyes widen in surprise. As if it's not bad enough that Marilyn is trying to orchestrate their wedding day, she now has the audacity to stick her nose where it most definitely does not belong. And to bring it up at Riley's workplace? How dare she!

It's all Riley can do not to send Marilyn on her way, banish her from the store forever. But it's her mother-in-law, she reminds herself. A certain decorum is required. Riley can almost hear her own mother's voice whispering in her ear: *Relax, honey. She means well.* As a matter of fact, Tom and Riley *had* fought before dinner. Over Marilyn! Riley had inquired if Tom thought his mom might be getting a teensy bit overinvested in their wedding day, especially since they'd always intended to keep things simple.

But Tom insisted that his mother was only trying to help, that she was excited, and shouldn't they be happy about that? Riley got it. It was hard to criticize Marilyn's efforts without sounding like an ingrate. Which was why she'd brought up the issue delicately over a glass of merlot before they'd headed to his parents' brownstone on Newbury Street last night.

"I mean, do you think Tom is doing okay?" Marilyn,

never one to intuit facial expressions, asks now. "Maybe all this wedding planning is stressing him out?" If the concern in Marilyn's face weren't so genuine, Riley would howl with laughter. Meredith's precious son has done almost nothing so far in terms of planning. If anything, Tom is doing *perfectly fine* as far as Riley can tell. Aside from looking at wedding invitations, he has shown little interest in the details of their wedding ceremony or reception, which Riley finds vaguely unfair and, at times, verging on sexist.

Marilyn's bright blue eyes, heavily lined in makeup, stare back at her expectantly. Undoubtedly Marilyn was a beauty back in the day and is doing everything she can to ensure that her looks persist well into her sixties. Her dyed chestnut hair is immaculately styled—Riley knows she gets it washed and blown out twice a week at a salon. In private, she and Tom have discussed whether Marilyn might have had a face-lift last summer, since her expression seems to have shifted to one of permanent surprise.

"We're fine, Marilyn," Riley says evenly now, invoking her mother-in-law's first name as she'd been instructed to do the first time they met. Riley hopes her voice carries an edge to it. Not that her mother-in-law would notice. "And so is Tom. Work has been a little busy lately, that's all. Thanks for your concern, though."

Marilyn smiles, then fiddles with the clasp on her purse. Riley momentarily considers the possibility that her mother-in-law might try to pay her off, get her to call off the entire wedding. She's well aware she's nothing like the poster girl Marilyn had in mind for her son. "Well, that's precisely why you two should let me do most of the heavy lifting with this wedding. Now that I'm retired, I have all this spare time on my hands. Whereas you two are already incredibly busy." She gestures to the empty store as if to emphasize her point, but instead it comes off as a pointed rejoinder, the implication being that Riley has next to nothing to do. Why Riley won't handle her bridal duties with the aplomb and dispatch Marilyn would expect from her future daughter-in-law is clearly driving her bananas.

When the doorbell chimes again, Riley spies a regular customer and relief washes over her. "Professor Halston, hello, there! What can I help you with today?"

Marilyn's impeccable brows arch in her forehead before she says quietly, "We'll discuss this later, dear." She winks at Riley, though Riley has no idea what's implied by it. On the way out, Marilyn points to a tub of roses sitting by the door. "By the way, those yellow roses would be divine for your wedding, don't you think?"

Professor Halston waits for the door to close. "A friend of yours?" he inquires.

"Future mother-in-law."

"Ah," he says, his eyes twinkling. "The dynamic relationship between daughters and their mothers-in-law. It's a feud dating back centuries, you know."

Riley grins ruefully. "Why am I not surprised?"

"I could write an entire book about it," he exclaims. "Perhaps I will!"

She lets out a small moan. "Let me know if you need more material. Now," she asks, "what can I help you with?"

Not until after Professor Halston has left the store with a bouquet of gorgeous periwinkle asters does Riley get a chance to text Tom.

Surprise visit from your mom at the store today. She's worried about you. Thinks you're stressed out. Ha!

A few minutes later, her phone pings with a response.

Sorry about that. I'll talk to her.

Riley feels a pinch of satisfaction. At least Tom is taking her side on this one. She hopes Marilyn will listen. Otherwise, the next twelve months are going to be unbearable. As in, she-might-have-to-flee-the-country unbearable.

FIFTEEN

On Thursday morning, the 10th, Claire wakes up with a start and grabs her cell phone from the bedside table. Ten fifteen. A fog envelops her mind, still caught in a dream. She was dreaming about Walt and his spiders. Or at least, that's how she'd come to think of them: Walt's spiders. He'd hated the things, had waged his own private war with an extended family that had taken up residence in their home. Various dusters and sprays were involved. And then, just when they thought the house was rid of them once and for all, the cobwebs swept away, the little guys would reappear, their webs spun in the deep of the night while she and Walt slept. Claire could cohabit amicably enough with spiders (mice were a different story), but Walt couldn't abide them.

When the store traps failed, he'd read up on the problem, learning that jars of peppermint oil left around the house could also serve as traps. Apparently spiders didn't like the smell...or maybe it was the taste. She can't recall exactly. Walt's spiders, however, didn't seem to mind the peppermint oil one bit. Sometimes she'd imagine them at night, backstroking through the bowls of oil scattered about the house, climbing out and dusting themselves off before heading out to cast another web. Undeterred by Walt's latest battle plan.

In the dream, he'd been cursing another gigantic web that had appeared overnight above the fireplace mantel. "The damn things won't leave us alone," he'd said, and Claire had suggested maybe they should think about moving. In real life, he'd sprayed a homemade potion—half vinegar, half water—along the house's perimeter, squirting the floorboards and the corners. (Every so often, when Claire bends down to tie a shoe or dust under the radiators, a whiff of vinegar will still waft over her.) When the vinegar concoction turned out to be a bust, he'd invested in eucalyptus shrubs, yet another supposed spider deterrent, and so now, every evening when she cleans the dishes, her hands soaking in warm, soapy water, Claire gazes out on the line of eucalyptus bushes hemming in the backyard—and thinks of Walt. Sometimes it seems he placed them there not so much to keep the spiders out but to keep her memory of him alive, as if he'd known all along what was coming.

He would have liked the Seafarer, she thinks, and a pinch of loneliness grabs her as she pulls back the curtains to the balcony window. Maybe not the balcony (he'd been deathly afraid of heights) but the ambience of the place, the sense of history. He would have liked that Churchill stayed here, maybe would have enjoyed a glass of scotch at the same bar. He would have loved the cherry bookcases lining the tavern, filled with histories of the Middle East and Africa, an entire shelf of *Peterson Field Guides*.

He would have also been able to adjust the hotel's room

temperature without having to call the front desk every day like Claire has had to do. She goes to fiddle with the thermostat now, but she can't seem to get the air conditioner to kick back on. Walt had been good that way, when it came to the more mechanical, scientific things. One day in January, she'd come home from work complaining that the defroster in her car was broken; she'd had to swipe at the front window constantly on her drive home, the heat cranked. But when she'd explained the problem to Walt, certain she had to bring the car in for maintenance, he'd smiled knowingly. "It's because of the temperature differential," he explained patiently. "The outside temperature is so cold, and you probably had the heat blasting, so all it does is fog the windows. It's better to start out with a cool temperature inside if you want your windows to clear." And Claire remembers thinking how useful it was to have someone around who knew such things, who could explain them to her without making her feel like a complete fool. Despite all his faults, Walt had been good this way.

She gives up on the thermostat and goes to slide open the balcony door. As soon as she steps out, the sea air grabs her, and the bright sun glances off the harbor in shards of light that cause her to squint. She stretches her arms above her head and watches the people down below, who remind her of tiny ants scurrying about. Her body is craving caffeine, but before grabbing a coffee, she makes herself recite the first US presidents aloud, her one daily ritual that has become as natural as showering each morning. The first five are easy enough: *Washington, Adams, Jefferson, Madison, Monroe*. There's a certain ring to them that rattles easily off the tongue. If pressed, she could probably remember a few others, like Lincoln and Cleveland (the only president to serve two nonconsecutive terms) and Teddy Roosevelt. Taft is in there somewhere, she knows; then there's Wilson and FDR, the war presidents. After that, there's a mix of Bushes and Reagan. Clinton and Obama. She refuses to acknowledge that other guy. And Biden.

At her doctor's suggestion, she has been performing these mental gymnastics every morning for the last several months. "It's never too early to start doing crossword puzzles or word searches to keep your mind sharp," he'd told her a few visits ago. If ever she can't recall the first five presidents, she'll ring him for some more of those memory pills.

She heads back inside to shower, then downs her medley of old-lady medication. There's one for vitamin D, another for calcium, two different capsules for omega-3 and a probiotic. A B_{12} pill. Two for blood pressure and cholesterol. From the looks of her dispenser, which tidily divides her daily medications for the week into *a.m.* and *p.m.* boxes, she could be a drug dealer. Nonetheless, the pill box provides solid evidence that she's taking charge of her health, determined to do whatever she must to keep her wits about her now that she's all alone.

When she types in her password on her phone, it dings with a calendar reminder, *Dinner with Marty. 6 p.m. @ Bricco* and Claire has to sit down for a second, catch her breath.

Perhaps that's why Walt came to her in a dream this morning, she thinks. Maybe somewhere in the ether, he knows what she's up to, trying to drum up a romance with her old boyfriend. But she understands that's ridiculous. Would Walt even care? Here she's imagining him being upset or jealous, when honestly, she can't say how he'd feel about her dating another man. They'd never discussed it. It hadn't seemed important, and Claire, for some reason, always assumed she'd be the first to go. If Walt wanted to fall in love with someone after she left this earth, she'd always figured more power to him.

But now it's she who's in this predicament. Because for the past seven or so months, Claire has been imagining those very words—*Dinner with Marty*—in her calendar, even penned them in pencil in her planner, as if by writing them they might come true. *Dinner with Marty.*

"Why don't you leave Dad, if you don't love him anymore?" Amber had demanded one Christmas years ago when she was home from college for winter break and newly in love herself. Claire had gazed into the eyes of her nineteen-year-old daughter, who, at the time, was taking courses on feminism and participating in sit-ins on campus. She debated how best to explain to her that it wasn't as simple as packing a bag, wasn't as easy as announcing you were through. That marriage wasn't only about the first blush of romance, that heady, fizzy feeling of infatuation. That there were other matters to consider. Companionship, for one. Family. That love matured in funny, unexpected ways.

Or, that her dad had looked good on paper when Claire married him. He was handsome, smart, self-assured and also, as Claire would discover over the years, emotionally reserved. Though she wouldn't say she'd been fooled by Walt exactly—she'd chosen him fair and square—she had been surprised by the turns in their marriage, the aloofness that had settled in after a few years, as if Walt could have married anyone so long as she made the meals and watched the kids while he worked. The exact life she'd been trying so hard to avoid with Marty.

Claire had shrugged. "It's not that easy, honey," she'd said. "Your father and I made a commitment to each other. We've been through a lot together." Then she added, "Besides, I didn't exactly imagine spending my twilight years all by myself." She'd been afraid to give voice to her fear of how lonely she'd be without someone else around. The thought of so much quiet in the house, especially with both kids gone, would have been unnerving.

But *Martin*, she thinks now. It's almost impossible to believe they'll see each other tonight. After all this time. She feels like stepping back out onto the balcony and shouting his name for all the world to hear. *Martin, Martin! I get to see Martin Campbell tonight!* Claire knows that if he'd wanted to find her, he could have reached out easily enough. With her byline plastered weekly on the *Providence Dealer*, she's a simple target, and at times, a certain disappointment that he *hadn't* tried to find her swooped over her. But now all of that can be remedied. After tonight, there'll be no more wondering. She'll find out what, precisely, he has been up to these past thirty years. And if, by chance, he's spent nearly as much time thinking about her as she has of him.

She dresses hurriedly, grabs her purse and makes sure to snatch the room key off the bedside table before heading for the elevator (she'd somehow managed to misplace it last night and embarrassingly had to request an extra from the front desk). Downstairs the lobby already hums with activity. In the concierge line, Claire waits to book a massage and then schedules an appointment for highlights at a nearby salon for later this afternoon. Exiting the hotel, she follows the main stretch of sidewalk on Seaport Boulevard across the bridge and over to Atlantic Avenue. Everyone seems to be walking with such purpose this morning—or maybe it's Claire, projecting her anticipation for tonight onto them. As she strides past one of the new luxury hotels (an article she'd read recently described it as an *architectural giraffe*, which seems even more appropriate now that she's next to it), something catches her eye through a window.

When she stops to look more closely, she sees it's the hotel gym. High-tech treadmills and elliptical machines are lined up in a tidy row, and on one treadmill an older man— probably in his early seventies, gray hair and glasses, dressed in a blue sweatshirt and baggy gray pants—stands behind an elderly woman. The woman walks with slow, deliberate steps while the man straddles either side of the machine, his feet firmly planted. Spread like a butterfly, his hands hover behind her back, ready to catch her, should she slip.

The tender image stops Claire. *This*, she thinks, *is what love looks like*. Standing behind your sweetheart on the treadmill to catch her if she falls.

Would Walt, she wonders, have done the same for her? Maybe out of obligation. What if it had become difficult for her to walk? Would Walt have patiently stood behind her while she logged miles of physical therapy? *Patiently* is probably too much to ask, but maybe out of a sense of duty he would have. Would she have done the same for him? The question lingers in her mind as she ducks into a Starbucks and orders a cup of coffee with frothed milk. The *New York Times* and the *Boston Globe* wink at her from the newspaper stand, but Claire resists picking up either one. She's promised herself she won't check the news for a week. While she waits, she plants herself on a stool by the window, and her phone rings with an incoming call. Amber.

"Good morning, honey," she answers. "Are you at work?"

"Hi, Mom. Yup, checking folks in." Every Thursday and Friday morning, Amber mans the front desk at the Providence YMCA. One benefit: Fiona can play in the Y's daycare for free while Amber scans members' cards. Still, Claire hopes once Fiona gets a bit older, Amber will be able to put her master's degree in anthropology to better use. "And now I'm checking in on you," Amber says. "How's it going?"

"Wonderful. I'm having the most fabulous time. It's a beautiful day here, and I'm about to take a walk along the Rose Kennedy Greenway. Yesterday, I went to the MFA. And later today, I've got a massage and hair appointment booked."

"Wow, that does sound pretty great." There's some noise on Amber's end, and Claire can hear the beeping of the scanner. For a split second, she almost divulges her plans for tonight. Martin's name has come up enough times over the years that the kids like to tease her about the fish that got away. But if they knew how much Claire's mind has drifted to him over the last year, now that Walt is gone, they might be shocked. *No, it's best not to get into it*, she decides.

"And how's my precious granddaughter?" she asks instead.

"Fighting a little summer cold, but otherwise, she's good."

"Tell her that her nana misses her."

"I will. We miss you."

"Well, only a couple more days till I'm back in your hair."

"Ha," says Amber.

"*Ha* back," says Claire. Her name is called for pickup. "Well, I'll let you go. Talk to you tomorrow?"

"You bet. Bye, Mom."

Claire collects her coffee and heads out, past Nebo and Rowes Wharf, the coffee warming her hands. Isn't it funny, she thinks, how daughters check in on their mothers, but sons rarely do? She hasn't heard from Ben since she left Providence on Monday afternoon. He'd come over Sunday night for dinner, hugged her goodbye and told her to call if she needed anything. Boys were funny that way. Men, too, as if whatever protective, worry gene women possessed hadn't been passed along to them.

A trolley car passes by and hoots its horn, causing Claire to jump. Years ago she and Walt had signed the family up for a trolley tour. It had been surprisingly educational. Their driver was flush with arcane knowledge, explaining such things as why the Beacon Hill brownstones had purple windows (precious glass imported from Europe had unexpectedly turned violet from the sun). The thought of that long-ago trip conjures up Walt, jarring in its immediacy, as if he's ambling along right beside her, commenting on the people, the sky, the rash of new buildings that have gone up since they last visited Boston. His image is so close, Claire can almost detect the scent of his cologne. Old Spice. She tries to shake it off.

But the thought prompts another memory, unbidden. There'd been that one year, when Amber had been in fourth grade and Ben in kindergarten, when Walt had seemed interested in her again. By then, Claire was back to working at the paper, Walt's hours at the firm had settled into a more reasonable schedule, and he actually made it home for dinner most nights. Claire remembers it distinctly because it was the year the Hillers moved into the neighborhood.

Originally from Manhattan, the Hillers were a nice enough couple. Their daughter was Amber's age, and their son one year younger than Ben. Like so many friendships those days, theirs was born of convenience—adults craving grown-up company when the weeks were mostly consumed by work and children. Claire had liked Trevor and Angie immediately, a breath of fresh air in their insular neighborhood. The Hillers listened to NPR, discussed politics and were always dropping off ripened tomatoes or fat zucchini from their garden. Like Claire, Angie worked outside the home in an administrative position at Brown University; their kids all went to the same after-school program at the elementary school down the block.

Angie was smart, funny, a fabulous dinner companion, armed with outrageous stories about goings-on on campus. She was also very pretty. Pale skin. Unusually large brown eyes and a thick, dark curtain of hair that she'd loop over one shoulder while she talked. Claire was completely charmed by her. It wasn't until a few months later that she realized Walt was equally charmed.

"You like her," Claire confronted him one night while they stood at the kitchen counter washing dishes after a cookout with the Hillers and their children.

"Hmm? Like who?" he asked.

"Angie." His eyebrows had flickered up.

"Baloney. Why would I like Angie?"

"Admit it," Claire had pressed. "You're attracted to her."

"Nonsense. She's married. The Hillers are our *friends*."

"Just because she's married doesn't mean you can't be attracted to her."

"Well, I'm not, okay?"

"But you think she's attractive, right?"

Walt sighed. "I suppose so. In a kind of old-fashioned, Natalie Wood way. But saying someone is attractive and being attracted to them are two entirely different things." He'd finished drying the last plate, placed it in the cupboard, and then, as if it were the natural next step in the sequence, he'd boosted her onto the countertop and shimmied her skirt up over her hips. Claire remembers being startled by that, Walt's unexpected boldness, returning to their marriage that night. They'd made love right there in the kitchen, his thighs slapping against hers, Claire's hands gripping his hair while the children slept upstairs. It had sparked a year-long stretch of intimacy, a spark that had dwindled shortly after the Hillers left town.

Yes, it had taken another woman, Angie Hiller, to insert the intimacy back into their lives. Was it her own jealousy that suddenly made Claire interested in Walt again and Walt in her? Was it the unspoken competition of trying to be as doting a couple as the Hillers seemed to be, always sneaking kisses behind corners, Trevor resting his hand lightly on Angie's wrist while she talked? Whatever it was, when the Hillers moved back to Manhattan and the dinner parties came to a halt, Claire and Walt's rekindled romance fizzled out as quickly as it had begun.

And then things returned to the way they'd been before or, as Claire thought of it, life returned to normal. They went back to passing each other in the halls more like roommates than husband and wife, Walt threw himself back into work, and the lion's share of responsibility for the kids fell to Claire once again. On the rare night when Walt did make it home in time for dinner, it was as if he barely noticed her. Once she'd counted the seconds while he rambled on about a situation at work and stared down at his plate. Fifty-four seconds passed before he'd glanced up and actually *looked* at her. Fifty-four! As if didn't matter who his audience was. After dinner she'd gotten up to load the dishwasher, actually taking the dirty spoons back out of the silverware holder so she could toss them in again and hear their satisfying racket, mirroring her own emotions. All clatter and bang.

To Walt's credit, when Amber was in high school he was the one who suggested they try counseling, and Claire agreed—by that point she'd have been willing to try aromatherapy, if it would work. Their therapist, Dr. Fallon, was a rotund, diminutive man. White beard and glasses, Santa Claus minus the holiday cheer. Each Saturday afternoon for a month, they filed into his office and sat next to each other, their legs almost touching on the doctor's shabby brown couch.

"I'm doing everything I possibly can to make sure our home runs on the few cylinders I have left," she admitted in their first meeting, fighting back tears. "The kids need so much attention, even now, maybe more so than when they were little. Amber's dealing with her eating issues, and Ben worries about *everything*. After I come home from work, I'm making supper, helping them with whatever the crisis of the day is. There's never any time for me to decompress." She felt a little selfish putting it that way, as if it were all about her.

But then a fire lit in her again. Because Walt wasn't there complaining about his lack of me time, was he? Walt was there because he thought their marriage had taken a decided turn toward the frigid, because Claire seemed angry all the time. Her response to Walt's complaints, albeit not helpful at the time, had been an eye roll. "Now, Claire," Dr. Fallon had said in a mollifying tone, "we want this to be a positive space without judgment."

And Claire had wanted to throw up.

Each visit left her feeling more dejected and hopeless than when she'd first stepped foot in the musty office with its corduroy sofa and weepy ferns. She imagined those wide fronds working overtime to absorb all the heartache that spilled forth. (Maybe, she thought during one particularly difficult session, the ferns were busily transforming patients' distress into something productive, like chlorophyll.) With each new session, the gulf between her and Walt grew only wider, their car rides home achingly silent while she seethed in the passenger seat. She'd thought the era of women being second-class citizens in their marriages was over, but she'd been mistaken. There was no such thing as an equitable division of labor when it came to kids and housework, unless, of course, they were well-off enough to hire a nanny and a housekeeper. Which they weren't.

At their very last session—before Claire quit—Dr. Fallon suggested she work past her anger if she and Walt were going to have any hope of reaching an understanding, and Claire had laughed, slightly hysterical. "Work past my anger? Work toward an *understanding*? Is that what this is all about?" She earmarked the word with air quotes. "Because I'm pretty sure I understand what's going on here. My husband is rarely home. My children miss their father."

Dr. Fallon set aside his yellow legal pad and folded his chubby hands on his knees. Claire still remembers the feeling that swept over her: a strange brew of relief and victory. And sadness. Because even Santa Claus couldn't cure whatever was troubling her marriage. She'd tried to track down Martin then, but it was the early '90s and the internet wasn't a thing yet. She'd heard rumors that he and Audrey had headed out to Seattle for work, that he had a few kids. But nothing definite. Their high school refused to share any details.

Martin, she thinks again, as she strides underneath the pavilion on the Greenway near the blue arc of the harbor. Mostly, she wants to lay eyes on him, hear his voice up close. Did a person stay the same after so any years? Are the seven freckles, scattered like a constellation across his abdomen, still visible, or have they faded with time? Does he still have his thick mop of sandy blond hair that she used to love to run her fingers through? Does he still try to sneak a cigarette every now and then?

And now here he is. In Boston. Will he have thought about her at all over the years? Claire realizes she's almost afraid to know the answer. Because what if it's no? What if Martin brushed her out of his mind as soon as she broke up with him on the steps of Faneuil Hall? What if she was no more than his first love, and once he found Audrey, Claire became a distant memory (except, of course, for that one time when they'd bumped into each other a few years later at Legal Sea Foods)?

Once you fell in love with someone did you ever stop loving them? Does Marty ever wonder what his life might have been like if Claire had said yes to his unspoken proposal? If they'd had kids together?

Of course, there'd be no Ben and Amber, which is impossible to imagine. But what if she'd had Ben and Amber with Martin? If they'd been *their* kids? Maybe Amber wouldn't have developed an eating disorder. Maybe Ben wouldn't have grown up to be such a shy and timid boy, always worried about disappointing his father. Maybe, Claire thinks somewhat ironically, she and Martin would have had enough money to hire a nanny, and she wouldn't have neglected her job for the first six years of the kids' lives.

What if? What if? It's an endless loop that she'll never know the answers to. But at least tonight she can stop wondering what Marty has been up to all this time. And maybe, if she works up the courage, if she has enough wine, she can bring up that other matter, too.

SIXTEEN

Jason wakes to a baggie of cold water resting on his hotel pillow. And a throbbing right hand. Throbbing as in, it feels like his thumb might have fallen off in the middle of the night. He slides his hand out from under his pillow. Nope, the thumb is still attached, but his hand is another story. It's practically unrecognizable. The knuckles, lined with scratches, are swollen to twice their size, there's a smear of caked blood on the web of skin between his pointer and middle finger, and in several spots, his skin has turned a shade of dark, midnight blue. *Serves me right*, he thinks.

When he remembers that today, Thursday, is his actual birthday, he lets out a moan. This is not how things were supposed to go on their vacation. Gwen, he knows, has been planning a harbor cruise for later this afternoon to celebrate the big thirty-three, but given the events of yesterday, she'll probably threaten to mutiny. Or maybe she's already can-

celed their reservation as punishment. Maybe she'll suggest
they head back home this morning, forget about the two
more nights they're booked for at the hotel. Jason wouldn't
blame her.

When he rolls over, she's curled up on the other side of
the bed about as far away as she can get, her back turned to
him, her honey-colored hair fanned out across her pillow. It's
the body language of someone who's still mightily pissed off.
Last night when they'd returned to the hotel, she'd fetched
an ice pack from the bartender and handed it over, saying
"Enjoy it. Because it's the last time I'm going to be nice to
you for the next five hours."

And Jason had thought *Understood.* A few cocktails followed, Gwen even agreeing to stick around for the first one.
"You told me you were going to get help," she'd said, slam-
ming down the shot glass on the countertop, as if they might
go at it right there. The bartender had sent Jason a look as if
to say *You've met your match tonight, buddy.*

"I know, and I'm sorry. I've been busy. But I will, I promise."

She shook her head, signaled to the bartender for another
and swiveled on the stool to face him. "I haven't asked because I didn't want you to think I was checking up on you.
But, honey, I can't keep watching you lose your temper with
total strangers like that all the time. It's insane. Not to mention terrifying."

"I know."

He understood she was shaken up—he was, too—but it
seemed a little unfair to characterize his random outbursts as
events that happened *all the time.* Especially when he could
count the number of times he'd lost his cool in public on
one hand. There was the guy at the MFA, obviously. Another loser at a bar in Portsmouth a few months back, who

kept spouting off about how great the Confederate flag was; and one or two other episodes, where sketchy guys had been lurking around Gwen. They'd only gotten a little warning punch to the gut, nothing serious. Yesterday's tussle was the most damage he'd sown in a long time.

The guy at the museum probably had a broken nose, maybe a few missing teeth. Jason wonders if they made it to a hospital. Gwen was worried that they'd track them down somehow, maybe trace their identity through the cameras at the MFA. But Jason thinks that's unlikely. Even if he was truly hurt, chances are Blue Eyes won't be eager to seek him out for a rematch. Besides, the guy was being a dick. He kind of deserved it.

"Seriously. That was crazy back there," she'd said, as if for emphasis, and downed her second Jameson.

"I know."

"You really did a number on that guy, and he didn't even touch you."

"Yeah, but when I saw the way he looked at you, and then later, when his buddy came over and he said something crude…" Jason shrugged. "I lost it."

"You have got to learn to control that temper."

"Yes, Mom," he'd chided, which was obviously the wrong thing to say. The alcohol was emboldening him in ways it shouldn't have. The best strategy, he knew full well, was to apologize profusely, as if he'd just burned down the MET, and keep on apologizing until his voice was gone. What was someone like Gwen doing with him, anyway? What was it that kept her coming back when he proved himself time and again to be such a colossal jerk?

She dropped her big, beautiful eyes and said in a quiet voice, "We've talked about this. It's not just random strangers I worry about." And it was this comment that had leveled him, punched him in the heart, because, of course, he knew what she was referring to. But he'd already apologized for those times! A random night when the world felt as if it was closing in on him and Gwen had snapped at him and he'd thrown a glass across the kitchen that shattered into a million pieces, narrowly missing her bare foot. Or, the morning when he'd gotten the call from his dissertation adviser saying he thought Jason might want to refocus his entire thesis. That had been a doozy. The fact that he'd only tossed his computer in the trash (and later retrieved it) seemed like no big deal in the scheme of things.

But he thinks of the other two lamentable incidents. The unmentionables. One last fall and one last week. He's pretty much pushed them out of his mind because thinking about them makes him feel physically ill, like he might vomit. But every so often, when Gwen sends him a deer-caught-in-the-headlights look, the memory resurfaces. The first time was at a football game last fall. They'd gone to cheer on the college team, the Raiders, and a few other teaching assistants had joined them. Jason was older than most by a good five or six years, but he tried to play it cool, taking a puff on a joint that someone passed him during halftime. Gradually, though, he'd grown annoyed with Gary, the other English TA, whom Gwen kept talking to. When another grad student yelled, "Hey, Gwen, you and Gary make a cute couple!" Jason's head had swiveled like the girl's in *The Exorcist*. The kid, quickly realizing his mistake, turned to Jason and said, "No offense, man. Obviously, you guys are together." And Jason had tightly grabbed Gwen by the wrist and led her back to the stands, where they'd watched the remainder of the game by themselves. Jason silently fuming, Gwen utterly humiliated. The purple bruises that encircled her wrist like a delicate bracelet the next morning had inspired him to buy her a necklace with a tiny diamond pendant.

His not-so-subtle plea for absolution.

"I know," he said again at the bar and reached out his hand, running it across her tightly knit fingers, those tiny silver rings of hers. "I know, and I'm sorry. I'm gonna get it under control. There's some stuff going on at work…"

"Stuff? What stuff?" Her eyes darted at him. "You keep insisting there's nothing bothering you, but now there's stuff going on at work? Which is it, Jason? Everything's fine or not fine. It can't be both."

"Nothing really important." He hesitated. "Well, kind of important, I guess, depending on your perspective."

"I'm waiting." He could feel her patience waning. The one person who believed in him—quite possibly the only person in the world who loved him at this point in his life—was having a crisis of confidence. *What was wrong with him?*

He twirled the Jim Beam in his glass. A little archipelago of ice chips had formed at the bottom. "I'm thinking I might quit."

He watched her eyes widen. "Quit?"

"Yeah, as in leave the university. I don't enjoy teaching anymore. The students are mostly entitled little punks, and my dissertation is going nowhere. I'm never gonna get my PhD."

"But you've been working so hard on it!"

His shoulders lifted. "Not really. I pretty much go to the library and take naps."

"Surely you're joking?"

Jason shook his head. "I wish I were. I'm blocked. Totally blocked."

"Babe." Something in her voice softened. "I'm sure it's a

passing phase. You know, end-of-the-year blahs. Give your-self the summer before you do anything rash."

"Maybe." He'd downed the rest of his drink in one swallow. He didn't dare mention the thing with Charlie, not until he talked to George. "Anyway, I'm really sorry about what happened back there. It's just that when I saw that guy hitting on you and then I thought he said something rude to his friend, a fire lit up in me, you know?"

But Gwen shook her head. "I don't know. I *don't* understand, Jason. Which is why I think you need to get help. And I don't mean maybe next year or six months from now but when we get back home. Look into it. Find someone who can help you sort through the stuff with your dad."

That she'd summed it up so succinctly surprised him, as if his whole persona could be boiled down to his complicated relationship with his father. Maybe it could.

"Okay, yeah," he said. "I'm going to get on it. As soon as we get home. Now, can we please talk about something else?"

She'd tilted her head, considering it for a moment. "You know what? I'm not really feeling it right now. I think I'm going to grab my book and go sit by the pool."

He checked his watch. It was seven thirty. "Are you sure the pool's even open?"

Gwen shrugged. "It's kind of immaterial. If it isn't, I'll find a spot on the porch."

Which he'd taken to mean that she wanted to get as far away as possible from him. Hell, if he could have escaped himself at that moment, he would have done the same.

He remembers now. He'd had a few more at the bar, alone, then gone up to their room and fallen into bed. By the time he dozed off, Gwen still hadn't returned.

Now he rolls onto his back, hands on his stomach, and stares up at the ceiling. She stirs slightly, her leg crisscrossing his. He's pretty much convinced himself that now might be a good time to start packing up, load the car with their bags. But then Gwen rolls over and moans, "Mmm…good morning, birthday boy." Her lips linger on his ear, her naked body, pressed up against his, is warm and smooth. The sheets rustle, and he can feel her hand searching beneath them until she finds what she's looking for.

And Jason, wonderfully surprised, lets out a soft moan. Of relief. Of wonder. Is it possible that she's forgiven him yet again? If that's the case, he'll resolve to be the best boy-friend ever for the rest of the weekend. He'll buy her flow-ers, give her hour-long back rubs, do whatever she wants. They can have dinner at the Capital Grille or buy theater tickets for tomorrow night. She can go to the spa, and he'll relax by the pool. He'll do whatever it takes.

He only wishes that the little voice in the back of his head would shut up. The voice that keeps whispering he's only a few short steps away from becoming his father. Because Jason will not let that happen under any circumstances. Not when he's worked so hard to escape his past! Not when he studied his ass off in college to graduate summa cum laude. *Genetics aren't everything* he has told himself a million times. Maybe he can't outrun his genes, but he can sure as hell shape them to the best of his ability. He will not become the violent man that his father was.

When Gwen crawls on top of him he wraps his arms around her, but his busted-up hand still aches with regret.

Friday, June 11, 2021

SEVENTEEN

Jean-Paul punches the button that will take him up to the tenth floor. He's on his way to meet with the police commissioner, who has summoned him for a few questions. As soon as he steps off the elevator, the yellow tape that cordons off the room under investigation draws his eye. Already, Gillian has seen to it that the guests staying in this wing—more than a few of them arriving any hour for the Saltonstall wedding this weekend—have been transferred to another floor or even another hotel (in this case, to the Four Seasons across the river). And, it's a very good thing. Because the tenth floor is currently overrun with men and women in blue. Jean-Paul steers his way over to the room in question, where a policeman stands guard and introduces himself.

"Hello. I'm Jean-Paul Savant, manager of the Seafarer. I understand the commissioner asked to see me?"

The officer shoots him an appraising once-over, says,

"One minute" and steps into the room. His black work boots are covered in what appear to be plastic baggies. When he returns, another man, hefty and red-faced, accompanies him.

"Mr. Savant," he says, extending his hand. "We met briefly downstairs, I think, right after the incident. Detective Lazeer. Thanks for coming up. The commissioner is busy at the moment, so he asked me to bring you on in."

Jean-Paul accepts the offer of his hand and shakes it. "Right, of course," he says. "Any idea what happened yet?"

"That's what we're working on. We were hoping you could take a look around, see if anything looks out of place to you. Or anything strange at all. We've already had the housekeeper by to see if anything struck her as out of the ordinary." He shakes his head. "Nothing."

"I'll try," says Jean-Paul. "Though, I don't know how much help I'll be."

The detective hands over two plastic baggies. "First, I'll have to ask you to put these on over your shoes. Can't risk contaminating the scene. And some gloves for your hands."

"Right." Jean-Paul takes them and slips them on, feeling the snap of the elastic across his ankles. Then he tugs on the yellow plastic gloves. Detective Lazeer ushers him into the room, where the bedsheets are pulled down and a suitcase remains open on the luggage stand at the foot of the bed. It's crazy, but Jean-Paul's first instinct is to be embarrassed. The room is in such a state of disarray that it looks as if Housekeeping has been negligent. There are trays of unfinished food leftover from room service, soiled towels scattered across the carpet. One chair, on its side, lies pushed up against the wall.

"Well, I can assure you that, typically, Housekeeping would have cleaned up all of this this morning, after the guest had left the room. That chair most certainly does not belong on its side." He steps over to right it before the officer stops him.

"Whoa, whoa. Hang on there. Remember we're treating this as a potential crime scene so we're not touching anything."

Jean-Paul nods. "Right. Sorry." Then he realizes the import of the officer's words. "A crime scene? Really? You think someone threw her off the balcony? Made her jump?"

The detective shrugs. "Right now anything is possible. We'll know more after the autopsy report."

Jean-Paul has been assuming all this time that it's a suicide they're dealing with. If it's a homicide, well, that will be another matter. Because there's no covering that up. He imagines the swift downtick in reservations if it's true and word gets out. The Seafarer, just back on its feet after renovations, having to somehow re-create itself yet again—a nightmare!

His eyes swiftly scan the room. A few different items of clothing lay scattered across the bed. The door to the balcony is pulled shut, but two officers stand outside. One has his back turned, and the other snaps photos, in particular, of a chair that has been pushed up against the railing. Jean-Paul's gaze lands on a white sweater, lying in a puddle next to the chair, and a pair of pink flip-flops. He swallows hard.

"Take all the time you need," the detective says. "It's never easy walking into these situations, especially when it's not your job."

Jean-Paul nods, remembers to breathe. There are a couple of abandoned plastic cups on the bureau next to the television. His eyes scour the room for any evidence of alcohol, but other than some half-empty water bottles, there don't appear to be any empties.

He pauses. "No suicide note, then?" Then hurries to add, "Since you're treating it as a potential homicide, I mean."

The detective seems to weigh whether or not to answer but finally says, "No, but that information doesn't leave this room, understood?"

Jean-Paul nods solemnly, gives him his word. Detective Lazeer continues. "Listen, I'm gonna want the video footage of the hallway from you. I need to see who entered the premises last night and this morning. And also any video you might have of the balcony—are there cameras out there?"

"We have a few," Jean-Paul says. "I'll have to check if they cover this room, though. As for the hallway footage, that's easy to secure." Already he'd been thinking the director of Security should be his next stop.

"Care to peek into the bathroom? See if anything looks off to you?"

"All right." Jean-Paul gingerly makes his way over. He doesn't know why he expects to see blood splattered across the floor (too much television probably), but that's what leaps to mind. Lots and lots of blood. Of course, the real crime scene is ten floors below. The bathroom that he walks into is floor-to-ceiling white tile, pristine.

On the vanity there's an assortment of items: a makeup bag, a comb, a tube of toothpaste. A jar of Vaseline. Nothing looks out of place, however. The magnifying face mirror is still on its swivel handle. A man's blue blazer hangs on the back of the door, as if someone was using the shower steam to get the wrinkles out.

"Nothing seems to be missing or broken," Jean-Paul says, stepping out of the bathroom, and realizes that the detective, who nods but says nothing, has been watching him the entire time. "Is there anything else I can help you with?"

Goose pimples have popped up on his skin, and he's feeling slightly queasy. There's plenty of work to be done, including writing up his official hotel report from memory.

He'd like to finish it while the timeline of events remains fresh in his mind. There are a million little details, a thousand headaches ahead of him.

Lazeer flips through his notebook and asks, "And remind me, Mr. Savant, where were you exactly when the deceased fell?" It's apparent that the detective doesn't care to identify the guest by name, which is fine by Jean-Paul. Somehow it's easier this way.

"I was in the front lobby, talking to Tabitha at the front desk. We were checking the band schedule on the terrace for tonight when we heard the crash—and then the screaming." His heart twists into a knot at the visceral memory of those screams.

The detective shuts his notebook, a long, narrow pad that flips open at the top, much like a reporter's notebook. "Right, okay. Well, thank you. You've been very helpful. Now, if you can get me the video footage and the hotel manifest of guests as soon as possible, I'd appreciate it."

"Absolutely." That part will be easy. Jean-Paul is good at taking orders. He's been on the other side of them for so long, it's almost comforting to be told what to do. "I'll get those for you straightaway." When he steps out of the room, the guard helps him remove the plastic covers from his wing tips and tosses them into a canvas bag. Jean-Paul yanks off his gloves, hands them over and offers his thanks.

On the elevator, he forces himself to count to twenty, taking deep breaths while he does so. But as he watches the floor numbers creep by, all he can think is that the elevator can't carry him away fast enough. Because what he wants more than anything is to be back home with Marie and Isabella, cradling them both in his arms. To smell the scent of Marie's shampoo, like apples, and the sweet baby smell of Isabella's skin. He wants to race up the stairs to their brownstone and double-bolt the door behind him so that nothing bad can get in. To keep the monsters out. To keep the news of this horrible day far, far away. He wants nothing less than the whole day to rewind and start over.

What if he'd stayed home today, he thinks? What if, instead of stepping out onto her balcony around twelve thirty, the victim had decided to go for a walk in the bright afternoon sunshine? There are so many maybes and what-ifs. If only he could get a do-over for today! A chance to get it right. An opportunity to keep a closer watch on his property. He thinks back to when he woke this morning, the foreboding feeling that had taken hold of him, as if something were off-kilter. Maybe the universe had been sending him a sign, and he'd chosen to ignore it.

But, no, Jean-Paul mustn't blame himself. It will get him nowhere. When he steps off the elevator, though, the impulse to keep on walking straight home to his wife and daughter is almost unbearable.

Earlier that week

EIGHTEEN

On Thursday night, Riley and Tom are stretched out on their sofa. Five cartons of Chinese food lay scattered across the TV table alongside an almost-empty bottle of Cabernet. Beef and broccoli for Tom, chicken lo mein for her, an assortment of dumplings and egg rolls. Typically, they save ordering in for Sunday nights, but after a long day, Riley suggested it as a stopgap measure for tonight's dinner. After Marilyn had left Smart Stems, there'd been a steady stream of customers at the store, and Riley hasn't had a moment off her feet since approximately eleven thirty this morning. Exhaustion rolled over her as soon as she walked in the door and kicked off her clogs.

"I'm sorry my mom ambushed you at the store," Tom says now, raking his fingers through her hair. She's leaning back against him while they watch Lester Holt deliver the news on their wide-screen TV above the mantel. "I don't know what she was thinking. Or what's gotten into her. It's like she's reliving her own wedding day or something."

After a glass and a half of red wine and a liberal helping of lo mein, Riley is feeling slightly more magnanimous toward her mother-in-law. The recent chain of events—from dinner at Tom's parents' house last night to his mom's unexpected visit at the store today to the already planned tasting at the Seafarer tomorrow afternoon—have been annoying, for sure. But maybe, she allows, it's not the worst thing having her mother-in-law so invested in their big day.

"It's okay. Do you think maybe she's having trouble dealing with the fact that her little boy is getting married?" This is the theory that Hannah floated past her after Riley had texted her about Marilyn's sneak attack at the store.

"Hmm...not likely," he says. "My mother has never been the sentimental type."

"But she was a teacher!" Riley protests. "A *second-grade* teacher," she says, as if to emphasize her point. "Aren't teachers supposed to be all touchy-feely and emotionally in touch with their students?"

He shrugs. "How am I supposed to know? All I know is that she was never the hugging type. More of a kiss-on-the-cheek mom."

Riley lifts her head to better read his eyes, see if he's kidding or not. But there's zero mirth there. "But that's so sad," she says. She thinks back to her own mother, whose love had been all-encompassing, almost to the point where Riley couldn't breathe. Literally. She remembers coming home from summer camp one year and having to tell her mom to stop hugging her so hard because her ribs felt as if they were about to break in half. Whenever Riley's friends would come over, Libby Thorton would settle herself at the kitchen table, fix them a sandwich and say, "Now, sit here a few minutes and tell me about what's happening in your life." The running joke in the neighborhood was that Riley's mom was the block's den mother. If you needed help— like a Band-Aid, a cool glass of lemonade or just a pat on the back—the Thorton house was where you went. She can't imagine growing up with a mother who didn't hand out hugs as if they were candy.

"I can't imagine," she says finally. "That must have been such a lonely childhood."

Another shrug. "I didn't know any better. And she's really not so bad once you get to know her."

Riley laughs despite herself.

"What?"

"Well, I've known her for almost a year now."

"And your point is?" His eyes are playful, almost jolly.

"And…well…I think I'll stop right there."

"Wise decision," he kids. "Honestly," he says a bit more sincerely, kissing the top of Riley's head, "you'll learn to love her. Trust me. She grows on you."

Riley reaches for the ravaged carton of pork dumplings on the table. There's half a dumpling left, stuck on the bottom in a congealed mess. Undeterred, she fishes it out with her fingers and plops it in her mouth. "Promise?" she asks, mouth full.

Tom nods. "Scout's honor."

"Does that even count if you were never a Boy Scout?"

He grins. "Couldn't tell you."

She tosses the carton back on the table, an old trunk they'd purchased at a flea market on a weekend getaway in Maine, and slides her feet over the burnished wood, inadvertently knocking the pink wedding manual onto the floor. It lies open to a page with another checklist, no doubt for something Riley was supposed to do months ago. But when she picks it up, she sees it's only an initial Q&A for the bride and groom, entitled "Are You on the Same Wedding-Day Page?"

"Okay, ready?" she asks, suddenly game, and grabs a pencil. *"If you had to pick a song for our wedding at the church, what would it be?"*

Tom doesn't even stop to think. "Guns N' Roses, 'Paradise City,' definitely."

She rolls her eyes. "You can't have Guns N' Roses at the church! That's equivalent to sacrilege. Not to mention it's not very romantic."

"Yeah, well, what else have you got?"

"I don't know." She's chewing on her pencil eraser, an annoying habit, she knows, and Tom reaches over to gently tug it from her mouth. "Maybe something from Broadway. Or James Taylor's 'How Sweet It Is'." She can sense his internal groan building. "Anyway, definitely something more romantic. Your mom would *die* if we played Guns N' Roses. I'll ask Hannah for some ideas." For the time being, she pencils in a question mark on the line next to *Church Music/Song*. "All right, moving on. *For the guys, suits or tuxes?*" She refrains from revealing that her decided preference is the more relaxed look of suits and is relieved when Tom replies, "Definitely suits. Tuxes are way too uncomfortable."

"Suits, it is, then," Riley says, thinking *See, I can be agreeable!*

"Band or DJ for the reception?"

"Tough one." Tom ponders it for a moment. "I like the idea of a band, but I'm sure it's more expensive than a DJ, so maybe just a DJ?"

She writes *DJ, cheaper?* on the line for reception music.

They continue on like this—*Chicken or fish or steak for an entrée? Wedding cake or cupcakes? Toss the bouquet or not? Bride and groom's dance song?*—for another fifteen minutes. When they get to the daddy–daughter dance, Riley pauses. What would her dad, who hates to dance, acquiesce to for a song? He's always been a Willie Nelson fan, and she combs her memories for his favorites. "On the Road Again," though, won't exactly hit the right note for a wedding dance. Then she remembers "Always on My Mind." She'll need to check the lyrics to be sure, but she pencils it in for the moment. The title, at least, fits. And the question jogs her memory: she should call her dad and check in on him. She hasn't talked to him since Sunday night when he'd sounded kind of down.

Lester Holt is wrapping up with the good-news story for the end of the day, Riley's favorite part of the newscast. To-night features a young couple who recently married across borders, the groom from Edmonton, Canada, the bride from Maine. "Wow, thank goodness we don't have that extra hur-dle to cross," she says. "Can you imagine if we were trying to corral our families and friends from different countries for this thing? What a logistical nightmare."

"Mmm." Without looking up, she can tell that Tom has checked out of their conversation. Over the past few weeks she has come to understand that if she wants his involvement in planning their big day, then she needs to include him in small, manageable ways, as if she's administering Novocain to a small child. Too much in one dose, and it will knock him out.

"Hey, what do you say we take this wedding-planning stuff into the bedroom?" she asks when the end-of-the-news jingle plays on the television.

Tom glances up from his *Sports Illustrated*. "I've got a bet-ter idea. How about we leave the wedding-planning stuff here and you and I go into the bedroom? See what happens?"

"Oh, really?" she says, playing it coy. "And what, exactly, did you have in mind?"

Tom pushes up from the couch and smiles wickedly. "I have no idea. Do you?"

NINETEEN

When she sees Marty for the first time in thirty years, the recognition is instant, a stab to her gut. A little grayer, a bit thicker around the middle, but wearing the same affable grin, as if he can't wait to see what's coming next. He's dressed in a blue blazer, a white oxford, faded jeans, a tan leather belt and soft suede loafers. He wears eyeglasses now, not the reading kind, but the permanent kind for distances, dark frames on top. *Still handsome*, she thinks—and vaguely professorial looking. Though they planned to meet at six, Claire has arrived ahead of time to enjoy a glass of chardonnay, alone, in order to better gather her thoughts. Calm her nerves.

Tanned and hale, Marty's face brightens as soon as he steps into Bricco and spots her in the far corner. The feeling that sweeps over her is similar to that when she rediscovered her late mother's lotus bowls hiding in the top kitchen cupboard. An odd comparison, maybe, but one that fits. The bowls were delicately hand-painted, and Claire had forgotten all about them. But because they represented one of the few items her mother had left her, they were exceedingly dear. Stumbling upon them a few years later had evoked such a tangle of emotions in her—surprise, delight, wonder, a sense of familiarity and sadness, guilt for not having found them sooner. This is how it feels to see Marty again after all these years.

"Martin," she says, the name as easy and familiar on her lips as if she has been waiting to utter it for thirty years (and she has, in fact, called it out in the middle of the night on occasion, climbing up from a dream). She waves him over, then clasps her hands together in an effort to stop them from trembling.

As soon as he reaches the table, she stands and lets herself be pulled into his warm embrace. His arms are big and strong around her, the swell of his stomach pressing against the roundness of hers when they hold each other. Like everyone else, they've both added a few extra pounds to their frame. He smells faintly of aftershave—and, regrettably, cigarettes. A long moment passes while they settle into their seats and he studies her, taking the measure of her, she supposes. Claire does the same. His mop of hair is almost entirely gray now, and modest creases bracket his kind, brown eyes. Those eyes, achingly familiar even now. "How is it," he says at last, tilting his head back, "that you look exactly the same?"

"Ha! Right." She cradles her wineglass in both hands, secretly pleased. "It's so good to see you, Martin. I didn't realize how nice it would be to lay eyes on you again."

He leans back and pats his stomach. "Not much to look at these days, I'm afraid." He laughs good-naturedly. "But you, Claire, you look fantastic."

She can feel the blush rioting to her throat, the compliment riding over her like a riptide. She's wearing the blue polka-dot sundress with buttons down the front, and her hair, freshly highlighted at the salon this afternoon, hangs loosely around her shoulders. It's probably the best she has looked in years.

"So, tell me, stranger, how *are* you?" he asks, resting his elbows on the table, his chin in his hands.

This ineffable quality of Marty's Claire has almost forgotten: making whoever is sitting across the table from him feel as if she's the only person in the room. "I'm doing all right. I can't get over the fact that it's been thirty-some years since we've seen each other, since that time we bumped into each other at Legal Sea Foods." She's staring, she knows, but it can't be helped when so many feelings are splashing over her. Is it happiness? Gratitude that he actually showed up? Relief? Love?

The white cloth napkin flutters in front of him as he shakes it out, places it in his lap. "I know what you mean. It's strange, isn't it? I'll admit I was surprised when I got your note." He pauses. "But happy-surprised. How did you find me, anyway?"

She shrugs. "I have my ways. I am a journalist, you know."

"Oh, I know. I read your articles in the *Dealer* from time to time. You've really climbed up the masthead there. Impressive."

Claire grips the stem of her wineglass more tightly. *So he has been following me*, she thinks. "It's kept me busy. It's been a good career," she admits.

"It's what you always wanted." A smile skirts across his lips.

"Is it?" she asks, surprised to hear him say it. But he's right—there's no sense in denying it. She was driven, back in the day. "I suppose so."

"So, I have to ask again. Why seek me out now?"

Momentarily Claire wonders: Should she play it coy or spill the beans immediately? She settles on a shrug. "Curiosity got the best of me, I guess." The real reason, she decides, can wait till later. "You are, incidentally, the one person on earth who doesn't seem to have a Facebook or Twitter account. If I can't stalk you, how am I supposed to know how you're doing?" She's only half kidding. Aside from his mention as the surviving spouse in Audrey's obituary, there'd been precious little available online. One photo, maybe from a decade ago, when he'd received a teaching award, but that didn't tell her much, aside from the fact that he was teaching seventh-grade social studies and, apparently, doing it very well.

A waiter appears to fill their water glasses and take Marty's drink order, a vodka and tonic. Claire orders another glass of wine for herself, clam cakes for an appetizer and chicken Alfredo. Marty requests the pasta Bolognese.

"Yeah, I've pretty much avoided social media as best I can. It's a real nightmare for some of our students. A lot of cyberbullying out there."

"Oh, right." She considers this for a moment, that his job still requires him to be current on what's going on with today's teenagers. Claire, on the other hand, has no idea about this particular slice of the world anymore.

Their small square table abuts a window opening onto Hanover Street, and drips of conversation from passersby drift through while they talk. Somewhere outside soft music plays, and Claire thinks back to all the celebrations they've shared together here: they'd toasted her twenty-first birthday in the North End; their college graduations; her first job offer at the *Globe*. How odd that they find themselves back in this place, staring at older, more wrinkled versions of themselves! And yet somehow it also feels preordained, as if they both suspected that one day they'd return to this very spot.

"Well, I'm glad you did," he says now. "Track me down, I mean. I always felt like things ended abruptly."

Claire feels her face softening. "Mmm... That's largely my fault, I'm afraid. I wasn't ready to take next steps."

"But you were ready for next steps with Walt," he points out helpfully. His eyes twinkle when he says this, though it doesn't come across as accusatory. More a statement of fact than anything else.

"True." She hesitates. Then laughs and says, "Well, what did I know back then?" The waiter arrives with their clam cakes, and they sit in thoughtful silence for a moment while they eat. "So, what have I missed?" she asks. "Bring me up to speed. I heard through the grapevine that you have a couple of kids?"

His face lights up. "Yeah, two girls. Can you believe it? That I ended up living with three women?" He laughs. "I'll tell you, though, those girls, they're the apples of my eye. I don't get to see them very much, unfortunately. Bridget's out in Seattle working for the EPA, and Gail moved to San Francisco when her mother died. About three years ago now."

"I was so sorry to hear about Audrey," Claire says softly. And she means it. "I read online about her passing." She knows how difficult, how utterly strange it is to lose the person you built a family with, whom you slept next to each night.

"Cancer," Walt offers. "By the end, we were glad her suffering was over. But it was really tough on the girls, Gail especially." Claire offers a sympathetic nod. "And I was sorry to hear about Walt," he adds. "Not even a year ago, huh?"

"It'll be one year in October. Heart attack. A surprise for sure, but we all seem to have adjusted." When the words sit out in the open between them, she's startled by how cava-lier, how frigid they sound. Martin leans back in his chair and meets her gaze with a curious look. "I mean, Ben and Amber seem to be doing fine," she elaborates.

"Oh, well, that's good, I suppose."

"And are you still teaching, then?" Claire, on her second glass of wine, is emboldened to change the subject. No sense dwelling on Walt tonight!

"No, not in the classroom anymore. I'm the principal at the local high school."

"That's wonderful! I always knew you'd go far."

"No, you didn't." He chuckles. "You didn't think I'd amount to much, actually."

She laughs. "Well, like I said, I didn't know much back then."

When their meals arrive, she begins to fill in the lines of her own life for him, about her family, her job. She tells him about Ben and his girlfriend, Liv. About Amber and Jeff and little Fiona, about her work at the paper (although, she leaves out the part about how the Providence Mafia might be searching for her this very minute). How she worries whether Amber will ever put her advanced degree to use. How Ben owns a health-food store and how he likes to verse Claire on the virtues of chakras and okra and other words ending with an -ah sound. She tells Marty it makes Thanksgiving dinner a royal pain in the ass, and he laughs.

"I think you'd really like Amber, though," she says. "She reminds me a bit of you, actually."

"Yeah, how so?"

"Oh, I don't know exactly. She's easygoing, like you, and she has a huge heart. She works at the YMCA and volun-teers at the local animal shelter. She loves kids."

He grins. "Hey, that reminds me. Let me show you a

photo of my girls." When he pulls up the picture on his phone, Claire inhales sharply. Shot someplace tropical, the picture frames the family amid skinny palm trees on a pink stretch of sand. Marty's daughters are remarkably pretty— long dark hair, big brown eyes, and tall. "Oh, Marty, they're beautiful."

"Thanks. Those pretty smiles of theirs cost me thousands of dollars' worth of orthodontia," he says, joking. But Claire can feel them both looking at Audrey. In the photo, one hand rests on each girl's shoulder and she's laughing into the camera, as if someone has just said something funny. She's thin, still attractive with a bob of auburn hair, a slightly older version of the woman Claire remembers. Martin's arm is draped around her shoulder.

Claire clears her throat and passes the phone back, suddenly feeling like a voyeur, peeking in on a prized memory with his late wife. She no longer has the heart to pull out her own family photos.

"I got lucky," he says now. "That's for sure." Claire's immediate instinct is to be jealous instead of glad, and she scolds herself for being so petty, so small-minded.

For dessert they order cappuccinos, and she prepares to launch into what she's come here to say tonight, such as she never really stopped loving him, that she regrets letting him go, and she wonders if, now that they're both single again, he might have room in his heart for her once more.

But before she can begin, his phone buzzes. "Sorry," he says glancing down. "I should probably take this. It's Gail. Do you mind? I'll just be a minute." Claire shoos him off, grateful for the interruption and the chance to organize her thoughts.

After he steps outside, she watches him through the open window. It's impossible to eavesdrop, but so many of Marty's gestures while he talks are familiar, as if it's a sign language she'd once learned and forgotten she had access to. She can tell he's happy. He reaches into his blazer pocket (*probably for a pack of cigarettes*, she thinks), and pulls out an empty hand. A second later, he lets go of a booming laugh that makes Claire smile. Oh, to hear that laugh again!

She'd almost forgotten how much she missed Marty's easy way of moving through the world. And that tiny, insistent voice in her head whispers again: How might her own life, her children's lives, have been different, if Martin had been her husband, their father?

Then he's back at the table. "Everything all right?" she inquires.

"Oh, fine. Gail likes to check in on her old man from time to time," he says and turns the ringer off on his phone before slipping it into his jacket pocket. "I told her I was having dinner with an old flame."

"Oh, really?" Perhaps this is Claire's opportunity. "Just an old flame?"

He tilts his head and shoots her a funny look as if it's the first time he's considered that what they're doing here might be something more than dinner, and for a brief moment, she wishes she could teleport herself right out of her chair. "I guess I'm not sure what you mean by that, Claire-Bear." A shiver travels up her arms at the mention of her old nickname. No one has called her that in ages.

"How about a walk?" she asks, handing him his cappuccino in a paper to-go cup. "Do you have time? There's something I'd like to talk with you about."

"Uh-oh. Nothing bad, I hope."

"Not bad," she says. "Just some, oh, I don't know, life news, I suppose."

"All right, then. We should probably pay the bill first."

"Already taken care of."

"You weren't supposed to do that," he admonishes.

"Why on earth not? I asked you out, remember?" She grabs her own cappuccino off the table. "C'mon, I want to stop off at Mike's Pastry for a, a whatchamacallit, before it closes. You know, the ones with the whipped cream inside."

Marty grins. "You mean a cannoli?"

"Cannoli! That's it," she cries, relieved he has come up with the name. She's had too much wine. "I can never remember those fancy Italian pastries. We only ever had doughnuts in my neighborhood," she kids.

Thankfully, the line at Mike's, notoriously long, stretches only a few people deep tonight, and within several minutes they've purchased a box of cannoli. "Just like old times." Marty takes a bite, sending the vanilla cream squirting out on one side. And Claire has to agree because there's something comforting about having the familiar white pastry box, tied up in its red-and-white string, tucked underneath her arm once again, as if they might be heading back to her dorm room to watch a movie.

They cut across the North End's winding streets and make their way over to Atlantic Avenue. Eventually they stop along a path tracing the waterfront. The nearly full moon bathes the harbor in an orange glow. "Remember how we used to take those harbor cruises?" Claire says now. "And how I would pack a picnic for Georges Island, but once we arrived, there was a whole colony of geese doing their business on the grass and both of us were too sick to even think about eating?"

Marty chuckles, another belly laugh. "That's right. I'd forgotten that. What did you call it again? You had a funny name for it."

"Goose Poop Island," she supplies.

"Ah, right. So romantic." When she begins to shiver, he

offers her his blazer, and she slips it on, but they both burst out laughing because she's positively swimming in it. Her hands have disappeared underneath the giant sleeves. Gently he pulls a wisp of hair behind her ear. "You're a funny soul, Claire O'Dell."

She waits a beat. "Do you ever think about us?"

"About us? Sure," he says, taking a step back. "Lots of times a memory will sneak up on me, make me laugh." But then a sigh escapes from somewhere deep inside him, and he leans over the guardrail, as if he might be tempted to tumble into the harbor. "But I'm worried you and I might have come to dinner with different expectations tonight."

"Oh." She's silent, waiting.

"I'm guessing you thought there might still be a spark between us." He straightens once again, spins toward her. "And you wouldn't be wrong."

Her hands grasp the railing so tightly that her knuckles have turned white.

"But I should tell you: I'm seeing someone. About eight months now." Claire's face must reveal her astonishment because he says, "I know. It feels weird to talk about. I still miss Audrey every day. But then I met Cora, and well, we're a lot alike, same interests. We both like to hike, and we even took a cooking class together. Anyway, she's a retired teacher, so she kind of gets me." He shakes his head. "It's so strange, but I think I might actually be falling in love again."

Claire steps back, as if he's just slapped her. She would like him to hit the rewind button on their conversation, back to the part where he'd mentioned the recurring spark between the two of them. While her mind might allow for the possibility that he doesn't want a do-over for their relationship, not once has it occurred to her that he might be involved with someone else! Already. So soon. Slowly, she walks over to a nearby bench and folds herself onto it. Marty follows, sits down next to her. A brisk wind blows off the water.

"I'm sorry," he says after a minute. "Maybe if you'd been in touch two years ago..." His voice trails off in the chilly air.

"No, no, don't be silly. There's no reason for you to be sorry. I'm glad for you. Really." Her throat feels as if there is a marble lodged halfway down it.

"Now it's your turn."

"Hmm?" she says absently.

"When we left the restaurant, you said you wanted to talk to me about something."

"Oh." She waves a hand in the air. "It was nothing. Just a little business venture I'd been thinking about, but now I realize it wouldn't work. You're too busy as it is."

His thick eyebrows knit together, dubious. "You sure?"

She nods, tears pricking at her eyes, and says, "Absolutely, positively," while managing a weak smile because it's the phrase they used with each other long ago. *Want to go for a drink? Absolutely, positively. Want to have sex? Absolutely, positively.*

Earlier, she'd promised herself that she'd tell him everything tonight. But how is that even possible now? Any mention of her own travails will sound too much like a plea for help. It will ring of desperation. How can she tell him that she's been having panic attacks and that she's pretty sure it's because she's afraid of being alone? That she has royally pissed off the Providence Mafia—and that now is a really bad time for her to be living in a house by herself. How she'd been imagining he might move in with her, or she with him. No, she won't do that to him. Not now when he's so clearly made a full life for himself, is already starting fresh. Nor will she humiliate herself further.

The realization that Marty has been over her for a very

long time seems so obvious—yet also utterly astonishing. Over the years, she has invented a relationship between them, as if they were characters in a book she could consult whenever she felt the urge. But it's clear that, for Martin, Claire has only ever reappeared on the margins of his thoughts.

She has half a mind to leap into the water herself, perform some desperate act that will make him jump in after her. To shake him awake and remind him of what they had! *But we were so good together, Martin*, she wants to shout. *I didn't realize it then. And I'm sorry. I blew it. Can't we try again? I know so much more now. I'm more patient. I'm happy with the little things in life. I'm not so greedy. My career might be over, anyway. Don't you want to spend the rest of the time you have left on this earth with me? Forget this Cora person!*

For a second, she believes she might have uttered her thoughts aloud and, panicked, she turns to see his reaction. But he's only staring out at the water, peaceful and content.

This is what she must reconcile with herself then, right here, right now. Whatever occurred tonight is nothing more than a lovely dinner between old friends, reminiscing together. Sharing the highlights of their lives since they parted ways some thirty years ago. Their story isn't one for the *New York Times*'s Vows section, as she might have hoped, but rather for the *Boston Globe*'s Connections column. Because what she and Marty share is a simple connection, based on a long-ago love story.

She clears her throat, checks her watch and pats his leg. "Well, it's getting late. Nearly ten o'clock." She laughs. "Whoever thought we'd be calling ten o'clock late, huh? Anyway, I should be getting back to my hotel."

"The Seafarer, right? Pretty ritzy stuff over there. Audrey and I stayed there once. Happened to be the same weekend that Jennifer Lopez was in town. She'd rented the penthouse. It was a bit of a zoo, but fun to people-watch."

He jumps up and offers her his hand. "Why don't you let me walk you the rest of the way? It's not far." And she demurs.

For the remaining several minutes they stroll along, hardly talking, the buzz of traffic on Seaport Boulevard filling the silences. When they reach the walkway in front of the hotel, Marty bends down and softly grazes his lips across hers. "That's for all those times I wanted to kiss you but you'd already left."

She's about to make a joke about how she guesses she'd better not invite him up to her room but thinks better of it. "I'm glad I got to see you," she says simply and elevates on her tiptoes to kiss him lightly on his whiskered cheek.

"Me, too." His hand squeezes hers before he turns to hail a cab. "And, hey," he calls over his shoulder, "now that you have my number, stay in touch, okay?"

"I will!" she calls out, climbing the stairs to the hotel porch and grabbing the wooden railing to steady herself, completely forgetting that she's still wearing his jacket. But they both know as they walk away from each other that it's the last time she'll be reaching out to him. To do so again, she thinks, would probably destroy her.

TWENTY

Before they step on the boat, Jason tells Gwen he has to take this call. Already George has sent him four texts since yesterday, and Jason has responded to none of them. The fact that his department head is now calling, not texting, must mean that the Charlie Problem, despite Jason's ignoring it, has not gone away. Gwen reluctantly steps over to the side of the small walkway that's meant to carry them onto their boat to wait for him.

"George," he says, struggling to sound as upbeat as possible. "Sorry, I haven't gotten back to you. Gwen surprised me with a little getaway for my birthday in Boston. I've been meaning to give you a call. What's going on?"

"It's Charlie Wiggam, one of your students? He's filed a complaint against the university and, more specifically, against you."

Jason clears his throat. "I'm sorry. Say that again?"

"A complaint, Jason. He's claiming that he saw you out at Old Marley's a few weeks ago, that you'd had a few and started giving him a hard time, and that, well, essentially you slugged him."

"What?" Jason can't believe what he's hearing. Old Marley's is a restaurant-bar a few miles off campus where students go when they're craving good food as opposed to the lousy stuff served in the cafeteria. Jason and Gwen have been there a handful of times themselves simply because there's a dearth of decent restaurants in their small town. "That's ridiculous," he says. "No way. Didn't happen. Not in a million years."

"I'm glad to hear you say that," George says. "When you didn't get back to me yesterday, I started to worry."

Jason sends Gwen, who's now shooting him beseeching looks from the gateway, a hurried nod. "C'mon, you know I'd never do anything like that. I flunked him in Introductory Russian History, and he's pissed. This is pure retaliation. He sent me a text the other day basically calling me an asshole."

There's a grunt on the other end. "Are you sure? Did you keep the text? Why didn't you tell me? It's university protocol, you know, to report it when a student sends any kind of harassing communication."

Jason kicks the edge of the sidewalk where a piece of loose cement has buckled up over the edge, and it goes skittering across the road. "I know. I was going to tell you, but I figured it could wait till I got back home. I thought the kid was blowing off steam. This whole thing is nothing but sour grapes."

"Well, even if it is, it's still a pretty serious charge he's leveling. Assault. The good news is that he's not taking it to the police. He's agreed to let the university handle it. But it's the kind of situation that, if things don't go your way, you could get kicked off campus for good."

If he weren't so incredulous, Jason might burst out laughing. George has no idea that this is what Jason has been considering for himself anyway, with or without Charlie Wiggam's help. Maybe, he considers, it's a blessing in disguise, the final shove he needs to convince him to wave goodbye to academia once and for all.

"Does he say when this was supposed to have happened? Because I'm pretty sure I'll have an alibi."

"Yeah, hold on a sec." Jason can hear George rattling through some papers on the other end. "May fifteenth," he says finally. "The complaint alleges that he was there with a couple of friends, that you guys met up in the parking lot and that you exchanged words. Something about how he better get his act together in class or else, and then—I'm quoting here—'Next thing the plaintiff knew, without any provocation on the plaintiff's part whatsoever, the defendant punched him in the stomach.'"

The irony is almost too rich to be true. Here Jason has punched a guy at the MFA, who arguably didn't deserve it, and now he's being accused of assault on a student whom he's never even laid a finger on.

"Jesus," Jason says, feeling the heat of Gwen's gaze on him. "I did no such thing, you gotta believe me. I don't think I was even there in May."

"I believe you, buddy," says George. "But it's your word against his, and well, I probably don't have to tell you this, but his daddy is Ryan Wiggam."

Jason is silent for a moment.

"Of Wiggam's Sporting Goods?" George says for clarification.

"No way."

"Yeah, big bucks there. But don't worry. If this kid is lying, we'll get it out of him. It wouldn't be the first time our department has been hit with a nuisance complaint by a disgruntled student."

"Well, he's full of shit. I mean, he barely passed the midterm. I told him he better do well on the paper and final exam, but both were a joke. He didn't even try. He earned that F fair and square."

"All right. I gotta say, I feel much better after talking to you. When are you getting back to town?"

"Um, tomorrow afternoon, I think?" Jason eyes Gwen, who's now waving her hands at him as if the boat is on fire. He better get over there if he doesn't want to miss the sunset cruise—or royally piss her off.

"Okay, well, stop by the office when you get back. I'll be there till six."

"You got it," Jason says. "Hey, George?"

"Yeah?"

"I shouldn't be thinking about, um, hiring a lawyer or anything, should I?"

There's silence for a moment. "Nah, the university's legal department should have it handled."

"Okay, cool. And thanks, man. I'm sorry again about keeping you waiting."

"Yeah, next time when I text you," he says, "you might want to get back to me on the same day."

"I will. For sure." And he clicks off. There's a part of him that thinks maybe he and Gwen should drive back up to campus tonight and stop this asinine accusation from spiraling out of control. How dare that punk try to weasel his way out of a grade by falsely accusing him! Jason has half a mind to show Charlie Wiggam what a punch to the stomach *really* feels like.

But, no, he knows that won't solve anything. Instead, he walks quickly over to Gwen and takes her hand, which, in turn, makes his own hand smart. It's still scratched and bruised from yesterday, and his right thumb has turned a deep purple. It's definitely sprained, possibly broken. *Slow down*, he tells himself. *Cool down.* "I'm starting to feel like a broken record," she says under her breath, clearly annoyed. "But is everything okay?"

"I'm not sure," he admits, debating how much to reveal. "That was George. Apparently, there's this kid—" he begins, but the shipman interrupts him, clasping Gwen's hand and pulling her onto the boat.

"Welcome aboard!" he says. He's dressed in navy pants, a white shirt with a blue square-knotted neckerchief and a white sailor cap. His floppy dark hair pokes out from underneath his hat. "So glad you two could make it."

"Sorry we're late. My bad," Jason says.

"Not a problem, mate!" The guy's fake cheer makes Jason cringe internally. "You're just in time for the sail-off."

He and Gwen make their way toward the bow of the boat, where a group of passengers, mostly other couples, already line up along the gunwales to watch the sunset. Their jolly sailor provides a quick demonstration on nautical safety, showing how to buckle a life jacket in the event of an emergency. Jason and Gwen exchange glances because it's pretty clear any fool could figure it out.

When the safety demo mercifully concludes, he leads Gwen over to the front, where she poses for the obligatory *Titanic* photo, arms outstretched at her sides, yelling "I'm the king of the world!" A few people snicker, but Jason could care less and snaps the photo. The sun, a vibrant orange-red, teeters on the horizon, as if it's ready to fall off the earth at any moment, and Gwen leans back in his arms to watch the show.

It occurs to him that his thirty-third birthday is almost over, and surprisingly, it hasn't been a total bust, save for George's phone call. After last night, he'd thought he and Gwen might be done. Kaput. But when he'd tried to raise it again this afternoon, say how sorry he was, she'd pressed her finger to his lips and said "*Shh*, I don't want to talk about it on your birthday. I am paying a small fortune for this vacation, and we are going to enjoy it." Jason was only too happy to oblige. They'd spent most of the day in bed, ordering gourmet hamburgers and ice cream sundaes off the room-service menu, making love, watching bad movies on the Movie Channel, even dozing off. In fact, they'd been so ensconced in their own little world that they'd almost missed the cruise entirely, waking up forty-five minutes before the sail-off. Their cab ride over to Long Wharf had been more of a sprinting roller-coaster ride (his stomach has only recently returned to its normal level) than a sightseeing venture.

Now the evening stretches before them like an enormous blanket, and for a brief moment, Jason wishes he could wrap the two of them in it, shielding them from the rest of the world, its screwed-up problems, its Charlies. He refuses to let that kid ruin his day. Just because he's filed a complaint doesn't mean he won't cave as soon as Jason calls his bluff. He doesn't care if the kid's father is Daddy Warbucks. You can't lie yourself out of a failing grade. Jason tells himself he'll deal with everything tomorrow. "Thank you, babe," he says in a soft voice. "For booking this for us." Gwen nestles more deeply into his arms.

"You're welcome. Happy birthday."

There's a sharp pinch of relief, as if maybe she really has forgiven him for, if not entirely forgotten, yesterday.

"Hey, what were you saying about George?" she asks.

But he shakes his head. It's not worth getting into right

now. "It's not important." Because regardless of whether Charlie decides to drop his threat, Jason's more certain than ever that he can't go back to campus now. Not to teach, not to finish up his dissertation. Only to hand in the key to his office. Because what's the point? He doesn't want to worry about disgruntled punks coming after him every time he hands out a bad grade. *Forget it*, he thinks. "Hey," he says, as the boat's engine begins to rumble and the crew hastens to untie the standing end of the line. "Think we'll see any whales?"

Friday, June 11, 2021

TWENTY-ONE

The flashbulbs wink as soon as he steps out onto the Sea-farer's grandiose, wraparound porch. Not that there's any need for them. The midafternoon sun splashes across the whitewashed porch so that he has to squint to peer out into the bright day. Maybe six to eight camera crews are gathered on the front lawn. Standing next to Jean-Paul is Boston's police commissioner, Hal Fisher, in his blue uniform, the sunlight glancing off his badge. Knowing that the commissioner is here to run interference gives Jean-Paul the shot of courage he desperately needs right now. Every word he chooses must be uttered with supreme discretion, since it will be rehashed and scrutinized on tonight's news. The commissioner, thank goodness, is much better versed in equivocation with the press than Jean-Paul.

"Good afternoon," Jean-Paul begins and leans in closer to the microphone, prompting a nails-across-the-chalkboard squeak. He steps back. "Sorry about that." He clears his throat. "My name is Jean-Paul Savant, and I'm the general manager of the Seafarer. Today we have experienced what can only be described as a tragedy." The commissioner takes a step forward, and Jean-Paul immediately panics that already he's misspoken during his informal welcome. "I'm going to read a brief statement first," he continues, "and then Commissioner Fisher and I will try to answer your questions to the best of our ability." He pauses and unfolds his formal statement, scripted by their czar of PR, Julie Morgan.

Already there are hands up among the crowd of reporters. A few call out his name, trying to get his attention. "Mr. Savant, Mr. Savant, is it true that the victim jumped?"

"Can you give us the victim's name?"

"Hold up," the commissioner says, raising a big, beefy palm in the air. "Let the man speak before you pepper him with questions."

His booming words seem to have the desired effect because the crowd quiets. Jean-Paul begins again.

"Today at the Seafarer, we have experienced what can only be described as a tragedy. A woman lost her life. At the present moment, we are cooperating with local authorities to find out what exactly transpired. We are in the process of notifying the family of the deceased, and our hearts and prayers go out to them during this difficult time. Once they've been notified, we can release the victim's name. In approximately one hour, we hope to give you an update on any recent developments. And with that, I'll turn it over to the commissioner. Thank you."

A barrage of questions from reporters follows, but the commissioner steps up to the microphone as soon as Jean-Paul finishes.

He speaks off-the-cuff, any pertinent numbers scrawled in

his notebook. He's a big man, probably six feet five inches, and has to straighten the microphone so that it stretches to his chin. "Good afternoon," he says in a commanding voice. "At 12:34 this afternoon, the Boston Police were summoned to the Seafarer Hotel. Upon arrival, a woman was discovered lying facedown on the terrace, where she appeared to have fallen from a considerable height. Emergency vehicles were dispatched, whereupon the woman was taken immediately to Massachusetts General Hospital, and where, at 1:05 p.m., she was pronounced dead.

"This is being handled as a death investigation, and as such, we're asking for anyone who might have information or who might have been a witness to the incident to please contact the Boston Police Department at the number below on your screen. If any of our first responders or other witnesses is in need of emotional support, there are therapists on hand at the hotel. Call the number on your screen, or reach out to me or Mr. Savant directly. We'll get you set up.

"Rest assured that we're working to determine what happened at this very public scene as quickly as possible. Just recently, our victim was identified, and, as Mr. Savant told you, we're in the process of notifying her family now. Once we do that, we'll be able to release a name to you all. Thank you."

They've agreed to take questions, but they answer only a few at the commissioner's discretion. The journalists want to know if there are any suspects. Could it be a homicide? Any evidence that she was pushed? Do they know which room she fell from? Is there video surveillance of the fall? Has anyone ever jumped from the hotel balcony in the Seafarer's history?

All excellent questions and ones that Jean-Paul desperately wishes he had the answers to. The commissioner graciously, boldly declines to answer. "Thanks, but that's all we have for now. Thank you." Jean-Paul follows him back inside the hotel.

"Well, I think that went as well as could be expected," he says, and Jean-Paul nods, having no idea how one measures a successful press conference. "The important thing is to keep the victim's name out of it until we can talk to the family, and we did that."

Again, Jean-Paul nods, says "Yes, right." His phone buzzes. It's Marie.

"Sorry, Commissioner," he says. "Mind if I take this?"

"Go right ahead. I'll catch up with you later."

Jean-Paul steps away into the alcove that houses the vending machines for a sliver of privacy. "Honey?" he says into the phone. "Honey, are you there?" He holds one finger to his ear in an attempt to drown out the buzz of the lobby.

"I just saw you on the news! Oh, how awful," she says. "Are you okay? Is there anything I can do?" He understands the flurry of questions, the compulsion to help, but there's nothing she can do. For a moment, he's seized by a sense of guilt: he's forgotten to call Marie. Shouldn't his wife's voice have been the first thing he wanted to hear after witnessing such a horrific incident? But, no, he reasons, there hasn't been a moment's peace until now.

"I'm okay," he says now. "A little rattled. Still stunned, I think. It was pretty awful."

"Oh, honey. Were you there? Did you see it happen?"

"Not directly. But I saw her." He pauses, the ruined face flashing across his mind again. "I mean, the victim. I saw her right after she fell. She was already gone."

There's a sharp intake of air on the other end. "How awful," Marie says again in a quiet voice.

"Yeah."

"Did she jump?"

"Don't know yet." He sighs and rubs his forehead. A headache is pushing at his temples; he'll have to remember to grab some Tylenol from the concierge desk when he gets off the phone. That and one of the Milky Ways staring at him from the vending machine. When was the last time he had anything to eat? he wonders. This morning? "Anyway, I'm not really supposed to talk about it. The police are handling everything now."

"Of course. I'm so, so sorry, love. I wish I could give you a hug. It's…it's just unspeakably awful." He can hear Isabella gurgling in the background. Incomprehensible baby syllables, wonderfully oblivious to the world.

Unspeakably awful. Those are the words that have eluded him. And again the compulsion to race home to his family and bolt all the doors washes over him. Because it *is* unspeakably awful. If only they could start the day over! Would it have made any difference? What if he'd been walking the grounds at the precise moment when the woman was up on her balcony? Would he have seen her? Would he have been able to radio for help in time? There's no way of knowing, and yet, how he wishes there was something he could have done to prevent it. Finally, his voice breaking, he manages to say, "It is. You're right. Unspeakably awful." He's struggling to regain his composure. His stomach rumbles. He needs food. "But I've got to go. I'll call you when I know more."

"Yes, do," she says before clicking off.

He fishes in his wallet for a crisp dollar bill and smooths it out before sticking it into the vending machine. If it shoots back out, so help him God, he will lose it. But, mercifully, the machine sucks his dollar up, and Jean-Paul punches in the coordinates: D,3. He waits, watching the coil spin around, working to push out the candy bar from the fourth row down. It inches forward to be released—and then snags on the coil, suspended in midair.

"Merde!" Jean-Paul says under his breath and kicks the machine, completely forgetting his station for a moment, losing his mind. He spins around, afraid someone has witnessed his outburst, but it's only Jean-Paul here in the snack alcove.

When he turns back, he begins to laugh, a slightly maniacal laugh. Because there, in the slot at the bottom, sits his Milky Way, dislodged by his angry, vicious kick to the machine's side. He reaches in and grabs it, practically biting off the wrapper and devouring it in a few solid, famished bites.

Earlier that week

TWENTY-TWO

What has she done? Oh no, oh no! is what passes through her mind as she stabs the elevator button to get back to her room on Thursday night. There's no one riding up with her, thankfully, but she wants desperately to get back to her room before she breaks down completely. "How stupid can you be?" Claire angry-whispers into the air. To think she actually believed Marty would wrap her in his arms and tell her he wanted her back, that he couldn't wait to spend the next years of his life with her. Outrageous! Verging on insane. For the first time, she wonders if maybe since Walt's death she has been living in some kind of alternate universe, only her children have been too afraid to tell her. To tether her back to earth, to the here and now. To reality.

For God's sake, Claire, she chides herself. *Why would you expect a man you haven't seen in thirty years to still be carrying a torch for you?* "Idiot!" she scolds herself when she steps off the elevator and strides fitfully toward her room.

The door shut behind her, she throws herself down on the fluffy white comforter and allows herself a good, long cry. She has been so stupid, so utterly foolish. Like a schoolgirl with a crush. When she'd stumbled upon Audrey's obituary months ago, she'd taken it as a sign. Martin was free, too! And the compulsion to find him had grown into a near obsession. Her heartbreak is gigantic, the floodgates breaking open. If she were home, she'd run into the woods behind the house and scream as loudly and as long as she could. She'd kick something hard, maybe hard enough to break a toe. She'd hurl a dish against the wall, throw an entire shelfful of books across the room. But she's in a hotel. That won't work. Still, she manages to sob into her pillow a bitter, crestfallen *Fuck you, Martin!*

Eventually, when she's pretty certain there are no tears left—at least not for tonight—she pushes up from the bed and goes into the bathroom to wash her face. The image that stares back at her is unfamiliar. Her eyes are swollen, her lips puckered from crying. She's a mess, a pathetic, brokenhearted disaster. She splashes cold water on her face and pats it dry, staring at the fine lines that she's quite certain weren't there earlier tonight. Or had she just missed them? Getting ready for dinner, she'd felt pretty for the first time in months. Now she understands it was all an illusion, a mirage. The urge to change into her pajamas and crawl into bed is overwhelming.

But no, she counsels herself. She won't do it. Instead, she summons all her strength and channels her inner Ruth Bader Ginsburg, who has become her own personal touchstone whenever Claire experiences a pang of self-pity. Because RBG tackled overt sexism at Harvard Law School, raised a baby while in law school, helped her husband fight testicular cancer while in law school, and on and on and on. Who is she, Claire O'Dell, to feel sorry for herself because of one disappointing evening?

With shaky resolve, she begins to start the process of re-applying mascara to her paper-thin lashes, a dash of blush, a smattering of face powder, a swipe of burgundy across her lips. It's only ten forty-five, she reasons. Plenty of time to head down to the hotel bar and drown her sorrows in another cocktail or two. Yesterday when she'd stepped off the elevator on the second floor by mistake, the cherry-paneled tavern had caught her eye. The place, lined with shelves of books, had reminded her more of a library than a bar. She'd been tempted to go in, but it was the middle of the afternoon—and drinking by herself midday seemed, well, unseemly. *Ha!* she thinks now. The joke is on her—she should have marched right in there and started downing whiskey sours straight through till tonight, in which case she would never have had dinner with Marty in the first place.

She brushes out her hair one last time and reexamines herself in the mirror. A little makeup, and she's almost back to her old self. She could, she thinks, pass for her late fifties, possibly early fifties in good light. On the bed, she plops down and straps on the Kenneth Cole sandals she'd gifted herself earlier today—when she'd been imagining Marty pulling them off later tonight. Now she sees them for what they are. Ridiculously expensive shoes with a too-high heel that she has no right to be wearing.

It reminds her of a summer night when she and Marty had dressed up to go into Boston—their junior year in college—and she'd worn heels so high she could barely maneuver across the cobblestoned streets of the North End. At one point her heel had gotten wedged in between the stones, and Marty had to yank it out. Except when he did, the heel ripped right off. Oh, how they'd laughed! (They were inexpensive sandals, so Claire didn't mind.) She'd tried hobbling along, one foot up in a heel, the other trailing along, but it was hopeless. Finally Marty ripped the heel off the other one and slipped it into his jacket pocket. For the rest of the evening, Claire traipsed around in her flat, heelless shoes, no one the wiser that a few hours ago she'd been three inches taller.

But what does any of that matter now? It doesn't. The fact that she's devoted the last few months to imagining the press of Martin's lips against hers, of climbing into bed to cradle his warm body, means nothing. For the first time maybe in her entire life, the sting of unrequited love has snuck up on her. And the recalculation of all that she's been counting on—now up in smoke—demands so much brainpower, is such a steep mathematical curve to reconfigure, that a sense of vertigo practically overwhelms her. How does she go from counting on Martin to fix everything to admitting that she is completely on her own?

She allows herself to consider that maybe Marty's relationship with this woman, this Cora (what a ridiculous name!), is short-lived. After all, they've been dating for only eight months. Eight months! Maybe they haven't even had sex yet. It's possible. And maybe in a few short weeks Marty will call to say that he's had a change of heart and wants Claire back.

But even Claire understands how unlikely this is, that whatever spark there used to be between the two of them has been extinguished. While they sat across from each other at Bricco, she'd sensed something was off. The only time the man's face had truly lit up was when he spoke of his daughters. Claire had searched his voice for that same radiance when he remembered their time together, but then it dawned on her that he'd already slotted her into another category: a fond memory. Tied to a particular space and time. When they'd both been younger, much different people.

She steps off the elevator, smooths her dress and crosses the foyer to the bar. The dark wood makes it seem even darker in the nighttime. Table or counter seating? she debates. Her eyes slide across the room to see if anyone famous might be lurking in the corners, remembering Marty's encounter with Jennifer Lopez. Maybe Robert De Niro or Meryl Streep, someone Claire would actually recognize. But there's no one notable, save for a youngish, attractive man in a sharp blue blazer and khaki pants sitting at the bar. When she plops down one seat over, he glances her way and offers a small smile. It takes her a second to determine where she's seen him before, but then it comes to her—he's the same young man who was playing tennis with his girlfriend yesterday morning.

"Oh, hello, there," she says and orders herself a martini. "I almost didn't recognize you. You clean up nicely."

He laughs, says, "Thanks. I think?"

And it's the beginning of a conversation that, given their disastrous nights thus far, neither of them could have predicted.

Jason doesn't know what to make of the woman who sits down next to him, who looks old enough to be his mother. For a second, he worries she might be hitting on him but then realizes she seems in need of a drink as badly as he is. Her eyes are red and puffy underneath the makeup. She's pretty, like she might have been a catch back in the day. Her ash-blond hair is cut to shoulder-length, and she's wearing a blue polka-dot summer dress, maybe back from a fancy dinner or the theater. Jason doesn't feel like striking up a conversation but finds himself in that awkward position of not being able to switch to a table without risking offending her.

Plus, she seems vaguely familiar. She surprises him when she says hello, tells him he cleans up nicely.

"So, how was your tennis match?" she asks, which is when it clicks. It's the lady from the elevator yesterday. From her martini, she plucks out the olive and slides it off the tooth-pick into her mouth. That she does this in such a matter-of-fact way, without a hint of seduction, intrigues him.

"I got my butt kicked," he says with a laugh. "Serves me right."

Her gaze settles on him for a long moment, so long, in fact, that Jason shifts uncomfortably in his seat. He won-ders if he's offended her. But she sips her martini thought-fully and finally says, "No offense, but I figured that might happen. Your girlfriend—or at least I assumed she was your girlfriend—looked much better prepared than you did."

"Yeah, that applies to pretty much everything we do. Al-though, she definitely has a leg up on me in tennis. She al-most went pro."

"Really?" It's clear that she's impressed. "Well, good for her. I come from a generation where when the gym teacher told us to run around the track once, we all looked at each other like he was crazy." Jason laughs. "I'm Claire, by the way," she says and extends her hand, her slender fingers stud-ded with rings.

"Jason," he says, taking it. "Nice to meet you."

"So, I don't mean to pry..." she begins. "Or, maybe I do." She smiles gamely. "But where *is* your girlfriend? Already turn in for the night?"

"Yeah, unfortunately, the sunset cruise we went on turned out to be more like the sunset blues. The water was a little choppy." He'd been surprised, especially because when they'd set sail the harbor had been exceedingly calm. But halfway into their three-hour excursion, the wind had picked up enough to start rocking the boat to and fro. Gwen and a few other passengers headed into the cabin to rest their heads on a table. When the captain turned the boat around for shore, she'd vomited all over the floor. Which prompted another passenger to get sick. It was, Jason thought, a little like being trapped inside that scene from *The Goonies*, where one kid after another starts throwing up.

By the time they finally stepped off, Gwen was still pretty wobbly on her feet. "Is it okay if I go back up to the room?" she asked. "I think I should probably lie down." So he'd helped her up to their suite, tucked her into bed and kissed her on the forehead, trying to ignore the sour smell on her breath. He's pretty sure there's still some puke stuck in her hair.

"Oh, I'm sorry to hear that," Claire says. "I've heard those cruises can be rough."

"Yeah, live and learn. How about you? What brings you here?"

"Hmm. Let's see," she says. "I guess you could say I came to the Seafarer for a little vacation. I wanted to get away from the rat race for a few days, and I've heard such great things about it. I'm a journalist." Then she adds, "My husband also passed away nine months ago, and I haven't gotten out much since then."

He inhales sharply and reprimands himself. *Boy, waded right into that one, didn't you, buddy?* "I'm so sorry," he says. "Nine months isn't that long ago."

She tilts her head and smiles faintly. "No, it's not. But don't feel sorry for me. I also came here with less-than-pure intentions. Something my own children know nothing about."

Now things are getting interesting, he thinks. "Well, you can tell me since chances are you'll never see me again." When she hesitates, he adds, "No pressure. Just, you know, if you were looking to get it off your chest."

"I like you Jason...Jason what-did-you-say-your-last-name-was-again?" Her words slur at the edges, and she scoots her glass and herself along with it onto the bar chair directly next to him.

He hadn't said but now he supplies it. "Wadsworth. Jason Wadsworth."

"I like that," she exclaims. "That's a name with character. *Jason Wadsworth*. Well, Jason Wadsworth, let me tell you something." She leans in closer to him, as if she's about to reveal her deepest, darkest secret. "I came here specifically to look up an old boyfriend of mine."

He leans back in his chair, surprised.

"I know," she says, wagging a finger at him. "I know what you're thinking. That I'm too old to have a boyfriend, right?"

"I didn't say that." It's exactly what he was thinking.

"This was the man I almost married a long, long, looong time ago." She drains the rest of her martini and orders another. "Get you another?" she asks, and Jason says, "Yes, please."

"And whatever he's having," she calls out to their bartender. "Anyway, we went to high school together and dated all through college. We were so in love. I was sure he was the man I was going to marry. But then, who knows what happened really? I started to get claustrophobic, I guess, thinking that he wanted me to be his wife and nothing else. But I had plans! Plans to become a famous journalist, you know. I was worried about subsuming my identity to a man." She pauses. "Is that the right word? *Subsume?* I think so. Anyway, long story short, I married someone else, and so did he. Then his wife died three years ago, and when my husband passed, I thought to myself, Hey, maybe he's lonely, too. Maybe there's an old spark we could rekindle."

The bartender sets down their fresh drinks before them. "Sounds reasonable to me," Jason says. He can feel the buzz working its way around his head.

"Does it?" Her gaze fixes on him, as if it really matters what he thinks. "I'm glad to hear you say that because honestly for the last hour and a half, I was pretty sure I'd lost my mind."

He laughs softly. "Nah."

"Anyway," she says, focusing back on her drink, "turns out there's no spark there, alas. Nada. Zilch. Or at least, it's only one-sided."

"Oh, man. I'm sorry. That's rough." Someone has dropped money in the old-fashioned jukebox, and a Peter Frampton tune drifts through the bar. A few more people have joined them at the counter so that they practically have to shout to hear each other now. Claire, he notices, is swaying slightly in her chair.

"So now what?" he asks.

"*So now what?*" she asks, as if she's not following.

"Well, you said this guy isn't into you anymore, so now what?"

"Oh," she says, and her expression dims. "I'm not sure, I guess."

"Well, come on, there's got to be someone else." There's no explaining why he's suddenly invested in her well-being—maybe it's the couple of Jamesons he's had—but it's almost as if he needs to know how her story ends. As if it will point him in the right direction, if only they can figure out how best to redirect hers. Here's a woman who has lost her husband, who has been jilted by an old boyfriend, and he can't get his act together for Gwen, the woman who is undeniably the best thing that's ever happened to him?

"Someone else?" She sounds surprised. "Oh, no. I don't think so. Marty was the only one left in my stack of cards. No one else." She drums her fingers on the countertop. "And Walt, of course. He was my husband. It's funny, I spent most of my life thinking he wasn't a very good husband. But now I can see that he actually was a pretty decent man. We made it work, you know? We raised two kids. That counts for something."

"I'd imagine that counts for a lot."

"And the last year with him, after he retired, was nice, too. We had some good times together. We kept each other company, and when you come right down to it, I suppose that's largely what marriage is all about. Someone to tell that the milk has gone sour. Someone to take a walk with, watch your favorite television show with."

"Although, you could do those things with a dog, too," Jason points out.

"Ha!"

He waits for her to go on but she's quiet. "It's funny, isn't it?" she continues after a moment. "How you can convince yourself that, if only you'd made another choice, your whole life would have turned out so much better? But then, that's not really the case, is it? We like to fool ourselves." She pauses to sip her martini. "But we don't know that a different path would have necessarily been better. It might have been worse. No, we all live the life we're meant to live."

The sudden philosophical twist to the conversation surprises him, and he finds himself wondering how it might apply to his own situation. Will he look back on leaving academia and regret his choice? Or is this new open-ended path, whatever it might turn out to be, the one he's meant to follow? Is he supposed to be with Gwen? If his dad hadn't been such a prick, would Jason still be inclined to his mad rages? It strikes him as a bit defeatist, believing everyone ends up where they are supposed to.

"Maybe," he says. "But doesn't that take free will and hard work and determination out of the equation? I mean, why even bother trying, if you're going to end up in the same place anyway?" He's enjoying their talk more than he could have predicted.

"Ah, you're a philosopher, I see."

"Nah, history professor," he says. "Well, almost. If I ever finish my dissertation."

She twists around in her chair, as if considering him in a new light.

"A smart guy, nonetheless." Her eyes narrow. "You make a good point, though—and I've had way too much to drink to refute it. You're right. You have to be motivated to achieve what you want in life. The argument I'm trying to make, though—and not very well, apparently—is that there's no point in regretting the choices you *have* made. You'll only make yourself unhappy wondering what could have been."

His mind feels as if it's spinning while he tries to follow along, but the whiskey is making it difficult.

"Anyway, I chose one man, and not the other. I thought if I married Marty I'd end up pregnant in the suburbs without a career. You know what's strange, though?"

Jason shakes his head.

"Turns out I ended up in the suburbs, anyway. A big white colonial with black shutters. And I got pregnant on our honeymoon. So things didn't really turn out that differently."

She drains the rest of her martini. "Listen to me! Poor you. Here I am rambling, and I've hardly asked you about yourself. Like what are your intentions with this girlfriend of yours? Are you going to ask her to marry you?"

Jason can only laugh at her boldness. The martinis have pulled off all the brakes.

"Sorry, I'm intruding again. I do that. It's the journalist in me. It's none of my business, and you should feel free to tell me so."

"No, it's not that. I just...I honestly don't know where things are headed with us. She's a great girl, and I'd be an idiot not to marry her, but—"

"Go on," she urges.

"But I'm not sure I'm good enough for her, I guess. That I deserve her."

"Ah." Claire falls back in her chair as if he's laid out an age-old conundrum. "You know what I say to that, Mr. Wadsworth?" He waits for her to tell him he's right, that he has no business dating Gwen, that she could tell from their first encounter at the elevator. Instead, she says, "Nonsense."

Jason bursts out with a laugh. "Why would you say that?"

"Let's just say that I've got a pretty good nonsense detector. And something tells me you're making up excuses for yourself."

"Huh. Maybe so."

A slight burp escapes from her. "Excuse me! Say, did I tell you I have a granddaughter? Fiona. She's three, and you've never seen such a precious angel. Anyway, I'm lucky. I've got my kids. Do you have kids yet? No, of course not. You're not even married. If I have one piece of advice for you, it's this. Have some kids if you can. Because when everyone else is gone, your kids will keep you company. Look after you. I've got a girl and a boy: Amber and Ben."

"Is that right?" He sips his whiskey. "So who does the better job? Of looking after you, I mean. Your daughter or your son?" He's purely making conversation now, asking whatever comes to mind. He's in no rush to get back to the room.

"Now *that*..." she pokes the countertop, slurring her words again "...is an interesting question. Amber would tell you that she takes care of me, that she's the one always checking in on me. But I'd tell you it's really Ben. He pretends to take a back seat, but Ben's really the one looking out for me. That mother–son bond is powerful stuff, you know."

He nods his head.

"Anyway, I think I should head home." She giggles. "Oops, guess I better pay the bill first."

But the bartender waves her off. "You're all set."

"But what about your tip?" Claire demands.

"Already taken care of. Automatic gratuity charged to your room."

"Oh, isn't that handy?" she says. "In that case, thank you very much. Your service has been impeccable." Although it comes out sounding more like *impickible*.

She wobbles getting down from her chair, and it's clear that she'll need some assistance getting home. "I got her," Jason says when the bartender shoots him a concerned look. "Come on, Claire, let's get you back to your room. What's your room number?"

"Another excellent question!" She giggles while he helps her to the elevator. "Ten-oh-eight? Or maybe it's ten-ten? I'm not really sure."

"We'll find it."

"If I didn't know any better, young man, I'd think you were hitting on me."

He grins and hits floor ten on the elevator panel.

As they leave the bar, a man sitting at a far corner table makes another call to his client. "Just wanted to let you know that Ms. O'Dell is headed back to her room for the night, and from the looks of it, she'll be sleeping in late tomorrow."

The voice on the other end says, "Okay. Thank you for letting me know. Check in with you tomorrow."

Friday, June 11, 2021

TWENTY-THREE

Riley is running late for their tasting at the Seafarer Hotel. It's twenty past eleven, and she's due at the restaurant no later than noon. Earlier this morning, she promised Tom that she'd be there in plenty of time. But then one of her all-time favorite customers, Mr. Seymour, had walked into the store, wanting a bouquet of irises for his seventy-year-old wife, who lives in an assisted-living home and has Alzheimer's, and Riley didn't have the heart to rush him. So now she's standing on the subway platform, saying a silent prayer that the train to South Station, and not the one to Alewife, will pull in first. If it's the Alewife train, it'll tag another fifteen minutes onto her commute.

A street musician, long-limbed and with the chiseled features of someone who hasn't enjoyed a full meal in a while, sits on a folding chair, strumming "Brown Eyed Girl" on his guitar. A small child, probably no more than two, bounces along to the song in his toddler-size Chuck Taylors, which Riley thinks might be the cutest thing ever. If she and Tom have kids, she'll definitely buy them little Chuck Taylor sneakers. She watches the boy's mom press a dollar into his hand and try to persuade him to drop it into the open guitar case lying at the musician's feet. But he's having none of it—he yelps and clutches the dollar tightly in his pudgy hand. The mother apologizes and fishes another bill out of her wallet—a five this time—and tosses it into the case. The small crowd gathered laughs and claps when the little boy finally relents and tosses in his dollar, too. When her train—not the Alewife-bound one—pulls up, Riley adds another dollar to the collection, grateful for her luck.

On the car she presses through a cluster of Harvard students who smell vaguely of weed and manages to find the one remaining seat. The train's wheels squeal as it heads for Central Square, then Kendall. Finally it bursts out of the tunnel into the sunlight and barrels across the Longfellow Bridge, the Charles River a bright ribbon unfolding below. On the left, the gentle curve of the Hatch Shell juts out, reminding Riley of all the runs she and Tom have logged on those paths. Probably more than a hundred. If they do buy a house and move to the suburbs one day, jogging along this river is one thing she'll miss.

The train plunges into darkness again as it pulls into the Park Street tunnel. Two more stops until she gets off. Riley braces herself for their luncheon. She tells herself it's no big deal, that it's only a tasting and ultimately it's up to her and Tom where the reception will be. But in the back of her mind is Marilyn's surprise visit to the flower shop yesterday and the disturbing sense that her mother-in-law-to-be has a very particular script for how she imagines her son's wedding day will go. Riley doesn't appreciate being steamrolled.

It's a fine line that she's walking today, probably the first of many. She sighs and checks her phone for any texts from Tom demanding to know where she is, but thankfully there's nothing. It's eleven forty—still room to make it on time. Once she's off the train, it's no more than a ten minute walk to the restaurant. Riley doesn't want to come across as ungrateful or indecisive or disagreeable this afternoon. But despite the holiday dinners (and occasional weekend or summer vacation) she has shared with Tom's family, she wouldn't exactly describe them as welcoming, like her own parents would be. Her father met Tom once when he flew out to Boston for a weekend, and they all enjoyed steaks and more than a few laughs at Del Frisco's. Had her mom been around, there's no question she would have swept Tom into one of her huge hugs, demanding to know everything about him. Conversely, Riley feels as if Marilyn tolerates her in small doses, like charity work she'd rather not be doing.

Tom tells her it's all in her head, that his parents adore her, that his mother has a strange way of showing affection. And it's okay, she tells herself, if his parents aren't in love with her nor she with them. It's Tom whom she's marrying, after all. But does it make her a bad person that a piece of her was hoping for a surrogate mom when she inherited a mother-in-law? That in losing her own mother, she'd be gifted the most fabulous mother-in-law because that's how the law of averages worked? Because the universe owed her that? It's silly, she knows, but somehow she'd been envisioning a mother-in-law whom she could meet for the odd midweek cocktail, with whom she could wander museums, maybe talk about her favorite books. Someone who would welcome Riley into her home and offer her a warm blanket and a good book to sit by the fire with while the chili warmed on the stove, as her own mother used to do. That

Marilyn, while perfectly nice, seems interested in doing none of these things hollows her out a little.

When she'd talked to her dad last night, he'd sounded back to his old self and had tried to talk her down from her wedding stress. "Honey, the wedding is more than a year away. You have plenty of time to plan it. And don't lose sight of the important thing."

"Which is?" Riley had waited for him to say something like *finding the perfect venue*, or *having a great band*, or *being willing to compromise*. What hadn't occurred to her was the response he'd actually given.

"The important thing, honey, is that you and Tom are in love and are getting married. That's all that matters. Don't get distracted by all the hoopla." He chuckled on the other end.

"What?" she demanded. "What's so funny?"

"I'm just remembering when your mother and I tied the knot." Riley had heard this story before. "We planned it for maybe a week. She was already pregnant with you, and we wanted it to happen before the bump started to show. So it was her, me, the minister, your mom's best friend and my brother. And our parents. Your mom wore a cream suit, if I remember correctly. I think I pulled out of my closet whatever jacket and tie I owned at the time. We were so poor back then! All that mattered was we were in love."

Riley has seen photos of this day, and it's true. Her mother wore a simple cream suit, her long dark hair straight and divided down the middle, like Ali MacGraw's, the style at the time. Riley seems to recall, however, that her dad wore a blue suit. But he's right: it was a simple affair. There'd been no worrying about flower arrangements or receptions or fancy invitations.

"I think we all went out for dinner at Ponderosa because that was considered fancy back then. And for our honeymoon, we drove over to Madison for the weekend and stayed at a Holiday Inn. I was back at work on Monday. But, honey, it was the most perfect day of our lives, aside from the day you were born, of course."

Her dad's description made her throat tighten, not so much for the reminder of the simplicity of her parents' wedding but more because the love he still so clearly felt for her mom infused every word. Her parents' marriage had been a true love affair. Forty-five years cut much too short.

The announcement for South Station comes over the intercom, and Riley pushes her way through the crowded car. Up the elevator and then up another set of narrow stairs and she's on Atlantic Avenue, several short blocks away from the restaurant. Already the air is swollen with humidity, and she imagines her long dark hair frizzing as she walks. At least, she thinks, they'll have the rest of the afternoon off. She and Tom have planned it this way. After the tasting they're going for a walk along the water, will maybe grab some gelato in the North End and enjoy a lazy Friday afternoon together. It's been a long time since they've done just that—linger in each other's company without being consumed by wedding talk. They've made a pact that post lunch no one can mention the wedding for the remainder of the day. And at the thought of this, Riley hurries a bit more quickly across the bridge and over to the stately white-clapboard hotel that is the Seafarer, host to dignitaries, writers, movie stars and— Riley thinks, mildly amused—florists.

TWENTY-FOUR

On her app, Claire locates the red zigzag mapping her route to the aquarium, about ten minutes away from the hotel. It's the only remaining item on her to-do list. It's already nine thirty, but sleeping in this morning had been a necessity. How her head had ached after her night out! In her dreams, Walt had been talking to her about those damned spiders again, and as she swam up from sleep, she'd reached across the bed to drape an arm over him, certain he was lying beside her.

That he hadn't been there left her feeling rattled. Is it only because Marty shattered her heart last night that Walt crept back into her dreams again? In the first few weeks after he died, Walt would make nightly appearances, reminding her where their tax returns were filed, telling her to pay the electric bill. But then, slowly, he'd faded away, showing up only occasionally in her dreams. Last night, though, he'd felt so close! He'd been wearing the same brown cardigan and khaki pants (of course, khakis!) that he'd worn almost every day last fall, when the evenings had turned unseasonably cool, the air sharp with the scent of fallen leaves. The same cardigan he'd had on when she found him in the TV room, a book on the Peloponnesian War tented across his stomach, his forehead cold to the touch and one arm dangling off the side of the couch, the bluish fingertips almost brushing the floor.

She thinks back to that awful October day, recalls the initial sweep of shock and anger. And sadness, too. Because regardless how far they'd grown apart as husband and wife, in the last year when Walt was retired, they'd begun to inch their way back to each other, to being companions, even friends. That he'd up and left during what were supposed to be their twilight years together had struck her as entirely unfair. How dare he die when they were just beginning to rediscover the things they'd enjoyed before! Activities like hiking and traveling the back roads of New England. They'd drive and drive, admiring the shifting golds and crimsons of the fall foliage, until they pulled into a diner only to discover that it had the best burger or blueberry pie they'd ever tasted. She'd let her guard down, enjoying Walt's companionship again. And look where it had gotten her.

Her stomach roils, though it's unclear if it's the thought of Walt and Marty combined or the unfortunate effects of her drinking last night. Thank goodness that young man had helped her back to her room! She wishes she could remember his name. James, maybe? Or William? It was something classic. She hopes she didn't make a complete fool of herself. If she runs into him today, she'll apologize profusely. But then again, she reasons, what good is a vacation if she can't have a little fun or, as it were, drown her sorrows in a cocktail or two? She hopes they solved the world's problems together—she remembers their conversation had turned profound at some point—but she has no idea what they actually talked about. Probably for the best, she thinks now as she crosses the street.

In the daylight, she can see her dinner with Marty last night for the fool's errand that it was. Of course, he didn't want to get back together. It was a ridiculous, nonsensical plan. As if thirty years gone by would make no difference in their lives. But she'd tricked herself into believing that having him back in her life would make everything okay again. She'd forgotten the oldest rule in the feminist handbook: it's up to her to make her life okay again.

She berates herself for not being the kind of person who can read a self-help book and register the same lessons she seems to get only from painful firsthand experience. In this case, the heartache (not to mention the humiliation) of seeing an old boyfriend up close. Surely there's a raft of books out there that would tell her reuniting with her ex-boyfriend less than a year after her spouse had died was a very bad idea. Anyone with any sense, she sees now, would tell her she'd sidestepped her grief for Walt by hyperfocusing on finding Marty. Maybe if she'd shared with Amber what she'd really been up to on this trip, her daughter would have spared her this disaster. Talked some sense into her.

Even at the ripe old age of sixty-one, Claire, it seems, is still having to learn new lessons.

And it dawns on her that during those hikes that she and Walt took last fall, each step had actually been a fragile step toward forgiveness. Forgiveness for all the times he'd gone missing from their marriage, her life. When the children were little. When they were not so little. When Amber had nearly starved herself to death. When Ben had so desperately craved his dad's approval somewhere other than out on the baseball field or the basketball court. When the numbers on a spreadsheet tugged at him more insistently than his own family, his wife. And one by one, his various transgressions, which Claire had cataloged ad nauseam over the years, began to drop away, like the falling leaves of a tree giving itself over to the inexorable pull of autumn.

Only Claire knew that when Amber was four and Ben one, she'd contemplated packing her bags and leaving her family behind. One night she'd gone so far as to stuff some shirts and jeans and underwear into a duffel bag, but Walt had walked through the door sooner than expected, and she'd shoved the bag under the bed. The next morning, she'd emptied it out, returning the clothes to their hangers and drawers. It was a dark time in her life, when she was fairly confident that the life she'd always imagined for herself—becoming a successful journalist—was out of her grasp.

On the day that she'd packed her bags, the kids were being particularly nasty to each other. Funny how she still remembers this—and how a seeming epiphany had swept over her. *They're better off without me. I'm not cut out for this. I'm not a good mom. Other people might be, but I'm not.* She couldn't imagine how raising two lively, independent children would ever go hand in hand with a journalism career. She loved her kids madly, but for that brief moment, she managed to convince herself that they'd do well to have someone else tying their shoes, running interference in their arguments. Thank goodness she'd stuck it out, if not for their sake, then for her own.

When she reaches the aquarium, a small crowd has already gathered outside the seal tank. An assortment of parents and children—some fully grown, others barely out of diapers—watch as if mesmerized. When an enormous seal glides by upside down, its pale belly exposed, the youngest ones squawk with excitement. Claire purchases her ticket and heads inside. It takes her eyes a moment to adjust to the dark space, which is cavernous and exudes a dank smell, a mix of fish and penguin guano. Kids zip around everywhere.

She bypasses the touch tank filled with sharks and stingrays and follows the corkscrew path up to the next level, where the massive ocean tank begins. Last summer she and Amber brought Fiona here, and her granddaughter had been fascinated by the enormous sea turtles, asking if she could take a ride on one. Today there's a funny-looking orange puffer fish that grabs Claire's attention; it's about the size of a tennis ball and swims against the current as fast as its little fins can carry it. She and a young boy share a laugh over its dogged perseverance.

Lining the walls are dozens of exhibits filled with snakes, lobsters and exotic fish, and Claire wanders over to check them out. There's a giant anaconda, its forked tongue darting in and out, and an octopus whose glutinous pink suckers inch along the glass. It's interesting enough, Claire thinks, but not as stimulating as the museum the other day. Probably having a small child along to make her appreciate the novelty would make all the difference. Which is when it occurs to her: she hasn't seen Fiona in a while. *Where has she gone off to?* A small tangle of fear begins to form in her chest. *Deep breaths*, she tells herself as something like a panic attack begins to wash over her. In the corner there's a bench, and she makes her way toward it. Even as she fights it, though, she can feel the heavy cloak of confusion descending over her.

All around her is a sea of unfamiliar faces, children everywhere. Where's Amber? Did Claire bring Fiona by herself? She can't remember. Everywhere she turns, there are more people, none of them belonging to her. Has her granddaughter run off somewhere? Is she with Amber? Or, God forbid, has Claire lost her?

She shoots up off the bench, panicked, searching for her granddaughter's familiar riot of red curls. Out of the corner of her eye, Claire spots a little girl standing near the sea dragon tank. "Fiona!" she calls out, a snap to her voice, but when the girl spins around, it's not Fiona. "Fiona?" Claire asks, bewildered.

The red-haired urchin stares up at her. "Mommy?" she asks, peering over her shoulder at a woman who's most definitely not Amber.

The woman turns and smiles at Claire. "I'm sorry," Claire apologizes. "I seem to have lost my granddaughter."

"Oh, no! Can we help? I'm sure she's around here somewhere. What does she look like?"

Claire tries to find the words to describe Fiona but draws a blank. "She's, um…she's little" is all she manages. Sweat gathers on the back of her neck.

"Ma'am, are you all right?" The woman frowns, furrowing her brow at Claire. The young girl reaches for her mother's hand.

"Yes, yes. I'm fine. Sorry to bother you. I'll find her. Thank you very much." Claire scuffles away and follows the winding path back down to the first floor. Her chest feels constricted, as if someone has tied it up in rubber bands. Where on earth has Fiona gone? Amber is going to *murder* Claire for losing track of her. And that's when it dawns on her: she should call Amber. She'll know what Fiona likes to see here, where she might have wandered off to. She pulls up Amber's number on her phone and dials.

"Mom?" It's Amber. Claire doesn't want to reveal that she's lost Fiona, but she has little choice.

"Amber, honey, I'm so sorry, but I seem to have lost track

of Fiona." She glances around at the teeming crowds. "She must be around somewhere, though. What's her favorite exhibit?"

"Exhibit? Mom, I don't know what you're talking about."

"At the aquarium!" Claire nearly shouts. Doesn't Amber understand that time is of essence? She doesn't want to alarm her daughter, but really, her reaction seems underwhelming, given the circumstances. "Does she like the hands-on area, the jellyfish, what? What does she like?"

"Mom." Amber's voice is calm, measured. "Mom, Fiona's right here with me. I brought her to work again. Remember? She has a little cold?"

Claire drops down on the bench closest to the gift shop. *Breathe.* "She's with *you*?"

"Yes, Mom. Right here. Wait a sec."

And then Fiona's squeaky voice is on the other end. "Nana? Hi, Nana. Where are you? You come visit me today?" And at the sound of her granddaughter's tiny voice, the panic leaks out of her like a helium balloon losing air. Of course, Fiona isn't at the aquarium! She's in Providence. With Amber.

"Not today, honey," Claire manages to say. "Soon, though, okay?"

But Fiona has already handed the phone back to her mother. "Mom, are you all right? Do you want me to come get you?" Amber asks. "You're scaring me."

Claire takes a moment to collect her thoughts while the world ever so slowly settles back into place, jagged pieces sliding back into their places like a jigsaw puzzle. "No, honey. I'm okay. I'm so sorry. I didn't mean to scare you. I just got confused for a minute. I don't know why I thought I had Fiona with me." She attempts a laugh.

There's a brief silence, then "Mom, I really think I should come get you. You sound confused."

Claire can feel herself inhabiting her own body again, as if it floated off for a short time and is now squeezing itself back into her skin. She knows exactly where she is, remembers that she walked here.

"No, really, I'm fine. I know where I am."

"And where is that?"

"At the aquarium. In Boston," she adds.

"And where are you staying?"

Claire thinks for a second. "At the Seafarer Hotel."

"What's your room number?"

Who remembers their room number? Claire thinks this is unfair. She only knows it's somewhere in the thousands. But she pulls out her room key and the paper sleeve that it's in. On the outside, it reads *Room 1018*. "Ten eighteen," she replies.

"Okay, good. That's right," Amber says, sounding relieved, though Claire has no idea how her daughter knows her room number. She must have given it to her earlier. "Do you remember how you got to the aquarium?"

"Walked here." Claire is confident of this.

"And you can find your way back to the hotel?"

"That's easy, honey. Of course. I have my Google Maps with the walking route right on it."

She can sense her daughter's hesitation on the other end. Amber will want to come and rescue her, but Claire wants no such thing. She needs to dissuade her somehow.

Fiona's voice pipes up in the background. "Mom," says Amber, "I've got to go, but I'm going to check in with you later, okay?"

"Yes, sure, that would be nice." A wave of relief washes over her because she has passed her daughter's test. Otherwise, Amber would be getting in her minivan to drive up to Boston this minute.

"You're sure you're okay?" Amber asks one last time.

"Yes, positive," Claire says, and she means it.

When she hangs up, the little redheaded girl, who has come down to the first level with her mom, shoots her a defiant gaze, as if Claire might be some kind of freak, a child snatcher. Claire directs a weak smile her way, but the girl spins around and tugs on her mother's hand to move on to another exhibit. *It's just as well*, Claire thinks. *Troublemaker.*

TWENTY-FIVE
Later that day

Just because there has been a tragic accident doesn't mean that everything comes to a halt. To the contrary, the show, as they say, must go on.

So after Jean-Paul checks in with Gillian one more time, he does a quick sweep of the rest of his staff: Housekeeping, Maintenance, Food and Beverage. Rumors have been circulating about the woman on the tenth floor. Was she part of a couple? Did she come alone? Was she on drugs? He calls a quick staff meeting in the wing beyond his office. When he looks out on the faces of his crew, so many of them personal friends, he has to remind himself to don his manager hat.

"Thank you all for taking a moment to meet with me. I understand the temptation to speculate on what may have happened this afternoon is great," he begins and waits for the crowd to settle. "But, please, I'm asking, indeed, *advising* you not to make that grave mistake. The police are working to determine what happened, and they don't need us mucking things up with our conjecture. Make no mistake: I understand that what occurred here today was a terrible tragedy, and such tragedies can take an emotional toll on even the strongest of us. Which is why I'd like to remind you—even encourage you, if you think it might be at all helpful—to take advantage of the counselors set up in our dining room. Your director will be happy to grant you the break time. In the meantime, let's remember to carry out our duties with the dispatch, elegance and care our guests are accustomed to. Remember, we have the Saltonstall wedding party arriving shortly this afternoon." He pauses for a moment and pulls his lips into a smile. "And, before I forget, let me thank you in advance for your help during what is sure to be a very busy weekend."

After they disperse, he checks his phone. Only ten minutes till four. The bride and her bridal party will be arriving any minute. He performs a quick check of the front grounds to make sure all looks presentable. The wraparound porch needs spraying down, as do the Adirondack chairs lining the south side. He gets word to the outdoor maintenance crew. As fate would have it, an order for eight dozen red geraniums due to arrive last week showed up this morning (of all days!), and so Louis, his head gardener, has been corralling his crew to plant ninety-six flowers before sundown. The last rows are just going in when Jean-Paul walks the lawns. The vermillion blooms, he notices, contrast nicely with the whitewashed porch. On the far side, the croquet matches have resumed, an encouraging sign that guests are slowly getting back to their normal leisure activities.

On the front lawn where the camera crews remain scattered, Jean-Paul takes the opportunity to make one last plea that they move their vans around to the side parking lot. "Imagine," he tells them, "if you were the poor bride who showed up here with a cavalcade of news vans waiting. Please, aren't the horrid events of today enough already? If you move your team, I promise you, we'll update you with the name of the victim as soon as we can. Or, better yet, go home to your families and hug them a little tighter."

Reluctantly, a few newscasters—mostly the women, he notes—begin to pack up their equipment and instruct their crews to move everything to the side parking lot. He's grateful for at least this modicum of sensitivity.

By the time he circles through to the lobby, the onslaught of new arrivals has already begun. It's five past four. There are guests who push up their sunglasses and stare out with puzzled looks, as if they might have stumbled into the wrong hotel. Jean-Paul welcomes a few, asks them to ignore the news crews and to please make themselves at home. He pulls aside Lydia, his restaurant manager, to enlist her help.

"Can you help with welcoming guests this afternoon? I could really use an extra person to defuse any tension around the incident."

"Not a problem, boss. Happy to help out."

"You know the drill," he instructs. "No mention of a dead body, just an unfortunate incident that the police are handling at the moment."

"Got it."

One man in a plaid sun hat, pink shorts and a T-shirt asks Lydia what's going on, and she answers right on cue. "We had an unfortunate incident on the premises earlier today, but the authorities are handling it. Come right in! Can I get you an ice water with lemon? Where are you all from?" Jean-Paul has forgotten Lydia's flair for idle chitchat. "If you're famished after your travels, please check out the Chantilly

Bar on the second floor with splendid views of the harbor. In fact, cocktail hour is starting right now! You can enjoy your favorite beverage along with prosciutto-wrapped scallops or maybe a lobster bisque. Do you like seafood?" Jean-Paul smiles with relief. Lydia has distracted him, this man in the plaid hat, who'd wanted to know what was going on and is now trying to decide between the scallops and the lobster bisque.

When a family arrives with a couple of budding teenagers in tow, Lydia is quick to mention the game room on the sixth floor. There are pool tables and Ping-Pong and some old-fashioned games for the kids. "No video games here!" she says with a wink. When a professorial man in jacket and tie arrives, she asks if he's here for the wedding, and when he answers in the affirmative, she swiftly steers him toward the check-in line they've cordoned off especially for wedding guests.

"Oh, and did I give you our bulletin of activities for the weekend?" she asks a young couple who stands off to one side. They're not here for the wedding, so Lydia rattles off a quick list of activities. "There's a croquet match on the front lawn at five. We like to make a few of the old Seafarer pastimes available to our guests," she explains. For another family with young children, she presses the Seafarer bulletin into their hands, exclaiming, "There are so many fun things for kids to do here! There's cornhole and a water-balloon toss at six o'clock. A three-legged race. Do you guys like horseshoes? There's a place you can play out back. And the pool, of course. And, oh, don't forget the Children's Museum, practically around the corner—so much fun! There are some fantastic new restaurants in the neighborhood you'll want to be sure to check out, too."

She's been grinning so hard, Jean-Paul thinks her dimples must hurt. Seeing her in action, he wonders why he's had her manning restaurant reservations all this time when clearly she should be working the front desk or the concierge counter. She's managed to deflect nearly every question about the camera crews outside. To another wedding guest, she says, "Relax, enjoy yourselves. And if you'd prefer to linger on the porch with a cool summer drink, please be our guest. Our staff is eager to provide you with whatever your heart desires."

He's not needed here, he realizes with a dart of relief. Lydia can handle everything at the moment. He's about to head back to his office when an attractive woman, her dark hair pulled up in a bun and dressed in white jeans and a black top, pushes through the doors with a baby stroller. Not until she removes her sunglasses, her warm eyes skirting the room before they land on him, does he make the connection. It's Marie, his wife's familiar, tender face inviting his gaze like the rarest of flowers.

And it's all he can do not to fall to his knees.

TWENTY-SIX
Earlier that day

When Jason gets out of the shower, Gwen's standing there with her arms crossed, like she's ready to ambush him. "So your phone dinged again, and I couldn't help but notice that it was George. Texting something about a Charlie kid?"

Her words have bite to them, as if she's waiting for him to let her in on some big secret. They're just back from brunch in the hotel dining room. Blueberry pancakes, omelets, fruit, mimosas. Jason was relieved to see Gwen eating after yesterday's cruise debacle. Over breakfast, they'd laughed about their jolly shipmate who seemed to take his job much too seriously, and afterward, they'd crept back up to the room to make love. He'd been thinking about his conversation with Claire last night, while the rain showerhead pounded on his back. *What was it that she'd said about him and Gwen? Oh, right, basically that Jason was full of crap and should get his act together.* He grins, thinking maybe he'll actually do it. Maybe before they head back to New Hampshire tomorrow, he'll propose. Of course, there's the matter of a ring, but he's pretty sure he could figure something out, maybe a stand-in for the real thing. But he'd had no idea of the tsunami building right outside the bathroom door.

"Oh, yeah, that," he replies now, as nonchalantly as possible, and reknots the hotel towel more tightly around his waist.

He goes to his suitcase to retrieve his boxer shorts, his jeans and T-shirt, pretending this is just the beginning of an ordinary conversation. But they both know it's not. "I think there's something you're not telling me," she says. "Like it's not only your dissertation you're having second thoughts about." She flops down on the bed, arms stretched out behind her. "What's going on, Jason?" She lifts an arm, holds up a finger. "And before you begin, let me tell you that it would be in your best interest to tell me the truth. All of it."

"What are you talking about, hon?" He's trying to buy himself a few extra moments while he shimmies into his jeans. How best to present the news that a student is accusing him of assault only two days after she watched him punch a total stranger at the museum. Only a week after he'd grabbed her so hard that a deep purple bruise had bloomed on her upper arm. Because regardless of the fact that the whole Charlie thing isn't true, he's scared she'll want to leave him if she finds out about it. And he can't let that happen. Not when he's just been thinking about how to get a proxy ring for a proposal.

"You tell me," she says. "By the way, I already knew that you'd bailed on your classes. That wasn't some big secret."

There's an angry edge to her voice, the flirt of earlier this morning entirely gone.

"You did?"

"Well, I didn't find out intentionally," she says. "A few weeks ago I went to your classroom with a sub from Downtown Deli. I thought maybe I could sit in and learn something and, afterward, we could have a picnic. I thought it would be a nice surprise. But you know who I found when I got there? A young woman, one of your students, sitting at a desk with her laptop. By herself. When I apologized, said I must have gotten the wrong classroom, she corrected me, told me that, no, this was Professor Wadsworth's room but that he'd canceled class a few days ago. She'd shown up, she said, because she was hoping maybe you'd change your mind and come back."

Jason is completely blindsided by this news. Whether it's because Gwen has been on to him this whole time or the fact that one devoted student actually kept showing up for his class, he can't say. He wonders who it was. Probably Molly. She'd been the only student who'd seemed half-interested in the Bolsheviks.

"I was going to tell you," he says, recovering, "but it never seemed like the right time. I wanted to get my own thoughts sorted out, you know? About my dissertation, about what I wanted to do instead of teaching, before I talked to you."

She sighs heavily, as if talking to him suddenly exhausts her. "So we're in this thing called *a relationship*?" she says condescendingly. "And usually people in a *relationship* talk to each other about what's happening in their lives. They help each other through stuff, you know?" She pauses to tug a stray string off the hem of a pretty yellow sundress she's wearing. "And it kind of feels like the past month you've been shutting me out."

He pulls on his T-shirt, rakes his fingers through his hair, then slides open the balcony door to let in some air. "It's complicated, hon. And unfortunately it's gotten a lot more complicated in the past forty-eight hours. I'm not sure you really want to know, to be honest."

"Try me. I'm a pretty strong girl."

He hesitates. "Can we at least go out on the balcony to talk about it? Please?"

She pushes up from the bed and rolls her eyes, as if that's not going to make the slightest difference in her reaction to whatever news he might possibly share with her. But she follows him out there, and they both peer out on the harbor that's as calm and flat as a pond today.

"So," he begins and takes a deep breath. "So, this Charlie kid that George has been texting about is one of my students."

"Uh-huh." Her lips are twisted into a knot, waiting for whatever's coming next.

"And, well, he flunked his final exam, which means he flunked the class."

"Wait, was he a senior?"

"No, freshman. So it's not like I kept him from graduating or anything. The kid deserved it, fair and square."

"I don't get it, then. What's the big deal?"

"A couple of things." He grips the railing while considering how best to frame it. "First, it turns out that his dad owns Wiggam's Sporting Goods."

"Shit."

"Yeah, so there's some money involved. Daddy's probably a big donor to the college. I don't know."

"And? What else?"

"The last one's a little more tricky." A long sigh escapes from his lips. He doesn't want to face Gwen when he tells her, but he knows he must. He turns and meets her gaze. "So, it turns out Charlie is also a gifted liar. He's filed a complaint with the university saying I assaulted him in the parking lot at Old Marley's back in May." The words come spilling out.

Gwen's eyes narrow. "And did you?"

"No!" he says a little too loudly. "Absolutely not. The kid's making the whole thing up. Says I punched him in the stomach completely unprovoked."

"But were you there, Jason? Is there anyone who can place you there?"

"No, because I *wasn't* there. It's his word against mine."

"Is he saying there were any witnesses?"

He has to stop and think for a minute. "I don't think so. Actually, I think maybe the complaint says that he was there with friends. I don't remember exactly."

"So if he was there with friends, presumably they would have seen something."

Jason shrugs. "I guess so. But I wasn't there, so it's not like they can confirm or refute anything."

She's leaning over the banister now, watching the people parading down below. She shakes her head. "Jesus, Jason. I don't know how you get yourself into these situations."

"But I didn't do it. That's what I'm trying to tell you. There is no situation. He flunked my class. What was I supposed to do? Pass him because he's the son of some bigwig? Which, incidentally, I didn't know at the time. Not that it would have made any difference."

On her upper arm, the smudge of the bruise now resembles a small birthmark. If he didn't know that this was precisely where his hand had grabbed her last week, he'd never guess it was a result of his fury. He'd caught her with that Gary guy again. Jason had come to pick Gwen up after class, and when she hadn't been waiting outside the building for him, he'd run in to let her know he was there. But when he'd rounded the corner to her office, she was leaning against the wall, Gary's head bent down while he talked to her, his arm outstretched above her. Jason had startled them both, and Gary had scampered off, saying, "Hey, Jason. Good to see you, man."

He can still remember the look in Gwen's eyes, fearful and pleading, when he told her he'd wait outside for her. He'd stormed back to the car, and a few minutes later, she'd come out of the building and climbed into the passenger seat. "Honey, I know what you're thinking, and it's not at all what it might have seemed like," she said.

He'd remained quiet, silently fuming the entire way home. When they got back to their apartment, he'd headed straight for the kitchen and slammed the pot down on the stove while he waited for the water to boil for spaghetti. When Gwen had come in to help herself to a glass of wine, he grabbed her by the arm. "What the hell do you think you're doing? Flirting with that idiot? Do you honestly expect me to believe nothing's going on?"

"Jason, please," she'd begged. "You're hurting me." But he didn't care. He was going to get the truth out of her, no matter what.

"Tell me. Just tell me the truth, and we can be done here."

"I swear to you," she'd said, trying to rip her arm away, and his fingers had pressed more deeply into her skin, "we were just talking. Gary has a girlfriend. He doesn't think about me that way."

"Then why was he leaning over you like he might kiss you?" The image flashed through Jason's mind, making him jealous all over again. Because the prospect of Gwen's falling in love with someone else—which he understood made complete sense in the natural order of things (she *should* have been with someone else, someone better than Jason)—had scared the hell out of him.

"That's ridiculous! He'd never do that. *I'd* never do that. How can you not know that? How can you not trust me?" And at that moment, the phone on the kitchen wall had started to ring. Something about the sudden noise jarred Jason from whatever rage had overtaken him. Just the simple noise of a phone ringing, as if he'd been jolted out of a dream. Kind of similar to the way he'd felt at the museum until he'd heard Gwen's screams and saw the guy lying at his feet in a heap. When the phone rang, his hand dropped, releasing her arm. She'd immediately pulled it away, run into the bedroom sobbing and locked the door. And Jason had thought *You idiot. What are you doing?* His dad's voice rang in his ears.

He thought for sure he'd lost her, that it was over. But no. There'd been heartfelt, tear-riddled apologies, makeup jewelry, makeup sex. He promised he'd never hurt her again. She said she loved him and wanted to stay together, so long as he got help. Jason promised he would. He still hasn't.

But this, this is different. He didn't actually do anything to this Charlie kid. *God, the irony is priceless*, he thinks. He's now in the position of trying to convince his girlfriend whom he *has* hurt in the past, who has watched him punch another man, that he didn't in fact hurt this kid. He feels like he's caught in the story of the boy who cried wolf, except that Jason is the wolf—and no one's coming to save the boy when he needs it most.

"Hmm..." she says quietly, suddenly thoughtful. "I'm not sure it really matters, are you?"

"Whaddya mean?"

Her shoulders lift in a shrug. "Just that it's your word

against his, and if his daddy is some bigwig, you're probably going to lose."

His eyes widen in surprise. "Geez, thanks for the vote of confidence."

"Maybe it's the push you need. You know, to cut yourself free from academia."

"Maybe." There's a ferry churning across the harbor, and Jason watches the frothy wake spilling out behind it. "Anyway, it'll all work out. It's not like he's pressing charges with the police department. He's not that dumb."

Gwen flips her hair over her shoulder. She's so pretty, sometimes it hurts to look at her because it only underscores for him the odd happenstance that they're together. She deserves someone so much better. Someone who will spoil her, who will give her the head-over-heels love she deserves and not get crazy jealous every time another male stands within six feet of her.

"I hope so. I hope it all works out for you," she says now.

The way she says it, though, makes him think there's more heft behind the statement than those eleven simple words. "Me, too." He waits for her to say more, something about how they've already been through plenty and this is a mere hiccup, that Charlie will disappear once Jason calls his bluff. But there's nothing. "It should," he adds. "I'm not really worried. We should be fine."

Which is when Gwen says something that sounds an awful lot like "Uh-uh."

"Sorry, what?" he says.

"Uh-uh, Jason. This one's not about us. I hope it all works out for your sake, I really do. But I can't do this anymore. It's exhausting. Wondering when you're going to lose it again." He thinks he sees her swipe at her eyes. "Because you will, you know. It's like I'm living on the edge all the time. And even though you promised me you were going to get help—and you said again you would this weekend—why should I believe you? Half the time you don't tell me the truth. Why would this be any different?"

"Babe, come on. You're making mountains out of molehills. I'm going to get help. Really. I mean it. Especially now that I'm handing my key in to the university, I'll have plenty of spare time on my hands. And you seem to be missing the key point here: *I didn't do it.*"

"Really, Jason?" She's looking at him with those big, sad blue eyes. "Is that the 'key point'? I really want to believe you. But remember I was there the other day when you leveled that poor guy who did *nothing wrong.* I've seen your anger in full swing. It's scary." She rubs at her arm in the exact spot of the bruise, as if pushing away the ghost of his hand.

"I know. And I'm sorry," he says, his voice softening. "More sorry than you could possibly know."

She nods her head slowly. "And I'm so sorry that it's not enough anymore."

A switch flips on in him, maybe one that's been dormant all this time, since the day his father threw him across the living room and punched him in the eye for the first time. Who knows? Maybe it's the same self-protective switch that kicks on anytime he's feeling threatened. The same one that flipped in the museum. Because Gwen can't leave him. She wouldn't do that. Not after they've just spent this mind-blowing week together. Not after they've worked so hard to get to where they are.

"What do you mean?"

She shakes her head. "I can't do this anymore. Your *sorrys* don't cut it anymore. Don't you get it? I'm *scared* of you."

She takes a step back from him, and he can feel his heart twisting in his chest. *Whoa. She's scared of him?* For a brief moment, he considers how to make this all better, how to reassure her that there's nothing to be afraid of. That he's the same old Jason, that he loves her like crazy and that she can't give up on him—on them—now.

Instead he says, "You're scared of me? Scared of the guy you made love to an hour ago? C'mon now, Gwen. Let's not get dramatic."

He gets that he can turn angry sometimes, but he'd never do anything to actually hurt her. Not really. Sure, he grabbed her arm a little too hard when he was upset, but it's not as if he beats her up, punches her in the face like those losers who end up in divorce court for domestic violence. Nothing like what his dad did to his mom. No, Jason's anger is usually directed at someone else, and typically on Gwen's behalf! Almost everyone he has ever laid a finger on has been someone who was being disrespectful of her. He's been protecting her. And now she's going to conveniently overlook that fact?

"I'm not." Her voice is so quiet he can barely hear her. "Being dramatic."

"Babe, I love you. You gotta know that."

"I do."

"So why do you want to break up all of a sudden?"

When she turns to him, her eyes are wet with tears. "All of a sudden? Really? This has been going on since that day last fall when you dragged me away from all my friends at the game because you thought Gary was hitting on me." She shakes her head. "God, that was so embarrassing. And you *grabbed* me. Hard."

"And I've apologized for that." His voice is measured. He's trying to keep it under control, but he can't quite believe she wants to rehash all of this again. It happened almost a year ago! "How many more times can I say I'm sorry?"

"It's not just that time, and you know it." Her eyes flash

at him. "Do I really need to list all the times for you? The broken glass? The computer? The guy in the bar with the Confederate flag? Last week with Gary? At the museum the other night?" She leans back against the railing. "Jesus, Jason. Don't you see a pattern here?"

"Mmm, not really," he says, but inside, he can feel something in him shift. From disbelief to incredulity to frustration to annoyance. "But if you want to go ahead and list all your grievances—"

"They're not grievances!" she shouts, and he takes a step back. "They're all about *you*! How can you not see that?" She's full on crying now. "I love you, Jason, and I swore to myself that I was going to give you another chance, but this can't work. Especially if you're hurting your students now."

"I already told you—I didn't do it." He's talking between gritted teeth because she's really pissing him off now. How many times can he tell her? How can he make her believe in his innocence? She's making him out to be some kind of creep when she knows that's not who he is. She should have seen his dad! This is nothing, this list of grievances she's apparently been carrying around with her for quite some time.

She takes another step away from him, turning her shoulder toward him, her face in profile while she gazes out on the harbor. And for a second, her beauty stops him—the delicate mole on her right cheek, the thick lashes, the aquiline nose that he used to tease her meant she'd descended from royalty.

"Gwen, be careful," he says gently, more softly now, moving toward her. "I don't want you to fall." And before he realizes what he's doing, his hand reaches out to grab her.

TWENTY-SEVEN

Claire watches the couples who wander lazily back to the hotel. The early-afternoon sun glances off the water like a machete, bright and dazzling. After her scare at the aquarium this morning, she's perfectly content up here on the balcony, feeling the sun warming her face, a Bloody Mary in hand, thanks to room service. *Hair of the dog that bit you*, she thinks. One of Walt's favorite sayings. Maybe she won't feel so hungover if she has a little cocktail. One or two little cocktails to calm her nerves. Scrub away the panic that had fallen over her like a second skin this morning.

She's just hung up with Amber. A call she'd made to let her daughter know that she got back to the hotel safely and not to worry about a thing. But Amber had suggested driving up to Boston later this afternoon when she gets off work. She'd pitched it as a fun girls' night out on the town (she could sleep over in Claire's room), but Claire, while forgetful, isn't dense. She knows full well that her daughter is worried, concerned that maybe her mother is losing her marbles. Already Amber has alerted Ben to her incident, as she called it, this morning. Claire knows this because Ben texted her a little while ago to ask if she's all right. Eventually, she knows she'll have to tell her daughter.

Because what Amber doesn't know and Claire does—and so does Ben—is that this isn't just a hiccup, another senior moment that will evaporate, right itself in time. Nor is it merely a panic attack. It's oh-so-much more than that.

They happened slowly at first, the senior moments. She'd started noticing them probably a couple of months after Walt's passing. Around the house, little things started to go missing. A container of ice cream returned to the fridge instead of the freezer. Her hairbrush left behind in the laundry room. A half-eaten pear abandoned on a bookshelf, as if she'd been called away to the phone and had forgotten to return for it. A neglected cup of coffee she'd reheated in the microwave only to discover it the next morning. Typical absentmindedness, she told herself, for someone who was recently widowed. She'd been guilty of the same forgetfulness when she was pregnant.

But then she'd started losing words, which had been more concerning somehow. At an editorial meeting back in January, she'd gotten stuck on the word *halo* while presenting. Imagine! Such a simple thing. And yet it was nowhere accessible in her brain when she'd faced her colleagues around the massive oak table, a place where she'd attended meetings for more than thirty years. She'd made a joke of some kind: *Oh, you know, that little circle thingy an angel wears over her head.* And right away someone guessed *halo*, and everyone laughed. Happens to me all the time, an associate editor fifteen years her junior said. And after that, Claire got skilled at playing off her memory lapses. *Just wait till you get old*, she joked. Or *There goes another senior moment.*

Eventually, though, the things that went missing around the house got stranger, grew more anomalous. One day in April, she'd found her toothbrush in the refrigerator. Another day a flip-flop in the basement and its match on top of the TV in her bedroom. It reminded her of that Norwegian memory game, Husker Du, that she and the kids used to play. A game that required finding two matching objects—a ribbon or a cat or a lamp—hiding behind a black checker-like circle on a game board. If the picture under the second black checker you picked up didn't match the first, then you had to return both checkers and wait for another turn. Claire had lost hundreds of times to Ben and Amber, who both had an uncanny knack for remembering where they'd last seen that ribbon or cat. Well, now she was playing it by herself in her own home.

When she stumbled upon something out of place, she'd struggle to remember where it was meant to go exactly. Some days it would come to her right away. *Oh, the TV remote belongs next to the television, not in the bathroom!* Or *Why on earth would this carton of orange juice be sitting on top of the piano? It belongs in the refrigerator!* Sometimes she let herself believe that it was Walt's spirit playing tricks on her, a mischievous elf hiding the very things he knew she'd be searching for later.

On bad days, though, when she couldn't figure out the appropriate place for an item, it would end up on her kitchen counter, where similar mismatched items had begun to collect. A random screwdriver. A coaster. A miniature sewing kit. A slipper. An envelope of coupons she'd been saving for something but couldn't remember what. Her kitchen counter had become the Land of Missing Stuff, much like the Island of Misfit Toys. Funny she had no trouble recalling that sad little jack-in-the-box in the TV Christmas special from years ago, and yet she couldn't fathom where her other slipper had gone yesterday.

One day last month she'd overhead two colleagues at the watercooler talking about her.

"Does Claire seem off to you?" one asked.

"Yeah, something's not right. Maybe she's coming down with that flu bug that's going around?" Claire had hovered just beyond the doorway, too afraid to move.

"No, this seems like something else. The other day I watched her at the copying machine, and it was so strange, like she couldn't remember which way the paper was supposed to go in." Claire, astonished to hear this, had nearly forgotten the episode herself. But when her colleague mentioned it, a wave of heat rode across her face as she recalled how flustered she'd gotten trying to make copies. She'd concluded the machine was broken.

And finally there'd been that time, just last month, when Amber stopped by on a Saturday night to drop Fiona off for their sleepover party, and Claire, already in her pajamas, had completely forgotten about it. It was a turning point, really. Amber and Jeff had been planning on a date night.

She didn't let on to Amber or Fiona, of course, but it had shaken Claire to the core, she who planned days in advance for every sleepover with her granddaughter, buying ingredients for homemade cookies and supplies from the crafts store. When she'd gone to check her datebook, sure enough, there were the words scribbled as plain as day on Saturday's square: *Sleepover with Fiona!* When she confessed to Ben the next day, he insisted she make a doctor's appointment to get checked out. "Just to be safe. It's not like you, Mom, to forget a sleepover with Fiona." And she had to agree. Maybe it was more than a few senior moments she'd been experiencing. But did she really want to find out if it was something more than old age? Something worse?

Ben promised he'd go with her, and he had, loyally pulling up in her driveway an hour and a half before her appointment at MGH so she wouldn't feel rushed. Some tests and then a follow-up scan had revealed troubling spots on her brain. When she reviewed the scan herself, the thickening plaques brought to mind the lit-up phosphorescence she'd seen in the ocean when she and Walt had gone snorkeling in Puerto Rico for their honeymoon. It was almost pretty, a work of art. She made Ben promise not to tell Amber, her most emotional child. Not until Claire was ready. But now, she thinks regrettably, her secret is out. How she wishes she hadn't called Amber at the aquarium! She should have phoned Ben when the fogginess first began to descend. But it was the matter of Fiona that had made her reach out to Amber instinctively. Amber, she'd reasoned, would know where to find her own daughter.

Claire sips her Bloody Mary (her second, but who's counting?), watching the tiny boats parade across the harbor. The doctor had warned her about these kinds of episodes becoming more frequent, though he couldn't say when, exactly, they might ramp up. *Mental eclipses* he'd called them, and Claire had clung to that lovely image, envisioning the moon getting in the way of her sunny brain for a brief moment before moving on to bother someone else.

Ben has been encouraging her to tell her boss, Julian, what's going on. Especially after the latest debacle, the flubbed article on McKinnon. But Claire hadn't been quite ready to do that. Her memory problems, she reasons, are her own. And she doesn't want anyone's pity. Not yet, at least. Because as soon as she tells Julian, pity will be all she'll get—

from him and her colleagues. Besides, how could she tell her boss before her own daughter?

But she'll need to have a conversation with Amber soon. Maybe even tonight, if she drives up from Providence. A talk where she'll reveal that the brain that has served her so well for sixty-one years is starting to let her down, shirk its responsibilities. It's disappointing. No way around it, she'll say, but crappy things happen in life—everyone's dealing with something, right? She'll do her best to downplay it so that her daughter, always a worrier, won't worry incessantly. Maybe she'll even ask her to return Marty's blazer that Claire rediscovered in her bathroom this morning, forgetting that he'd lent it to her last night. Because Claire doesn't have the strength to reach out to him again.

She sighs. It won't be easy talking to Amber. She's been dreading this conversation, which is probably why she has postponed it for so long. Amber has always been her most apprehensive child—and her most responsible. Maybe because Ben is Claire's baby, when something needs doing it's typically Amber who has risen to the challenge. Even when the kids were little, this was the natural order of things. But Ben, her quiet, reserved child, has surprised Claire these last few weeks, shuttling her back and forth to appointments, shouldering the bulk of responsibility when it comes to her health.

And while the doctor talks, Ben takes copious notes, asks thoughtful questions. At each appointment, he calmly files away any new information as if it's the same as keeping track of the flurry of baseball statistics he used to memorize as a young boy. It's astonishing how much he reminds her of Walt during these sessions! So matter-of-fact, respectful. Not one mention of chakras or crystals. The doctor said she might have anywhere from one to several more years to enjoy, years when the graceful contours of her children's faces will remain familiar to her. When Fiona will visit and Claire will remember her sweet granddaughter's name and might even recall her favorite kind of cookie—chocolate-chip oatmeal—and will know that the dollhouse Fiona loves to play with (Amber's old toy house) is upstairs in the guest-room closet waiting for her. Even though the more mundane details of daily life—like remembering whether or not she has showered, turned the kettle off, returned a phone call—might begin to slip away. Naturally, the doc can't make any promises.

It's the thought of not knowing, not recognizing the people who are most dear to her that breaks her. She can handle losing a word here and there. She can even come to grips with leaving her job. And an *episode*, while terrifying when she's in it, is short-lived. Somehow she knows that if she's patient enough, she'll reach the other side of it. But once those episodes become permanent, when she's not even aware that she's staring blankly into the eyes of her own children? Well, that part she can't let herself consider right now. Not fully. It's simply too terrifying.

Her secret, though, is one that she knows she won't be able to hold on to much longer.

When the man dressed in a hotel uniform knocks on the door of room 1018, the guest who opens it smiles gamely at him. She's holding a glass with a celery stick in it that could be tomato juice or something stronger, perhaps a Bloody Mary.

"Hello," she says and tucks a piece of hair behind one ear. "Can I help you?"

He's immediately struck by how young she appears up close—and how attractive she is. He's been told she's sixty-one, but the past few days he's been following her from afar so it's been hard to tell. Her skin is smooth, and her eyes are a bright, bright blue. The effect is almost startling. She's wearing a yellow sundress with daisies embroidered along the bottom. He nearly forgets his speech. "Sorry to bother you, ma'am," he says. "I was checking to see if you needed a set of fresh towels?" He holds out a stack of crisp, white towels.

"Oh, no thank you. I have too many as it is. Thanks, though. I appreciate it."

"No problem at all. Is there anything else I might get you?"

She tilts her head, as if considering, then says, "No, don't think so. I'm all set. Thanks, again."

"You're welcome. Have a nice day, ma'am." When she shuts the door, the man moves swiftly to the elevator and punches the button for the ground floor. As he exits the elevator, he tosses the fresh towels into a rolling cart of soiled linens and heads out to the Seafarer's front lawn, where he places his call at exactly 11:45 a.m.

"Hello, sir. I just checked in on your mother. She's safely back in her hotel room, as she told your sister. She had a drink in hand, perhaps a Bloody Mary?" He listens to the response. "Yes, she gave us a bit of a scare there, didn't she, among the fishes? But she made her way back to the hotel all right. I would have intervened, if needed." He hesitates. "I should add that your mother appeared to be in good spirits and had her wits about her when I spoke to her briefly." He waits for the response on the other end. "Very well. I'm glad to have been of service. I'll stay until your sister arrives at the hotel, then. Once I see that Ms. O'Dell is with her, I'll conclude my services. You're very welcome. Take care. And, sir? My best to your mom. She seems like a lovely person."

TWENTY-EIGHT
Later that evening

Riley watches the evening news from the comfort of her couch at home. She's changed into her gray sweatpants and a Jessica Simpson T-shirt, which Tom loves for some reason that's probably twisted up in teenage fantasies and other stuff Riley doesn't care to know about. When the newscaster announces the story of the woman who jumped at the hotel today, she calls Tom in from their study, where he's working. Though, how he can be getting any work done after the afternoon they've recently endured, she can't imagine.

"The story's on the five o'clock news," Riley says, pointing to the TV, and Tom sits down next to her. On the screen, the hotel manager stands off to one side while the police commissioner addresses the reporters. Riley and Tom listen to his every word.

"What's a 'death investigation' mean, I wonder?" she asks

when the report wraps up. "Could it be a homicide, then? Like maybe someone pushed her? I kind of assumed she'd jumped."

"I'm not sure," Tom says. "I think it means it could go either way."

"Ugh. It's so awful. I can't believe we were there." She curls up closer to him and rests her head on his shoulder. "Do you think your poor mom will ever recover?"

After being questioned, they'd found Marilyn sitting in the hotel lobby with Gillian, the wedding coordinator. Riley had never seen her future mother-in-law looking so pale. "Hello, there," Tom said, helping her to her feet. "Thanks for your help, Gillian. We'll take it from here. Let's get you home, Mom."

After they'd arrived back at Newbury Street, Riley brewed Marilyn a cup of tea and sat down across from her at the dining-room table. The view out her in-laws' second-story brownstone was gorgeous this time of year. The tree-lined street was bursting with bright green leaves, a stark contrast to the somber mood in the room. "That poor woman," Marilyn said into her tea. "Do you think she had any family?"

"I don't know." Riley was being honest and wasn't sure what Marilyn wanted to hear. Would it be worse if the woman had family because there would be people left to grieve? Or would it somehow be better if she didn't? Her death an isolated incident without any ripple effect.

But everyone had family of one kind or another, didn't they? Even if the woman hadn't been old enough to have her own children, she was somebody's daughter, probably someone's sister or aunt or fiancée. "It's so hard to understand why anyone would jump from the balcony of one of the most expensive hotels in Boston. Do you think she was trying to make some kind of statement? I mean, assuming it was a suicide."

"Maybe she was on drugs," Marilyn had said. Her mother-in-law-to-be was always preaching about the danger of drugs, which Riley had come to accept as part of her teacher's quiver. Not that she'd talk about drugs with her second-graders (Riley hoped not!), but it fell onto her list of potential hazards, things wrong with the world.

Now Tom shifts on the couch and wraps his arms around Riley. "What are the odds that we'd be there for the whole thing? I mean, it's pretty incredible when you think about it. We were sitting at the table closest to the window, too."

"Do you think it's a sign?" Riley traces little circles on his forearm with her finger. "You know, like we're not supposed to get married?"

He tilts his head so that their eyes are level. "If anything, I think it's a sign that we should get married as soon as possible."

"Ha, right." She rolls her eyes.

But he's still staring at her. "No, I mean it, Ry. Seriously."

Her eyebrows shoot up. "Do you mean we should elope to Vegas or something?"

"Maybe?" He shrugs. "Though, I don't know that we even have to go that far. I hear a justice of the peace can tie the knot just as easily—and a lot more quickly."

Riley can't believe what she's hearing. The news has switched over to a story about a train derailing on the Green Line, but she can't focus on it at the moment because she thinks her fiancé might be suggesting that they get married within the month, maybe even next week. That they might be able to stop thinking about wedding invitations and eight-piece bands and meal tastings and all the other headaches that come with a guest list of two hundred.

"Are you serious?" She's gauging his expression, trying to judge if he's kidding or not. "Your mother would *kill* us if we did that." She cringes when she hears herself. "Sorry, bad choice of words."

Tom shrugs again. "So what? My mom isn't getting married. We are. We should be able to marry however we want. Besides, I don't think she's going to care as much about a huge wedding after this afternoon. We can cross the Seafarer off the list, that's for sure."

Riley tries to fight back her grin because it's not funny. A woman has died today, and as a result, she has felt like crap all afternoon. But, yes, she agrees that the Seafarer, and preferably all the other fancy places where Marilyn might feel comfortable but Riley wouldn't, should drop off the list. "Don't tease me like this, because if you're kidding, I might have to scream. You realize that you're pretty much describing my dream wedding? Beautiful wildflower bouquets with a few friends and family. No fuss."

He nods. "Mine, too."

"But my dad!" Riley slaps a hand over her mouth. "My dad has to be there. He'd be so upset if he weren't there to walk me down the aisle, even if it's at a courthouse."

"Not a problem," Tom says. "With all the money we'd save on the wedding, we ought to be able to afford a plane ticket out from Michigan. How does sometime next week sound?"

He speed-walks into the study and comes back with his laptop before opening up a link to a travel website. Her hands are shaking. "You're really serious about this."

"Never been more serious in my life. The longer we sat there at the hotel, the more I realized that our wedding was turning into the wedding my mom always wanted but never got. And then, when that lady jumped, it seemed like the universe was shouting at us to get the hell out of there. I'm fairly certain that's not where we're supposed to get married." He pauses, and Riley waits for whatever's coming next. "And I've been sitting in the study, trying to work today, but all I can think about is what we saw and how sad it makes me, but also how I'm kind of glad we were there because it makes me realize that I don't care about all this wedding stuff. I never did. All I want to do is marry you as soon as possible and enjoy every minute we have together."

Riley is speechless for a moment. *He gets it*, she thinks. *He really gets it.* And here she'd been thinking she'd lost her fiancé to his mother's niggling requests. For a second she considers how it might feel *not* to have the big wedding they've started to plan—will she be disappointed? But no, not even a flicker of regret rises in her at the thought. Instead, it's more of a buoyant sensation, as if she might be able to actually breathe again.

Her lips graze Tom's before she grins and says, "Yeah, I think I could get behind that."

TWENTY-NINE
Earlier that day

Jason has got to get out of here. There's no time to waste. What was he thinking? He's stuffing his clothes into his black duffel bag, but his hands are trembling. He goes into the bathroom to grab his dopp kit, his toothbrush, the tiny tube of Crest that he and Gwen were sharing. Quickly he wipes the counter down and tosses the tissue in the toilet and flushes. His eyes scour the bathroom for anything else that's his but there's nothing.

Back in the main room, he races around to organize a few magazines on the table. He's about to toss the empty cups and leftover trays from room service last night (he'd ordered a late-night snack after he got back from dropping Claire off at her room) but then thinks better of it. That's what maid service is for. The bed's still unmade, and he ruffles through the sheets to make sure there's no stray underwear or a T-shirt left behind. Then he checks under the bed. Only some random Kleenexes. Gwen's stuff is still all over the place—discarded clothes that she'd rejected for one reason or another for the cruise last night—but there's not much he can do about that now.

His heart careens around in his chest, like a train that might torpedo off the tracks any minute. He looks around again for any last items, locates his wallet on the bedside table and slides it into his back pocket. He's not thinking clearly, he knows that, and struggles to slow his thoughts down long enough so he doesn't screw things up even worse. But the only thing that comes to mind is his own voice saying *Dude, you have got to get out of here.*

What was supposed to be an incredible birthday getaway has turned into the worst possible nightmare. But he can't dwell on that now. Where will he go? Who will take him in? Maybe his sister, Ruthie, in Manhattan? Can he catch a ride on a bus? He recalls seeing a bus station over on Atlantic Avenue. Maybe he can hightail it over there, buy himself a ticket. He rakes his fingers through his hair. *What else? What else is he forgetting?*

Then it hits him. *A note.* He should leave a note for Gwen. Something apologetic. Something that says he loves her and always will and he's an idiot and he's going somewhere far, far away. That he hopes she'll forgive him. That he can't believe she has put up with him for as long as she has. When he pauses to think of what he's done—the memory of him grabbing her so hard and shoving her like he *meant* to hurt her—he has to race to the toilet and vomit. He wipes the seat down, flushes again.

On the bureau where the TV sits there's a pad of paper and a pencil. Jason grabs the pencil and begins to write. *Dear Gwen, Words can't begin to describe how very sorry I am...* He's written almost two pages by the time he's finished. They're small note-sized pages, but still, he's surprised he has this much to say. If the note is going to serve its purpose, though, it has to end on an upbeat, a nod toward the future. It can't just be about how sorry he is. That's not good enough.

He chews the tip of the pencil and thinks. He knows precious seconds are ticking by. Finally he writes *I really hope that one day you'll consider taking me back. That we'll look back on this day as a turning point, when we realized we needed to take a break from each other, but that it was all for the best. I love you, Gwen. Always will, Yours, J.*

He slides it under the table lamp next to the bed, someplace visible where it won't be missed. Then he quietly pulls the heavy door shut behind him and heads for the stairs that will carry him down ten flights. It's not until he's sitting in the last seat in the back of the bus to New York that he realizes he's forgotten his phone back in the room.

THIRTY

As soon as they reach his office, Jean-Paul shuts the door and pulls Marie into a fierce hug. "Let me hold you a minute," he says. "I can't tell you how much I've needed this." Isabella squawks to be let out of her stroller, but Marie ignores her for the moment and squeezes Jean-Paul back. Hard. When they finally pull apart, he drops onto the couch, pulls off his glasses and rubs his eyes, trying to organize all the thoughts swirling around in his mind. Marie, meanwhile, stoops down to push one of several buttons on the baby's stroller that light up with a song. "Mary Had a Little Lamb" begins to play, and Isabella startles for a second, then resumes crying. Marie shrugs and fishes the pacifier out of her pocket before plopping it into the baby's mouth.

That there is so much life in front of him when only a few hours before he was confronted by death seems like such a giant disconnect that Jean-Paul can only shake his head at

Isabella, now sucking away on her binky. "How wonderful," he says, "that she's so easily soothed."

Marie glances at him as if he might have lost his mind. "You know this is short-lived, yes? Soon she'll be screaming again."

"But she's here. You're here. All the people I love most in the world." He understands he's rambling, that his stream of consciousness makes no sense, but given the last several hours he has endured, it makes perfect sense to him. "She's so full of life," he says and almost laughs.

"Yes, she is. Full of life," Marie says. "And she won't let you forget it."

She sits down next to him and begins to rub his back in tiny circles, like she used to do when they were first married. Is it possible, he wonders, that he's in shock? That he hasn't had a moment to realize it till now? "That poor, poor woman," he moans.

Marie shushes him, says, "Don't worry. The police will figure out what happened. Your job is to keep the hotel running."

Jean-Paul nods, but a thick cloud of exhaustion threatens to overwhelm him. "That's assuming I still have a job."

Her eyes widen. "Of course, you still have a job. Why would you even say that?"

His shoulders rise and fall. "Not exactly a good day for publicity."

"But there's nothing you could have done to prevent this, Jean-Paul! Certainly you know that. And Mr. Manley knows it, too." She squeezes his forearm, her slender elegant fingers wrapping around it. "You mustn't worry."

"And we have a wedding this weekend." He pulls his arm away and rests his head in his hands, the first time he's allowed himself this small gesture of capitulation the entire day.

"I was wondering about that on the way over," she says quietly. "The poor bride. Will they still go on with it, I wonder?"

"I think they have to. I haven't spoken to the bride, but Gillian has been in touch with the bride's mother. She says so long as any access to the terrace is blocked off and there are no camera crews around for tomorrow, they'll keep the wedding here."

"Well, that's good, then. I like a woman who's practical."

Jean-Paul lifts his head, surprised by his wife's sudden pronouncement. He would have expected a more sentimental response from her, something along the lines that the wedding reception couldn't possibly take place here now. "Yes, well, I'm not sure she has much choice in the matter. You can't exactly switch your venue at the last minute. And needless to say, an exorbitant amount of money has already been invested."

"Which is exactly why you need to get back out there and keep your ship skating."

A smile flits across his face. He's almost forgotten that Marie was a motivational speaker back in Paris, that she's prone to silly metaphors that don't always translate well into English. "You mean *sailing*?" he asks.

"Yes, yes. Whatever the right word is. *Sailing, skiing*? You know what I mean. Get back in your boat. Or your canoe. Or whatever." She pauses. "Your crew needs you right now."

"And I'm here," he retorts. "I'm just taking a few minutes to appreciate my wife and my daughter, whom I've been missing all day."

"I'm sorry, honey." She rubs more circles on his back. "I don't mean to upset you. We've been missing you, too. When do you think they'll release the name? When will they know what happened?"

Jean-Paul shrugs again. "Soon, I hope. We already have a name. From the room that's been cordoned off. It's only a matter of time before the police release it, once they've spoken to the family."

Her dark eyes widen again in surprise. "So you know? You know who it is?"

He nods his head. "Yes, I know," he says. "I know and wish I didn't."

He's about to say more when his cell rings—it's the commissioner. They exchange a few words, and when he hangs up, he tells Marie he has to go. "They've found a phone," he explains hurriedly. "And it's not the victim's."

THIRTY-ONE

She'd googled it. Of course, she'd googled it. Nearly six million Americans were suffering from Alzheimer's disease, but fewer than five percent of those were diagnosed with *early-onset* Alzheimer's. Five percent. She'd sat with that number for a while. Roughly 250,000 to 300,000 people under the age of sixty-five. It struck her as both an impossibly large number and an incredibly small percentage. The more she read, scrolling down the pages, the more it seemed maybe she'd gotten lucky with a diagnosis at sixty-one. Some people developed it in their fifties or forties. Even their thirties. At least, Claire thought, there was some solace in knowing that she was officially on the other side of middle age, staring down her retirement years. Not as devastating as if she'd been a young mother or had just been getting back to work at the *Dealer* and had been handed the diagnosis.

So much can go haywire in a body! she thinks. Things

like MS or ALS, other ailments with tidy but fearsome acronyms. She'd never spent much time considering it until she'd gotten sick, but now it seems a small miracle that something else didn't knock her out of the world a long time ago. Her doctor had said anywhere from a year to several years for the disease to progress. But what she really wants to know is the exact day when she'll lose it all—the ability to recognize her friends' faces, her children's voices, the door to her own house. She'd read about a young woman who'd been diagnosed two years after she'd first begun noticing vague symptoms, things like blurred speech, missing words. Her loved ones had commented on it, and she'd blown them off. Now a part of Claire wonders if Amber is already onto her secret but is too afraid to ask.

For doctor's appointments, Ben has been her rock, no question, but that doesn't mean he has shied away from homeopathic-healing suggestions for her. And even though Claire puts about as much stock in homeopathy as she does in astrology or Ouija boards, she figures what can it hurt? If it helps Ben feel better about her situation, then she's on board. Her cupboards at home, when she remembers to open them, are filled with specialty teas, her fridge stocked with fresh blueberries and other produce rich in antioxidants. Twice a week, Ben delivers bulging bags from his health-food store directly to her fridge. And although Claire doubts that any of it will actually halt the disease from creeping across her brain like kudzu, she eats those damn blueberries, every last one of them, as if her life depends on it.

Because the part that terrifies her most, that she won't often allow herself to think about, is the burden she will become to her kids once her memory truly slides away from her. Several years ago, Claire had visited an older friend in a home for Alzheimer's patients because she'd promised the woman's children she would. It was one of the most awful, depressing places she'd ever set foot in. The antiseptic smell, the intermittent moaning, the beeps of nurses' call buttons. But the worst were the blank stares on the patients' faces, their mouths hanging open. One woman, her hair in a rat's nest atop her head, had approached Claire and asked, "Are you my sister?"

She'd looked so full of hope, it was all Claire could do not to lie. "No, I'm sorry, but maybe your sister will be here later?" The woman had nodded and wandered off, her slippers slapping against the cold, tiled floor.

No, when the time arrives, Claire will *absolutely not, no way* put her children through the agony of caring for her. Not will she allow them to watch her wasting away into nothingness, becoming a shell of herself, someone who no longer recognizes them at visiting hours. When the time comes, as it inevitably will, she'll inquire about options, about a magic pill. Maybe she'll have to enlist Ben's help, but she's counting on him to understand. It's Amber who will try to talk her out of it. But no matter, because Claire has already made up her mind. *If a person doesn't have the presence of mind to appreciate life, then how is it living?* she'll insist. In the end, it's her life. Her choice.

Never before has religion assumed a large presence in her life, but lately she has found herself thinking a lot about God, about heaven and where she might go. A few weeks after her diagnosis, she'd wandered into a Unitarian church during her lunch break, the hard wooden pew pushing against her back, and asked herself why, exactly, was she here? What was she searching for? Hope? Absolution? A cure? They had always been more of a holiday-churchgoing family, and she and Walt had brought the kids to a Protestant church on occasion. Every Easter and Christmas Eve, she'd comb the

kids' hair and cut their fingernails in anticipation of services, though if Walt had had his way, they'd have avoided
church altogether. But Claire insisted they go. If only to in-
troduce Ben and Amber to the idea of it. *Well, here it is, religion, should you need or want it. You have a holy place to worship,
a Holy Being to pray to.* And some holidays Claire would feel
her pulse begin to slow when she cracked open the hymnal,
a sense of serenity unexpectedly falling over her while she
recited the Lord's Prayer.

When she'd visited church on that weekday, she'd been
surprised by the handful of parishioners already present, their
heads bowed in prayer. One woman's hands threaded through
her rosary beads. A few rows ahead, a man rocked back and
forth, as if the rhythmic swaying of his body alone might
grant him peace. She wondered if, like her, they'd come
looking for answers. And as she sat there that day, she'd been
surprised to find tears sliding down her cheeks, salt licking
at her lips. It was the first time she'd allowed herself to cry.
Not even when she'd received the diagnosis with Ben holding her hand had she cried.

*Lord, please watch over Amber and Ben and Fiona. Please
watch over Jeff and Liv. Lord, please give us the strength to get
through this with grace. And if this whole thing happens to be a
huge misunderstanding—if, say, the doctors mixed up my charts
with someone else's, I'll be mad but okay with that. I know you can
work miracles, God. If you could spare one for me, I'd be grateful.*

Claire has been very clear about her last wishes: no extra
measures to be taken, no pumping oxygen to her brain if
it means living without awareness for the rest of her life.
But how does a person dictate her last wishes if her facul-
ties are fading away in bits and pieces? "Please don't keep
me around when I can no longer recognize you," she'd told
the kids years ago before she had any idea what early-onset

Alzheimer's even was. "Just slip something into my drink or smother me in my sleep."

She was only partially kidding. She reminds herself of the doctor's prognosis, that she might still have a decade left before things start to get really bad. Unlikely, but possible. When she talks to Amber tonight, she'll answer her questions as best she can, hold her hand, let her cry on her shoulder. All the things a mother would do for her child while she's still able.

She'd hoped that maybe Marty could be convinced to join her on this final leg of her journey, but it's not to be. And now, while she looks out on the water, she realizes that having him by her side isn't what she would have wanted, anyway. Because it's her family whom she wants right now, no one else. Turns out that waving good-night to Marty on that chilly, fateful night so many years ago was not the biggest mistake of her life. She hadn't been turning down a chance at a family at all. It was Marty she'd said no to.

The realization comes barreling to her through the salty air: Marty was never her one true love. All this time, all these years, through the ups and downs, it's been Walt. She realizes now that it's Walt who would have stood behind her on the treadmill to catch her if she fell.

And it's not just the Bloody Marys talking. Or the last few days. She's known it all along.

She resolves to stop asking herself the *what-ifs?* of life. Because what's the point? Now more than ever, it's critical that she begin planning for the rest of it. She'll resign from the paper. Maybe she can spend more time watching Fiona so Amber can get a full-time job. Maybe she'll ask Amber if she can move in with her and Jeff and Fiona. Not forever but while she still has her wits about her. So she won't be all alone. Above all, she's glad that her children will have each other when she's gone.

She slides her bare feet out of her flip-flops, pushes out of her chair and walks over to the banister. The harbor twinkles in the noonday sun—she'll have to remember to bring Amber out here tomorrow morning so she can enjoy the view herself. How many others have stood on this very balcony, in this very place? she wonders. If the hotel dates back to 1886, then the number of guests who've considered the same view must be in the thousands. Hundreds of husbands and wives, perhaps newlyweds. Shipping captains who've stood in this spot, planning their next sojourn at sea. Claire's fingers trace the wooden railing, the white wood freshly painted, all the way back to the corner where the banister meets the building. There's a ledge that juts out from the building, about three feet by three feet, and above that hovers a gargoyle, some kind of mythical creature. A Pegasus? A griffin? She's never been good with mythology. It has enormous wings, a horse's head. If she slides her chair over, she thinks she could probably climb over the banister and onto the edge of the balcony.

It's a crazy idea, she knows this. But what's the worst that could happen, given that the universe already has other plans for her? She drags the chair over, which makes a high-pitched scraping noise, and pushes it up against the banister. It's almost as if an invisible voice dares her to climb over. Maybe she'll just test it out, she thinks. See if maybe, when the time comes, this might be a better way to go. A fall. She wouldn't have to enlist Ben's help for a magic pill. She'd be no one's responsibility, no one's guilty conscience.

Gripping the back of the chair first and then the railing, she stretches one leg over, and then the other, until she can scoot her bottom onto the railing. There's a good six inches of balcony floor on the other side of the railing, so that when she slides her feet down, her toes land firmly on it. She grips the railing on either side of her. She realizes she hasn't thought this through very well, though, because she's not facing the water, which, ideally, would be the direction she'd want to go. Gingerly, she pivots on her toes so that her body faces the harbor and begins to walk, placing one foot in front of the other, her hands grabbing the railing on her right. There's plenty of room to set her entire foot down on these narrow six inches.

She remembers herself as a young girl walking the balance beam in gymnastics and how her coach would insist she point her toes and always look ahead, not down. Claire conjures up her ten-year-old self now, a remarkably poised girl who had no idea of the myriad trials—and celebrations—that awaited her. A young woman who kept her eyes trained on the end of the balance beam, confident that if she did so, she wouldn't fall.

Well, there have been a few falls, for sure, but none so terrible that she hasn't been able to get back up. She thinks of Ben and Amber when they were younger, how they'd grow angry over something small—a broken toy, a slight by a friend, a forgotten assignment—and she'd try to persuade them to focus on the bigger picture. *Although your problem might feel Godzilla-size right now,* she'd say, *in the scheme of things, it probably won't matter much tomorrow.* Up here, with nothing but air surrounding her on all sides, she reminds herself to take the faraway view, to see the bigger picture. Her eyes focus on the water beyond, not the ground below. This disease will not be what defines her, how she is remembered. Rather, it's her life's work—her pursuit of truth through journalism, her enduring marriage, her remarkable children, her brilliant grandchild—that define her.

It's odd, but she's not at all scared up here. Because what's to fear when she's already facing the end? She should probably go back and pull herself up over the banister. Her chair, she knows, awaits her. If only Walt could be here now so that she could show him.

"See, Walt?" she says out loud, her words getting swallowed by the wind. "There's nothing to be afraid of." The sky is a swath of pure blue, the harbor a warm oasis in the sun. And without warning, a flood of unexpected tranquility rushes over her, one that's so sublime she wishes she could share it with her children—this sudden certainty that everything will be all right.

She's at the front of the balcony now, her hands gripping the railing behind her. She lets her left hand go and takes a tiny step forward, as if she might grasp a piece of the sky in her fingers. Amber's face flashes before her, then Ben's. Then Walt's. And Walt is saying something to her that she strains to hear. *Don't worry?* Maybe that's it, she thinks. But no, it's something else. She feels a flutter of annoyance that she can't make it out. But next thing she knows, Walt is extending his hand to her and she could swear he says *I've got you.*

She balances on the edge of the balcony for a moment. Walt's always been there, she realizes. Even all those times when she'd doubted it. Her right hand lets go of the railing to reach out for him.

And then suddenly the image of her granddaughter—red curls bobbing, her sweet face delighted to see her nana—dances before her.

And she cries out, "Oh, no, Fiona! Stop!"

But it's too late. Claire's foot is already slipping.

THIRTY-TWO
5 o'clock, Friday

Jean-Paul stands next to the police commissioner on the side porch of the hotel, as far away as possible from the wedding guests, who have been arriving nonstop in the lobby for the past hour. The Seafarer's atrium brims with the rush and excitement of young love, of a weekend that promises to be filled with romance and music, family and friends. Gillian has offered a complimentary cocktail hour to all wedding guests in the Chantilly Bar on the second floor, while the maintenance crew hurriedly transfers the remainder of tables and chairs that will be needed for tomorrow's reception from the dining room into the Churchill Banquet Hall, located on the opposite side of the hotel.

The young Miss Saltonstall had been distressed to learn of the tragic events on the premises this afternoon, but she hadn't let it sway her in terms of going forward with her wed-

ding reception. When Jean-Paul shared the victim's name
with her, she'd insisted that flowers be sent to the victim's
family with sincere condolences from herself and her entire
family. It struck Jean-Paul as a class act. Straightaway, Gillian had arranged through a local florist, Smart Stems, for a
lush bouquet of lilies to go out to the O'Dell children, along
with another enormous mixed bouquet courtesy of the hotel.

The number of news trucks present at five o'clock has
dwindled slightly from earlier this afternoon, but four or five
still remain with their camera crews in tow. The commissioner addresses them first this time. Jean-Paul is only here
to be his wingman, to fill in any details as needed.

"Good afternoon," Commissioner Fisher begins. "It's been
a long day for all of us, but we promised you folks that we'd
have an update for you on the victim's name later today. As
I mentioned earlier, this is being treated as a death investigation, and we've now been in touch with the family, who
is understandably heartbroken. However, they've given us
permission to release the name of their family member who
passed away so tragically earlier this afternoon." A hush falls
over the reporters while they wait. "That woman's name is
Claire O'Dell. I'll spell it for you. C-L-A-I-R-E O-'-D-E-
L-L. I understand that she was a well-regarded journalist at
the *Providence Dealer*, where she worked for the past thirty-
some years. We can also tell you that Ms. O'Dell, a resident
of Providence, was sixty-one and, according to her family, was visiting Boston on holiday. She is survived by her
two children, Amber Halifax and Benjamin O'Dell, and
her three-year-old granddaughter, Fiona, all of Providence.
Ms. O'Dell's late husband, Walter O'Dell, passed away last
October.

"This is an ongoing investigation, and so at this time,
I'm afraid I can't comment any further except to say, for the

moment at least, there doesn't appear to have been any kind
of foul play involved. Our condolences—and I know Mr.
Savant and the Seafarer join the Boston Police Department
when I say this—our sincere condolences and prayers go out
to Ms. O'Dell's family on this tragic day.

"Now, if you wouldn't mind giving the hotel and its guests
some well-deserved space for the remainder of the weekend, I
know that the folks at the Seafarer would really appreciate it."

Jean-Paul nods beside the commissioner, relieved that
nothing is expected of him at this press conference. Because
he's not sure he could offer anything more. He is totally and
completely spent, as in he-could-lie-down-and-sleep-for-
twenty-four-hours spent. The news reporters shout out questions about whether this means it was a suicide, if Ms. O'Dell
was alone when she fell, if the police have any other theories.

"Thank you. That will be all for now," the commissioner
tells them. After talking with the family, both he and Jean-
Paul had agreed not to mention Ms. O'Dell's early-onset
Alzheimer's. It seemed the news had come as a surprise to
her daughter when the son first mentioned it to them. Nor
did it seem pertinent to address the phone that had been discovered in the jacket pocket of the blue blazer hanging in
Ms. O'Dell's bathroom. It belonged to one Martin Campbell, who, when the commissioner located him at his place of
work, explained that he was an old friend of Ms. O'Dell's and
had met her for dinner last night. Apparently, he'd lent her his
blazer on the walk back to the hotel and had been searching
for his phone all morning. The news of Ms. O'Dell's death
appeared to truly upset him. The hallway cameras further
confirmed his story that he'd never set foot in Ms. O'Dell's
hotel room last night or this morning, and so he'd been ruled
out as a potential suspect.

The commissioner and Jean-Paul also agreed not to allude to another incident that occurred shortly before the fall. The press hadn't gotten hold of it yet, and it didn't appear particularly relevant.

But somewhat curiously, around noon today, a young woman had stepped off the elevator and hurried to the concierge to report that she'd sprained her wrist. Maybe broken it. She'd asked if he could please fetch her a ride to the hospital. Jean-Paul had been summoned and had been surprised by how stoic the woman seemed, cupping her wrist in her other hand like a broken wing. When he'd inquired what happened, she said she'd tripped and landed on her wrist. But when he'd asked where exactly—for purposes of the accident report he was required to file—she'd been vague. "On my balcony, or near it," she'd said. Jean-Paul chalked it up to her pain. He could ask her more specifics when she returned from the hospital. But now he's thinking they'll absolutely need to double-check all the balconies for safety. Yet another task to add to his to-do list.

When they head back into the hotel, he finds Marie and Isabella waiting for him in the lobby. They're sitting on one of the new seafoam-colored linen couches, and a handful of guests has crowded around the baby, cooing at her, telling Marie what a gorgeous baby she has. Jean-Paul watches his wife's face beam under their compliments. There is something about a plump, happy infant that helps to fill the enormous gap left today, and Isabella is playing her part perfectly. He watches his daughter gurgle and smile and kick her bare feet, as if she has finally come under the spotlight she so naturally deserves. Perhaps this has been her problem all along: Isabella has wanted a larger audience than what he and Marie can offer.

When he catches Marie's eye, she offers him a shrug and

a smile, as if to say *Who knew our daughter was a natural entertainer?* And Jean-Paul nods and smiles back. Maybe, he thinks, Marie will have to start bringing the baby to the hotel more often, not only for Isabella's sake but also for Marie's and Jean-Paul's sakes. For all their sakes, really. Because if today's tragedy has underscored anything for him, it's that life needs to be celebrated. That even when death surrounds them—maybe most especially when death surrounds them—they need to push on and celebrate all that they hold dear.

He's been a fool, he can see that now, to neglect his wife and new daughter for his responsibilities at the hotel. Of course, the Seafarer will continue to demand his attention, but Jean-Paul can work to create slices of time for only him and his family. Oliver can help. And Gillian. And Tabitha and Rachel. And a host of others on his staff. The pressure he has felt to ensure a successful reopening of the Seafarer has been immense. But there's more to life than this hotel. Much more.

Those simple pockets of joy, he thinks again. Pockets of joy that they can share with one another, if only they take the time to look for them.

And he goes to sit down next to his wife and daughter, Marie scooting over to make room for him.

★ ★ ★ ★ ★

AUTHOR NOTE

December 2020

Dear Reader,

If you walk down the streets of Boston's Seaport District today, you'll see new luxury apartments and hotels, upscale restaurants and nightclubs, and stores like Lululemon and L.L.Bean. There are lovely parks to linger and play in. The Harborwalk fronts the majestic federal courthouse and, farther down, there's the Institute of Contemporary Art. The newest kid on the block, so to speak, the Seaport District has become the place to see and be seen.

It wasn't always this way. Originally a shipping port back in the late 1800s, the area fell into disrepair a century later. Aside from two landmark restaurants, Anthony's Pier 4 and Johnny's Harborside, there was little to see except parking lots and abandoned warehouses. But with the launch of the Big Dig project in the 1990s, which connected the Seaport District to downtown, and a four-billion-dollar cleanup of the Boston Harbor, the seeds for a spectacular rebirth were planted.

A few summers ago, while my family and I strolled along the waterfront and marveled at its transformation, I began to wonder, What if a hotel had existed here over a century ago? Would it still be around? Would it have attracted the famous and fabulous, like those who once flocked to Anthony's Pier 4? The questions got my mind spinning.

I'd also been wanting to write a modern love story, one that centered on four different couples who were in various stages of a relationship—the promising first blush of new love, the more staid love of a couple trying to find their way back to each other after having a baby, the troubled roller-coaster love between two academics and the stirrings of a thirty-year-old romantic flame in one woman. What better place to bring them all together than at an illustrious hotel?

I knew that the book would begin with a tragedy, one that could unite the guests. I debated if a woman plummeting to her death would be too gruesome, but the more stories that popped up on the nightly news of someone slipping or falling or otherwise meeting their untimely demise from a great height, the more it seemed that such a tragedy, at the very least, would be plausible. It also got me wondering how someone stares down the edge of death. Would drugs or alcohol be involved? How would the witnesses to such a tragic event be affected?

The result is *Summertime Guests*, a mix of summery romance and mystery. I hope the novel will keep you turning the pages as well as give you a welcome escape from these exhausting, challenging times. As I write this, a COVID-19 vaccine is making its way across the country, and my fingers are tightly crossed that soon we'll be able to return to our favorite places, maybe a hotel not so unlike the Seafarer, where we can relax poolside and enjoy a refreshing drink with friends—without giving a single thought to a crisis, care or worry.

My warmest thanks for reading, and all best wishes for a wonderful, healthy summer.

Fondly,
Wendy Francis

ACKNOWLEDGMENTS

This book has come to fruition thanks to the hard work of many people, not least of all my wonderful agents, Annelise Robey and Meg Ruley, who believed in the story from the very beginning. To my marvelously talented editor, Michele Bidelspach, thank you for your multiple readings of the manuscript (which improved it each time), and all while you were managing a newborn baby at home during a pandemic. Fingers crossed you can now get some rest. Thanks to Vanessa Wells for bringing a gimlet eye to the finer points of grammar and catching any inconsistencies that snuck into the manuscript. And thank you to the entire team at Graydon House, including Susan Swinwood, Melanie Fried, Monica Espinoza Chavez, Pamela Osti, Heather Connor and Lia Ferrone, for taking such good care of my books. To Jonathan Knudsen, my heartfelt thanks for answering my flurry of emails about hotel management and my questions about how things actually work at a top-notch establishment. Your insights and knowledge were invaluable. Any mistakes about the world of hotels and/or hotel management (particularly during times of crisis) are my own. And thanks to Ryan Bergin for stepping in to help out during those final weeks of writing. Nicholas enjoyed all of his "big brother" time!

There were a host of articles and books that helped me gain a better understanding of early-onset Alzheimer's, both fiction and nonfiction. Lisa Genova's *Still Alice* (Gallery Books, 2009) stopped me in my tracks when I first read it several years ago for its utterly convincing and heartbreaking portrayal of a woman who slowly succumbs to early-onset Alzheimer's. Then there's Wendy Mitchell's *Somebody I Used to Know* (Ballantine Books, 2018), an illuminating, wonderfully candid memoir about the author's own experiences. This book gave me valuable insights into how a person lives in the aftermath of such a diagnosis. And more recently, Tom Keane's heartrending articles in the *Boston Globe* about his late wife's battle with younger-onset Alzheimer's has struck a chord with countless New England readers, including myself. His honest portrayal of how devastating the disease can be for victims and caregivers alike offers another important window into the illness.

Finally, to my family, who listened to all my complaining while they were stuck at home with me during a pandemic, thank you, thank you for tolerating me. There's no one else I'd rather be cooped up with during lockdown. Mike, Nicholas, Katherine and Michael, Jr., thanks for making me proud every day. Here's to hoping we're on the other side of COVID by the time this book is out in the world.

SUMMERTIME GUESTS

WENDY FRANCIS

Reader's Guide

GRAYDON
HOUSE

1. The Seafarer Hotel is a fictional hotel built in Boston in 1886, full of wealth, sophistication and decadence. In *Summertime Guests*, the lives of four very different characters collide there with very dramatic consequences. The hotel almost feels like a character in the book. Why do you think the author chose to set *Summertime Guests* at a hotel like the Seafarer? These characters are all at different places in their lives. Why did the author choose this moment to bring them all together?

2. Riley and Tom's relationship seems to be ideal...until they start planning their wedding. Why do you think Marilyn becomes so involved in helping Riley plan the wedding? What do you think of the way that Riley handles Marilyn's involvement and opinions? If you were in Riley's situation, how would you manage this relationship? Do you think that her own mother's untimely death has any effect on Riley's relationship with Marilyn? Why or why not? And why do you think wedding planning so often causes tension?

3. The relationship of Jean-Paul and his wife, Marie, seems to have changed after their daughter's birth. How would you characterize Jean-Paul and Marie's relationship at the beginning of the novel? How has Isabella's birth changed their dynamic as a couple? And how do you think their relationship changes as the story progresses? Why do you think the author chose to tell the story from Jean-Paul's perspective but not Marie's?

4. The first time we're introduced to Claire O'Dell, she's driving by the house of Marty, her boyfriend from thirty years ago, anxious to see him again. She acknowledges that Marty "has continued to take up space in her mind, like an old, comfortable recliner she can't bring herself to throw out." Why does Claire think of him that way? How does seeing him and catching up in person change the way she thinks of him now? How has time colored her memory of Marty? And how have those memories affected her relationship with her husband, Walt?

5. Claire has very different relationships with each of her two children. She's in more frequent contact with Amber and they seem to be closer, yet she's entrusted her big secret to only Ben. Why do you think that is? Claire muses at one point, "Boys were funny that way. Men, too, as if whatever protective, worry gene women possessed hadn't been passed along to them." Why then did she tell only Ben the truth about her secret? If you were in Claire's situation, would you do the same? What role does gender have in the relationship between parents and their children?

6. Claire seems to believe that Marty is "the one that got away" for much of her marriage to Walt. How did that impact her marriage and the way she saw her husband? Do you think Jason and Gwen will think of one another that

way? Why or why not? What is the allure of "the one that got away"? Has there been "one that got away" in your life?

7. Why do you think Jason has kept from Gwen the fact that he stormed out of his class and hasn't gone back since? And why do you think he's continued to lie to her about writing his dissertation? He worries that she "might be too good for him." Do you think that's true? Why or why not? And what do you think Gwen sees in Jason that makes her stay?

8. Throughout the book, the four main characters are forced to confront their pasts, time and again, in order to move forward to their future. For example, Jason is determined not to become just like his father, so much so that he has missed the warning signs that the one thing he fears most may be coming true. How do you think the past has shaped these four characters, for better and/or for worse? Do you think the cycle of the past can be broken? Which character exemplifies your beliefs the most? And the least?

9. The author brings these characters together at different moments in the story, whether the characters consciously realize it or not. For example, Jason and Claire are both at a pivotal moment in their lives when they meet at the hotel bar and they're more honest with each other as strangers than they are with anyone else in their lives. Why do you think this is? Claire suggests that "we like to fool ourselves.... But we don't know that a different path would have necessarily been better. It might have been worse. No, we all live the life we're meant to live." Do you agree with this statement? Why or why not?

10. In Claire's last scene in the book, she thinks to herself, "It's odd, but she's not at all scared up here. Because what's to

fear when she's already facing the end?" Why do you think Claire climbs out onto the railing of the balcony? What do you think she intends to do? And what do you think is the significance of Walt's words to her? Do you think Claire's realization about the truth of her relationship with Walt has any effect on what happens?

11. Letting go of the past, forgiving and embracing love—any kind of love—is at the heart of this story. How do Riley, Claire, Jean-Paul and Jason accomplish this? And how do they fall short? Which character did you feel the closest to and why? Which character was the most unlike you? Did anyone surprise you at the end?

The Seafarer is a fictional hotel with a long, colorful history and a sterling reputation, *the* place to see and be seen, and it feels like a major character in the novel. Is it inspired by a real hotel that you've either stayed at in the past or have read about? What about a hotel like the Seafarer interested you?

The Seafarer is an amalgam of hotels, real and imaginary, that I would love to vacation at. The hotel probably closest to it in terms of aesthetics is the jaw-dropping Wentworth by the Sea in New Hampshire. Built in the 1870s, this stately white expanse perches on the small island of New Castle. With its own rich history, including hosting several presidents, Wentworth by the Sea offers ocean views, golf courses, swimming pools and tennis courts, elegant dining, and a spa. What more could you ask for? As for my interest in older hotels, I've always been drawn to those places that harbor their own histories—and stories. It's fun to imagine the people who came before you, who once sat in the exact same spot where you sit now, enjoying a summertime beverage.

Summertime Guests is full of twists and turns. When you began the story, did you know exactly how it would end? Were the characters' journeys solidified in your mind before you started writing? Did anything—or anyone— surprise you as you were writing?

This was a different, and challenging, book to write because, for the first time, I actually knew the ending: a woman dies. What was less clear was how the characters' stories would intersect around that event. I knew the novel would be set at a tony hotel in the Seaport District of Boston, and I knew I wanted to explore various stages of love through four main characters. It took several drafts before the plotline and relationships came into full view, though. Plenty of people surprised me in the narrative, probably Jason most of all.

Throughout the story, the reader gets an inside perspective into four very different relationships. Between Riley, Claire, Jean-Paul and Jason, which character's perspective did you enjoy writing from the most? The least?

Claire's and Jean-Paul's characters were the most engaging to write—Claire's because hers was such an intricate, difficult journey to plot, and Jean-Paul's because I could empathize with this poor man who's doing his level best to keep everything running smoothly at work and at home. Riley's experiences were a little more distant in my memory (all that young love!), and Jason's darker side forced me to write outside my wheelhouse.

Many of your books are set during the summer. What about the summer intrigues you? Why does it lend itself so perfectly to the backdrop of a book?

Summer has always been my favorite season. For me, it represents that almost sacred time when kids are out of school and work slows down a bit. My childhood summertime memories are wrapped up in family vacations, trips to the beach, lazy days reading on the back porch and eating too much ice cream. Throw in some sunshine and the scent of sunblock, and I'm at my most content. Something about summertime also immediately says relaxation, and these days that sense of slowing down, of allowing ourselves the time to appreciate those "pockets of joy" with the ones we love most, seems especially important.

Claire's last scene in the book is incredibly poignant. Why did you choose to end Claire's story the way you did? What significance did Claire's revelation about her feelings for Walt have on her death and the timing of it? Why did you choose to have her granddaughter, Fiona, be the last face she saw?

Thank you. It was certainly one of the most difficult scenes to write. Without giving too much away, I wanted the book to end with Claire maintaining her dignity even in the face of incredibly difficult circumstances. As for Walt and Fiona, I think I'll leave it up to the reader to decide how those two may have influenced Claire in her pivotal moment. I will say that I wanted the ending to be hopeful.

The characters in this book feel so vibrant and alive. How do you create your characters? Do friends and family ever find themselves—or parts of themselves—in the characters you create?

I love character-driven novels, and so my own writing tends to lean that way, too. I also spend a lot of time (probably too much time!) thinking about what's going on inside other people's heads. So, putting those thoughts down on the page seems like a natural extension of what I'm imagining every day. As I write, though, the characters inevitably take on lives of their own and become much more complicated and nuanced than anything I'd imagined. And yes, my family absolutely worries that they'll end up in my fiction (especially because there's so much material there!), but I try to keep them out of it. I won't lie, though: a few conversations with my husband and kids have turned up in my books.

What are your favorite books about romantic love? Which authors capture the feeling of love for you?

Oddly enough, the first thing that comes to mind isn't a book but a movie: When Harry Met Sally. This classic, starring Meg Ryan and Billy Crystal, is a valentine to both New York City and their relationship. I love the witty rapport between the characters, the humor, the darned wagon-wheel table (if you haven't yet watched, you must!). As for fiction, Sue Miller's Monogamy, which I recently read and adored, offers a brilliant depiction of a modern marriage, warts and all. Dani Shapiro's deeply honest portrayal of her marriage in Hourglass is another favorite, and for summer romance, there's nothing quite like an Elin Hilderbrand novel. As my husband will tell you, I'm a hopeless romantic, but I'm not a complete fool—I understand that life sometimes gets in the way. But that brand of love—forged in hard times and embellished in good times— gives rise to some of the best love stories out there.